CHILD OF THE SKY

VANISHED, BOOK 5

B. B. GRIFFITH

Griffith Publishing
Denver

Publication Information

Child of the Sky (Vanished, #5)

Copyright © 2023 by Griffith Publishing LLC

Ebook ISBN: 979-8-9874270-2-6

Paperback ISBN: 979-8-9874270-3-3

Written by B. B. Griffith

Cover design by Damonza

All rights reserved. No part of this book may be reproduced in any form or by any electronic or mechanical means, including information storage and retrieval systems, without written permission from the author, except for the use of brief quotations in a book review.

This is a work of fiction. Names, characters, places, and incidents either are the product of the author's imagination or are used fictitiously and any resemblance to actual persons, living or dead, business establishments, events, or locales is entirely coincidental.

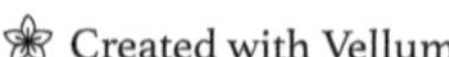 Created with Vellum

*For Murphy.
A spirit warrior from day one.*

"In pursuit of old age and happiness I follow the scent of rainfall and approach the place where the lines of rain are darkest."

- Diné Bahane'
The Navajo Creation Story
(Paul G. Zolbrod, trans.)

1

GRANT ROMER

I nudge open the gate to the Arroyo with the grille of my truck. The rusty chain that used to keep the swinging doors hooked to the pine poles on either side drags a thin line through dirt made soft by early spring rain.

Somebody always manned the gate, back in the before time, when we had something to man. Usually, it was the Smoker, who would eye you up and down for the length of a cigarette before decidin' to let you through or not. Now, they swing whichever way the wind tells them.

Beyond is the Arroyo—or what's left of it. The half-moon lip of the canyon used to glow like a river in the moonlight. Campfires would burn here and there. Gennies powered soft lights inside thirty or so trailers all spread out the same way they'd been for decades.

Eight months ago, a hundred or more people called this place home. It was alive. Now, it's more like the kind of ghost town you come up on way off the map: a few structures here and there are falling apart by degrees, leaning relics. Blowing trash is bleached by the sun and wind.

Echoes of what was.

The ground shifts underneath my tires, and I spin out more dirt than I'd like. It's not the tires. It's the ground— more sand than old hardpack these days. The weird damp is chipping away at this place, and there ain't no foot traffic left to hold the ground together right.

Finding Joey isn't hard. His car camp and the elder twins' double-wide next door are all that's left, beacons of soft light in the dyin' afternoon. I try to come out here at least once a week. Maria still takes care of the twins, God bless her, and Joey takes care of all three of 'em, but nobody checks in on Joey. And sometimes, Joey needs checkin' in on.

He took it hard—the loss of the Arroyo. Because that's what it is, gone. The people that lived here were stolen, but they walked out themselves, followin' a medicine man from another world called Jacob Dark Sky.

The roots of the Arroyo are its people. When most all of them left, the land started to slide away bit by bit, back into the desert. And then these rains came, which made things worse.

So I'm checkin' in on Joey, yeah. But I'm checkin' in on the Arroyo too. Every time I nudge these gates open, I half expect to find nothin' but flat desert, and if that ever happens, I really don't know what I'm gonna do with myself.

In the passenger's seat to my right, Chaco shivers. He's not a fuzzy little blob anymore. But he's not what you or I would call a full-grown crow either. He's that awkward in-between: a bit patchy, a bit glossy—big feet, small wings.

"Damp cold in the desert. Makes no sense," he says.

He's talking to me, mind to mind, but he's also talking to himself, tellin' himself what some old part of his endless soul remembers about this place. He's a new bird, but he comes from a long line of old, old birds, and they're all in there somewhere, even if they can sometimes be hard to find.

I gotta agree with him. "Can't say I ever seen it this wet before."

He inches up closer to the vents, closing his eyes and letting them blow hot air over the fine feathers of his head. He's only about the size of my hand, so he's gotta reach to feel the air, and he almost topples to the floormat.

"Can't say I've seen the Rez like this before either," I say. "Dark. Quiet. Like we're just tryin' to get it over with. But what, I got no idea."

"The rain and the quiet are connected," Chaco says, trying to sound deep, like thirteen-year-old me lookin' to impress Kai with my zen brush strokes on the float committee back in high school. He's tryin'.

I can't help but smile. "No shit?"

"Not even a bit of shit," Chaco says, fluffing up everything he's got for that heater vent.

He's not like he was. But he's not different, either. He's new. And he'll get there—back to the weird desert wizard he was—just like he'll be able to zip across planes again, to be a guide for us when we're lost.

But not yet. Right now, it feels like he needs us as much as we need him. Like how I gotta put my hand out to keep him from donking his little bird head on the dash when I brake. But all said and done, I'm just happy to have him here with me in the car, trying to steady himself in that weird bird way as the tires slide and grip. Him and me work. And in this place, people gotta hold on to things that work, things we're grateful for. They're what gets us by.

A trail-worn Bronco with mud splashed up to the windows is parked next to Joey's van on blocks. I recognize that Bronco. Everybody in the Rez does.

I shut off the engine and sit there in the whispering silence the rain makes on my windshield. I wasn't expecting company.

"What's the problem?" Chaco asks. "Sani Yokana is just doing his job. I know this."

"I know, I know."

Chaco's longtime chief of police is one of the few remaining threads that hold strong 'round here. He's been at it since Ben's time.

"Problem is he's looking for answers we can't give," I say.

I hop out and walk around to get my bird. He steps onto my palm and hops off at my shoulder. He can fly for short distances, but he doesn't really like to. He prefers the crook of my neck, which is alright by me.

The kerosene lantern underneath Joey's flagpole is lit up, as usual, but his car camp is dark, and his Navajo Nation flag hangs limp in the rain. Looks like everyone is next door at the twins'.

Joey and I replaced the old wooden front staircase to the elder twins' double-wide with a ramp around midwinter because they're way past the age of walkin' up and down cinderblock stairs to get in and out of their home. The ramp helps, especially since Maria still sweeps it and keeps the fake yellow daisies in the window box clean and bright. She's the one that opens the door for me and gives me a big hug. I feel it full on, and for a second, it fills that space in the middle of me where the bell was.

That hollow spot is a strange place.

Sometimes, I forget the bell is gone. If I'm with Kai or working on the trucks or walking the Rez with Chaco, sometimes I can go a whole hour without thinkin' about it. But then I always remember. The feeling is a strange ache, like I slept on my neck wrong, but deeper inside, near my heart.

The worst thing is that the longer I go without it, the more I realize I'm glad it ain't there.

The bell and me, we got what you might call a complicated relationship.

"Come, come," Maria says. "They're all out back."

"In this shit?" I ask, holding my palm out in the never-ending spit of rain, and when Maria gives me that look on account of the language, I follow with a quick "Sorry."

Maria sniffs and puts her hands on her hips. "They won't come in. Maybe you can talk sense into them," she says.

I pass through the twins' double-wide, which takes about four steps, and walk out the back to what you might call their backyard although, truth be told, the whole Arroyo is their backyard now. There ain't nobody else here to say otherwise.

The twins are in their old folding chairs. I have no idea how they're still holding up except to say maybe Maria wove some steel into the seats when they were asleep. Sani sits on a painted stump next to them. Joey is leaning against the low wooden trusses that make up the back fence, watching the canyon beyond as if the people he lost might pop back up from inside any minute.

A fire burns in the pit between the twins, as always. The pine smoke is sweet and beats back the grim damp, which makes me feel like I'm not getting rained on for the first time since I can't really remember.

They're talking in Diné, but when I come in, the Diné drops off.

"Grant, welcome in," Chief Yokana says, offering me a seat on the painted stump next to him. "Maybe you can help shed some light on things." He's got a beat-up old notebook in one hand and a chewed-up pen in the other. His hair is long and full, the silver strong and bright in the gloom. His black hat sits on his knee, marked at the brim where he's been taking it on and off for at least a decade but clean as a whistle otherwise. He's still broad, if a bit thinner these days. Overall, he don't look his age, which has to be near seventy by now. But his hands don't lie. They're spotted even underneath the desert tan, gettin' knobby, and they shake a bit.

"Shed a light? On what?" I ask even though I know damn well what.

Chief Yokana licks a finger and flips through his old notebook to an earmarked page. He holds it up. "One hundred and eighteen missing."

Each name is written out, given its own line. He has to flip the page three times to get through them all.

Joey chimes in, "Chief, we told you—"

"A hundred and eighteen," Yokana says again, cutting him off. "Forty-one cars and trucks and trailers in an impound lot over in Grant. Most of them loaded up with every earthly possession these folks had—but not a one of them claimed. Going on seven months now."

Tsosi picks up another piece of pinewood and lays it carefully on the fire. The pop and hiss sounds flat in the soggy air.

"I called in a favor with the bureau over in Gallup.

Usually, the feds don't give two shits about missing Indians, but they owed us big for that mess with the impersonated agents all those years ago. I got them to sweep the whole mountain with one of their choppers, look for heat signatures. Even if they're all dead, a hundred and eighteen bodies oughta be hard to miss from the air."

He's waiting for us to chime in, but we ain't got nothin' to say that won't make us look like we're wrapped up in how the Arroyo folks went missing. Which, of course, we are.

After a minute, Yokana closes his notebook and stares into the fire. "Nothing, then?" he asks.

Chaco chirrups at my side. I repeat what he says before I can stop myself. "They ain't dead, Chief. They're just lost."

Joey looks at me warily. Yokana eyes me much the same. I clear my throat and look elsewhere. I shoulda kept my mouth shut.

Joey bails me out. Again. "We've told you the truth, Chief," Joey says. "Jacob Dark Sky took them. They followed him to the Turquoise Mountain, and he took them away."

Yokana stands. "Where? Where did he take them?"

"We don't know," I say.

I'm being honest. We've been looking on our side. Ben's been looking on his. We got nothin'.

"But we're going to find out," Joey adds.

Tsasa speaks up, gesturing across the fire like it was the whole of the night sky, shrouded above. "Of a time long, long ago these things are said."

With Chaco's help, I get most of his story.

"In those days, the people were apart from one another. Men and women, apart. On two sides of a deep river. And being apart pained them. When the pain became too much, three women jumped in and tried to swim across. A mother and two maidens."

The fire flares here and there where raindrops hiss into the coals. Yokana rubs at his face like he ain't got time for this, but he's old school and won't interrupt the twins.

"The mother made it across. But the maidens disappeared. For three days, the people searched and found nothing. But on the fourth day, they listened to the gods, who told them to look deep in the water. There, they found Big Water Creature. He had stolen the maidens and put them next to his own two children. Hidden them all in his house of four rooms deep below."

Tsasa settles back, watching the fire, coughing a dry cough. Eventually, Maria moves a metal cover with a smoke hole over the fire, to protect it, and the rain starts to ping off it.

"I don't get it," I tell Chaco, mind to mind.

Chaco flares the tiny feathers on the hood of his head and huddles deeper under the brim of my hat, close to my neck and out of the storm. "Me neither," he says. I can tell he's disappointed with himself. "I should get it, but I don't."

I surprise myself by speaking up in broken Diné. "Did they take them home? The two maidens?"

Tsosi and Tsasa and everyone else looks up at me. I can't think of a time I've really addressed the twins directly. Joey looks impressed, which I'll take to the bank.

"Yes, they took them home," Tsosi says. "But while they did, Coyote snuck in and stole the children of Big Water Creature."

"Dumb move," I say, switching back to English.

Chief Yokana cuts in. "Grandfathers, with all due

respect, I'm looking for real people who have gone real missing. If you know anything—"

Joey cuts in. "What happened then?" he asks in that way he has that says he knows exactly what happened then.

"A flood," says Tsosi. "A terrible flood."

Chief Yokana stands, his joints popping. "I got a hundred and eighteen bodies to find," he says. The word *bodies* seems to hurt him physically. "If anything comes to you that might help the cause, please give me a call."

He pulls his collar up against the rain and looks up at the sky like it's a stranger. Then he heads out to his car without another word. Joey watches after him, his face heavy. The twins stir the ashes through the smoke hole until the flames lick at the new log and the hood steams in the rain.

Tsasa looks out at the Arroyo, which is fading to black in the way rain can bring on an early night. Maria helps him to stand then does the same for Tsosi.

Together, the twins walk to the edge of their yard, where a wooden fence stands. There they lean, with Joey and Maria and me right behind. All five of us stare out at the vacant sky, hollow like a footlocker and empty except for the strange way the rain moves the air about in shades of gray.

After a minute, I notice what the twins are eyeing. A thin stream of water is running outside the fence, and the way they're lookin' at it—like it was some sort of rattlesnake sliding past—makes me think it's water where there ain't really been water before.

With my eyes, I follow it as far as I can into the dusk. It's streaming slow and steady into the canyon itself.

Joey sees what I see. His face is grim. "This isn't the work of Coyote," he says in Diné.

"It's the work of Dark Sky," I say. "And Black Bear."

The twins grumble to each other and shake their heads. "The people who were stolen are what matters," says Tsasa. "More than the people who did the stealing."

Tsosi nods. "Return the people, and the balance is restored."

Joey leans hard against the fence, making the wet wood creak. "What if we can't find them?"

The twins watch the water. Maria fusses over them with raincoats, but they seem not to feel the rain—at least not yet. Tsosi covers Joey's hand with his. It reminds me of the way Chaco leans against me when he can tell my mind is in a dark spot.

But Tsosi's answer brings no comfort at all. "If we cannot find them, then the flood comes."

2

———

THE WALKER

The Arroyo people are missing. They were taken by a dick named Jacob Dark Sky. Maybe unto death. But the funny thing is, I'm the physical manifestation of death, and nobody told me about it, which leads me to believe things aren't what they seem.

Chaco, my bird friend, used to be able to jet all over the place, through every plane, in and out like a flying magician. He could find anyone. But then Chaco... Well, Chaco kinda died. He's back, but he's in his tweens again and going through a bit of a phase, and right now, he can't even really be counted on to fly in a straight line, so the only thing that has any sort of vision across the lands of the living and the dead is me.

My whole life, all the elders of the Rez told me my people were expert trackers. I heard stories of wayback folks that could sniff out a deer by the smell of their horns molting. I remember a legend of some great chief who once caught a whole mess of deer by tracking the mountain lion tracking the damn deer and tripping up the lion in a drop trap. He got the deer but let the lion go—so that he could *track it again*. The point is this "finding things" shit is supposed to be in my blood—or the memory of my blood, given that I'm long gone.

My people are supposed to be trackers, and this is my tracking task: find the Arroyo people. Craft a plan to get them back home. Get things back to normal. Return the balance. And when that's done, sit and watch the sunset.

Simple, right?

Well, it turns out I can't track for shit.

I should have known. I found this memory way in the back of my head of Joey and me trying to use our "tracking skills" when we were teenagers. It's not a super clear memory, partly because it's so old but also because we might've been a bit drunk on trash beer Joey rustled up from God knows where. In the end, I think Joey eventually caught a field mouse for, like, five seconds in a box-and-stick trap. All I caught was a sore ass from Gam's sandal.

So when that's taken into account, maybe it makes sense that I'm going on seven months now following Dark Sky but all I ever seem to catch is echoes.

I'm sitting on a stretch of river along the border between California and Arizona where a bunch of soul stories told me a man named Jacob Dark Sky once lived. The river is gorgeous. Slow and wide, it's a sweeping brush stroke through the canyons, scruffy with bright green at the edges where the real daring bushes and trees give life a go.

He was here once, Jacob Dark Sky—or someone much like him. But he's not here now. The soul stories don't have what you'd call a concept of time. Maybe centuries ago, Dark Sky walked this riverbank. Now the place is home to birds soaring the thermals and little chipmunks darting over each other along the tiny edges of the red rock banks.

And one squirrel in a tree, staring at me like a waiter hanging around for a tip.

Sometimes this happens. Animals run the spectrum just like people do, and I occasionally come across one that looks like it knows too much.

"What?" I ask.

They never answer. Nothing living can truly see me or hear me. Stuff like this makes me miss the old Chaco, the way he would just drop in on me like a houseguest I never knew I needed. Hell, I'd even take the new Chaco. He's got no filter, like me. Dying does that to you. You should hear the mouths on some of the souls I escort. Life is the filter, and once that's gone, people call it like they see it.

Finding this place took me a while. I had to do some deep digging in the soul map, some real dusty work, and it's making me feel a little strange, like maybe I oughta just sit here on the bank of this river and rest for a while. I'm having a hard time remembering what I had to do today, other than the relentless day job, of course. But I can pull little bits of myself away to do that and still sit here.

The squirrel lets loose a long string of spastic chatter that snaps me back. I come around and find myself in the river up to my ankles. I make no mark in the living world, but I do feel it. It's more like a memory than anything, but it is there, the soft pressure of the water pushing at my legs, the sinking feeling of my feet in the mud.

I have no memory of stepping foot into the water. If that squirrel hadn't caught my attention, I might have sleepwalked for days. When I do that, I can come around again weeks, months, or even years later.

The squirrel is up on an overhanging branch, staring

daggers in my general direction. It does that little clicky growl again and butts the air with its nose a few times.

"Thanks for snapping me out of it."

The squirrel seems more interested in chewing at the wood now. Maybe I'm giving it more credit than it deserves. Either way, whenever I start daydreaming like this and talking to the squirrels, I know it's time to get grounded again back at the Rez, to shake free some of the cobwebs.

I swirl open the soul map and step inside.

THE FIRST THING I notice is the rain. The Rez can get a bit of rain from time to time, but this is different. This is angry rain. The old-timers would call it male rain—heavy and loud, with arc lightning that jumps around the low clouds and thunder that rumbles itself to a snap, over and over again.

Usually, the few times we get male rain, it's quick to shout and quick to burn out, and what follows is a soft and quiet misting, what the old-timers call female rain. The clouds usually pass quickly. Then the sun comes blazing back to the high desert.

But judging by the state of the Arroyo, this storm is stuck in. Little rivulets of water cut the dirt and drain down into the canyon. The water has the run of this place now that the car camp is gone, and the few structures that remain aren't putting up any kind of fight. The rain looks like it's eating away at the dirt around the cinderblocks the deserted Yageezi family trailer is perched on. It's teetering already, and it's not the only one.

First things first, I gotta check in on Joey, Maria, and

the twins. I feel Chaco nearby, too, which means Grant is here as well. The bird tracks me as I come up on the twins' double-wide, blazing out into the night like a lantern in a swamp.

"Good to see you, Walker," he says. His voice is a pitch higher than it was before he died, and the subtext is clear: *"Thanks for showing up this time."* He's got a lot of the old Chaco in him like that. Subtle jabs are how the old bird kept me honest when I would lose time.

It's also a lot of lip for a seven-month-old bird the size of my hand. And another reason I like him.

"What the hell is this?" I ask, arms out.

"I'm still pretty new here, but I believe it's called rain."

I smile. My job spans the breadth and width of this planet. I talk with every type of person who exists when they're on the way out, and I can't do anything else. It's a big prison I walk, but it's still a prison, and Chaco is my only tin-can phone to the living. When he left us, I thought that string had been snipped clean forever, and I guess I'm still riding high on being able to talk with a thing that exists over here, even if it does take me coming to him these days. He's not such a good flyer yet—dinky wings.

"'Evil rain' is probably closer to the mark, Fuzzball. But what I'm asking is why the hell are *they* out in it?" I point at the twins, sitting in their customary spots underneath waxed deerskin that rolls the rain off like glass beads.

One holds an umbrella while the other feeds the hooded firepit, which still burns somehow.

"I'm trying not to come visit these two in a professional capacity anytime soon, if you know what I mean."

"I'm working on it," Chaco says.

"Right," I say. "I forgot you're a rookie. Can I speak to your manager, please?"

That gets what I think is a bird laugh. And I'll take it.

Chaco shivers water off the tips of his fluff, and Grant turns toward him. They talk to themselves in their brains, then Grant looks in my direction.

"Hey, Ben," he says.

I'm a little hurt by hearing the disbelief in his voice. He's still shocked every time I show up. Like it's nowhere near a sure thing. I'm not sure what I gotta do to get him, Owen, and Caroline to trust that I'll keep coming back, but I can't say I blame him. I did bail on them for, like, five years. Didn't mean to, but I did. Doesn't matter that it felt like a blink of an eye to me. It was bad for them.

Maybe they'll never trust me again. But I think the only way I've got a chance is if I keep showing up on the regular. So that's what I'll do as long as I can.

Joey walks my way with his big arms held wide. He knows he'll never touch me again—at least not until I take him across the veil—but he still tries blindly every time, and I love him for it.

Joey and I go way back. We broke through betrayal and back to trust long ago. We shattered it all and repaired it. What's between us now is stronger. Maybe too strong. I love Joey, but I think he could benefit from having a best friend that isn't dead.

"You all need to get inside," I say. "This isn't a good rain."

Chaco translates. Grant takes his hat off and tips the water. "The twins won't go," he says. "And nobody goes without the twins."

I put my hands on my hips and stare at the elder twins. They're still watching their fire, the stubborn old men. They know better than anyone on this planet that steady rain and arroyos don't mix. It's a recipe for a flash flood. Everyone could be wiped out in minutes. And now, I'm getting pissed because without them we *really* have nothing. All because two elders with more tribal knowledge in the tips of their huge old-man ears aren't sensible enough to get to high ground at Boxes or, better yet, up at Wapati Casino. The Council would never let that place flood. They would chuck themselves into the water first.

I take a deep breath then let it out.

Nope. Still raining. Twins still here.

"Did they say *why* they won't go?" I ask.

Chaco flutters again and tucks himself closer under Grant's hat. "They did not. And this is night two."

Typical. Also typical that Maria and Joey wouldn't leave them. Grant neither.

Behind me, in the dark, where the water is falling in sheets now, something makes a noise.

I walk to the fence, still the same old hitchin' post it's been for decades. I probably leaned against this exact log more than a few times when I was alive. The thought gives me a strange inner vertigo. That, combined with the way the darkness turns the rain into a wall of water, makes everything seem very thin here, thinner than usual.

And something is definitely out there—movement in the soup.

"You see that?" I ask Chaco.

"It's the animals," he replies. "They're... restless."

I reach out with the part of me that walks the map, the part that sees the souls' threads and holds the shears that cut them. And I see what he's talking about. A herd of mule deer is skirting the far edge of the canyon, making their way east. The rain hides them, but I see their soul threads pulsing in time with their rapid heartbeats. Above us, the threads of probably twenty bats wheel and cut. Up high, the threads of a pair of red-tail hawks glimmer as they work to stay aloft, course correcting with the wind.

"Night flying," Chaco says, tut-tutting after them. "Tricky stuff. Don't like to do it unless I have to."

"Where are they all going?" I ask.

"Some are looking for higher ground. Some are waiting," Chaco says, "like the crows." He nods toward the far reaches of the fence, where two crows join a line of three others, all of them with their backs to us. Five fat black blobs in the rain.

"They look like they're waiting for the headliner to come on stage," I say.

Chaco tics his head my way. "The crows usually time these things pretty well."

"We gotta get everyone out of here, bird."

Grant relays our talk around the firepit. "Chaco says the animals are freaked out. Ben—the Walker says we should get gone."

The elder twins look at each other.

Tsosi says, "The animals can leave if they wish. We cannot."

Tsasa passes the umbrella to his brother and pulls his deerskin higher. "If we do, all is lost. Our people will have no home to return to."

Chaco turns back to me. "See? I told you. They won't go."

Joey leans against the double-wide under the lean-to and crosses his arms. The little uptick at the corner of his mouth might as well be for me. He's sayin', *You know how they are, brother.*

And he's right. The Arroyo is all the twins have ever

known. Reminds me of folks who refuse to evacuate in the path of the hurricane. They turn away the firemen who come knocking, then they turn away the rescue boats, each time saying they're 'gonna wait it out.' These folks are usually old, too. A lot of times, the next person knocking on their door is me. And on their way out, they all tell me the same thing: *I couldn't leave my home. Where would I go?*

But there's more to this refusal than old habits dying hard and the stubbornness of the elders. I can sense it, and I think the others can too. The elder twins are working right now, working hard. They're holding on tight to the Arroyo in ways we can't see.

And I don't want to see what happens if they lose their grip.

Maria looks fondly at the twins. She was always a mainstay around the Arroyo, but only after I died did I get the full picture of how she got here. A runaway, she took off from home at twelve, figuring she'd chance the Arroyo rather than the horrific situation she had at home where her mom's scumbag boyfriend kept her mom high enough to take advantage of them both.

Things could've gone bad for her here, too, except that the twins found her back when they used to take regular walks around the half-moon canyon lip. They gave her food and a warm fire and asked no questions, and she inched closer to them from then on. She's getting up there in years herself, but living around those two, she's always gonna be the young one, which has kept her soul string strong.

"I'll go brew some tea and try to scrounge up another umbrella then. Maybe some trash-bag ponchos, eh?" Maria says as if she simply had another drop-in for supper and the Arroyo wasn't falling apart all around us like rotting drywall.

Tsasa looks at the blackness gathering like a bruise in the distance and gently jostles his lawn chair farther back under the lean-to that juts from the back of their trailer. Tsosi does the same then takes his knobby staff, hooks it on the lip of the shade above, and pulls it out as far as it can go. The shade squeaks until it stops, but it only covers about half the fire. That and the hood will help keep it burning, but by the looks of these clouds, it won't help for long.

Chaco leans into Grant. "This is a spirit storm. It comes from the other side. That's all I know. What I *feel* is that it's gonna get a lot worse before it gets better. And when it gets worse, it'll get worse here."

Grant tries to convey all that to Joey with a glance, but I know Joey, and even if he got it, he would still do exactly what he does: shrug and move closer to the fire. The sky grumbles, rumbles, then cracks loudly enough to make the puddles shimmer. The crows on the line all bob their heads and chitter like they just saw a big firework. The rumble lingers long after the lightning. I think the Yageezi camper finally went over the edge, way out there in the dark.

A slick of water washes across the back yard. The twins' matching rubber boots are in an inch of standing water now. And I've got a bad feeling there's a lot more on the way.

3

CAROLINE ADAMS

If you think Rice Krispies treats are good, try Rice Krispies treats when you're seven months pregnant. I don't know when they turned into an addiction, sometime between when I said RIP to my ankles and welcomed in my cankles. But that's why I'm shoveling a saucer-sized treat into my mouth while leaning sideways over the sink in the CHC breakroom like some sort of fat rat who stumbled onto a cheese wheel.

When I'm done, I pat my rotundness fondly with one sticky hand. "What do you think about that, huh?" I ask my tummy. "Your mom's an RKT addict. I bet you'll be one too. Studies show."

I push myself to standing. That was the last of this week's tray. I'll not so subtly leave out another box of cereal and bag of marshmallows and stick of butter on the counter when I get back tonight for Owen to not so subtly take the hint. He makes them better than I do.

"Oh, don't worry," I say. "It's not bad. Not like crack or anything. And I already passed the gestational diabetes test, so..."

I talk to my spark all the time. Since that day at Mt. Taylor, we've basically been having one long conversation that started in my head then moved out of it around the time I stopped sleeping more than four hours a night. Funny how that works.

Man, I could go for a latte. Just a real hot latte. The weather has been weirdly rainy and dreary, and I've been exhausted. That's one of the things they tell-you-but-don't-tell-you about pregnancy. The books all say you'll be tired, but they don't *really* tell you. They don't say you'll get slammed from all sides. You'll get winded walking down a hall, exhausted from tossing and turning all night, trying to sleep with a weird puffy snake pillow between your knees. They don't tell you your thoughts can make you tired.

My OBGYN told me spinach and almonds would help with energy—for real. I laughed until I realized she was being serious then covered it up with some lame joke about how maybe that's why all the squirrels around here are all nuts.

"I could go for another RKT too" I say, threading my hands beneath my tummy and yawning. Something, maybe a foot, rolls softly against my palm—a little touch, so faint. But it gets me every time, like a cat resting its paw on you for just a sec.

"I know, I know. Back to work. It'll take my mind off RKTs."

My list of things they tell-you-but-don't-tell-you about being pregnant gets longer by the day. I know it sounds like I'm complaining, but I'm not. This is just good-natured preggo banter, back-and-forth between a mom and her spark, and I wouldn't want to change anything, wouldn't want to miss a day of it for the world. Sure, it sucks that, at forty, there ain't no force on Earth short of a plastic surgeon that is ever gonna get that flat tummy back or wipe these stretch marks away, but I don't care if I walk around a bit stretchy and poochy for the rest of my life because when I look at myself, my body will remind me of her.

It'll remind me of my baby girl.

"Because she's a her," I say, testing the words out again in the air around me.

It's such an obvious thing when said aloud, and I wonder how it could still possibly be as mind-blowing as it is. But it is.

I can tell by her smoke. Not the color so much—from what I've seen, boys and girls and everything in between and around can have any color—but the way the smoke moves gives hints. The Navajo believe that rain can be boy or girl rain—well, technically, they call it male or female, but I'm in a baby mood, so I call it boy or girl. I know this because it's usually dry around here, and on the rare occasions we do get rain, Dee and Nascha and all the other Navajo that work with me would always talk in the break room about whether the rain had male energy or female energy because that would change the way they were going to plan their weekend. That is something I totally get now. In the beginning, I'd have stared blankly at the convo, but I've been here ten years now, and I get it.

The gist is boy rain comes from on high, makes noise, and drives hard. It drenches and booms. Girl rain is low and slow. Soft, it envelops like mist.

That's what I see in the smoke coming from my tummy. It's low and slow, and it mists.

I told Owen as soon as I figured it out. He and I decided months ago that we weren't cut out for a gender surprise. He likes to picture the future, likes to hold it in his mind as a goal, something to work toward. The clearer the picture, the easier it is for him to keep the train moving, to keep doing what needs to get done in order to get there.

I had to know because my anxiety would eat me alive otherwise. I hate surprises and much prefer prepared lists. From everything I've read, baby girls and baby boys are basically the same sort of blob for a while, but certain considerations have to be made—the color of the blanket, for one. The way I write out their entire life story in my head from birth to the moment I pass away with them holding me gently in their arms is another.

Also, a name.

Names are big, but they're especially big here.

The CHC phone holding on for dear life around my balloon hips buzzes. I'm getting paged by Dee at the front desk, which is good because I was starting to sweat while thinking of the name issue, which does keep me up at night and is an area in which I could totally blow it and ruin my unborn daughter's life right out of the gate. But anyway.

The notification must be something about my last appointment for the day. I wouldn't mind a cancellation. My ankles are down there praying to God.

I waddle my way up front, where the waiting room is empty. Our patient load recovered once Dark Sky skipped town, but this weather has been doing weird things to the clinic—more house calls and fewer drop-ins. Dee is tapping her acrylic nails rapid-fire across her old computer.

"Looks like your five is another no-show," Dee says. "We've been having a lot of these."

I pull out my notes and look at the five o'clock slot. These days, if I don't write out patient notes beforehand, I walk into the exam room totally lost. I'm one-hundred-percent reliant on ink to page these days. If it's not written down, it's gone.

"David Bitsui," I read from my notes, "managing COPD and high cholesterol. Tried a different statin. Working on getting maintenance inhaler approved. Had a six-month follow up. Had to push it..."

Damn.

"He's Arroyo," I say.

Dee stops tapping. Her face falls. "Shit. I thought we'd gone through and cleared them all out of the schedule."

"They could be back," I say quietly.

Dee clears her throat and wrinkles her nose. She's worked the front desk as long as I've been here. You need to be thick-skinned to work front desk at an HIS clinic. But the loss of all these Arroyo people still hits hard.

"I meant *rescheduled*," she says, tapping again at nothing on the keyboard.

She thinks they're gone forever. And why wouldn't she? Things that go lost in this country usually stay that way.

I've got enough of a thumb on the pulse here to know I can count the people on the Rez who think we might see the Arroyo again on one hand: Me, Owen, Grant, and Joey. The rest of the Navajo have been burned too many times by too many missing to think that anyone gone more than a few days will ever be seen again.

One of the things they don't tell you about when a lot of people who don't have much to their name suddenly drop off the map is this: nobody goes around notifying the rest of us still here. Owen did a ton of medical outreach in the Arroyo before they disappeared and got a lot of appointments booked, but the booking system doesn't know if the name on file walked through a portal to nowhere. It pings our front desk all the same. Then nobody walks through the door.

David Bitsui is the third this week.

"That's it for you today," Dee says, clearing her throat and popping in a fresh stick of gum. "Go get off your feet, you crazy woman. We need you as long as we can have you." She lowers her glasses and looks at me like she's sizing up a cow at an auction, but she's smiling again.

"Two more weeks," I say.

That was my rule: eight months. Will I feel guilty about it when literally nobody is there to fill my space? Yes. Will I blame the toxic culture of health care piled on top of all the insanity that is the Indian Health System? Yes. Will I eat plate after plate of Owen's RKTs, knowing he is basically working for two while I'm eating for two? Also yes. But a girl has to take a stand at some point. Or a sit, in my case. Super pregnant women on the job aren't good for anyone.

"This place is gonna go to shit," Dee says, looking down and typing away.

That's as close as Dee gets to saying what I know she means by the color of her smoke. She thinks I'm a key player. By now, I know I am, but really believing it took my developing a sixth sense. I wish everyone could know like I know, because I'm not the only one. Dee thinks everyone still showing up is a key player, and she's right. When I go on maternity leave, things are gonna get tight.

I have no idea how long I'll be out or how we'll manage coming back with a newborn. I can't even fathom the idea at the moment. Right now, I just need to get back to the A-frame and put my cankles up.

I shoulder my bag and size up the weather outside the front door. My breath fogs the glass. The clock says it's only five in the afternoon, but at first glance, you would think it was nighttime. The lights at the Quik-N-Go across the street show how bad the rain really is. Four halogen shoeboxes are glowing like they're on fire amid all the water pouring down.

I'm driving Grant's old truck these days. He won't let me go anywhere on the Rez without it. I think it's his own way of looking after me and her. It's parked only about fifty feet away, but that's still drench territory.

I cup under my tummy. "We're gonna have to hoof it," I tell her.

As I'm taking a few breaths, arranging my hair to be fine at maximum flatness, I realize she isn't really talking back to me.

I mean, she doesn't really *talk*. She's the size of a squash and still inside me. But she's listened. Her whole tiny life, she's listened. And in her own misting way, she's made it clear she's heard me.

But this feels different. This time, her canary-yellow mist is flat. *Message not received.* And I can't help but wonder if that last little nudge I felt in the break room was some sort of farewell.

I break into a cold sweat, and every sort of worst-case scenario storms right into my brain. I have to shout something, anything to keep all these awful thoughts away, so I just yell, "Nope!"

Behind me, Dee asks, "You okay?"

No, I'm not okay. I need to figure out what's missing, to compare before to now in my brain, list them side-by-side, to see what, exactly, feels so different. My girl is... I don't know. She seems to be retreating. Where to, I have no idea. But if that place is not in me, it's not good.

"You need an umbrella?" Dee asks.

"Uh, yeah, that would be great."

I stare into my tummy. The smoke is still there, but it looks far too still. *Why didn't I benchmark the misting?* I should've taken notes, measured depths. I try to imagine how much a squash could mist, and that's when I realize I'm on the edge of a panic attack.

The facts, Caroline: she's still here, which is good, but she's not quite right.

"What's going on?" I ask her.

The smoke stills. My heart catches in my throat until the smoke mists again, very softly.

"Here you go." Dee scares the hell out of me by thrusting a beat-up old umbrella into my face. "I'm gonna need that back, though."

I mumble thanks and take it in both hands. I'm sure I look like deer in headlights. But Dee just nods and walks off, so maybe looking like a stunned deer is sort of my status quo.

I cup my little girl over my tummy. "Just hold on. Let's get home. Owen will know what to do."

I step outside and pop the umbrella. The rain batters down with the sound of a waterfall. Big fat drops feel like they'll punch right through. My first step sploshes me right into a little river running down the street. The water is cold and quick. My shoes are soaked in an instant, so I just keep walking, but everywhere I step has more water. It's beading together, glomming from the gutters and the sidewalks into rivulets that cling together into bigger streams, all of them heading out into the street, heading south, down toward the Arroyo.

"Hold on, baby!" I tell her, yelling loudly.

Above, something flutters. Bats are moving in and out of the halogens at the Quik-N-Go, probably looking for an inch of something dry just like I am.

I get to the truck and lumber myself inside, but as I try to shut the janky umbrella, something catches my eye. A deer wades its way through the cones of light and stops to stare at me. Its honey-colored head steams, and its eyes glow for just a second. Then, head down, it steps its way north, walking right down the middle of the street.

"Tough night to be out!" I call after her, buckling low and crossing the belt high.

The truck starts on the first roll of the engine, and I pull out into the night, windshield wipers flicking like maniacs, on my way back home.

4

OWEN BENNET

I'm finishing some leftovers when Caroline comes back from her shift. She closes the door, hangs up her dripping coat, scuffs off her rainboots, sets them carefully on the mat by the door, turns around, says, "Hello," and starts to cry.

I forget I'm holding a spoon, and when I stand, chicken chili dribbles all down my shirt. "What is it?" I ask, brushing off and walking over to her. "What happened?"

"Something's wrong with her," Caroline says, sitting on the couch and holding her head in her hands.

"Who?" I ask even though I know exactly who. There's only one *her* in our world at the moment.

"The baby," she says. "Something's wrong."

That chicken chili rumbles in my stomach, and I swallow that last bit back down again. Baseline pregnant Caroline is still what most might call a bit neurotic, but for the past seven months, she's been very levelheaded about things—astonishingly levelheaded, given her proclivity for spiraling. She has not cried wolf here, not once. So if she's feeling something's not right, I'm afraid something really isn't right.

"What is it? Where does it hurt?"

She wipes her eyes and stares longingly at her bump, which is more of a hill now. "No pain. She's just... quiet."

I furrow my brow. "Quiet? Honey, a lot of babies go long stretches without moving. Maybe she's asleep."

"I felt her move a couple of hours ago," she says, looking miserable.

"Well, that's good! That always makes you feel better."

She flutters her fingers over her hill, searching. "But she's changed since then."

Ah. I understand now. It's her smoke. And in matters of smoke, I become universally unqualified. I'm not all that qualified in matters of gestational health, either, but I can at least fake it enough to try and calm us both down.

I sit down next to her and put her hands in my hands. "What do you mean *quiet*?"

She's trying very hard to keep her tears respectable and not ugly because she's thinking if she starts to really cry, that means things are really wrong. She's willing this to be a blip, just a tough day. "There's less of it, her smoke. And it's not misting out like it's supposed to."

"How's it supposed to mist out?" I ask.

She wipes gently at her eyes. "She usually goes *floof.* Like a little fat cloud, you know?"

I do not know, but I nod.

She clears her throat and scrunches up her nose like she's trying will back tears the way she might a sneeze. "I just know something's not right."

"You want me to get my stethoscope? Listen to the fetal heartbeat?" I ask.

She nods.

"Alright, you stay right here."

I find I'm shaking when I pull my bag down from the chair by the door and root around inside. Shaking won't do. Caroline does not need to see shaking. I take a few deep breaths and wipe the last bits of chicken chili from my front before I come back to the den and kneel down to listen. There, underneath her heartbeat, I hear the baby's. I squeeze her hand and give her a look of reassurance. I have to tune out the ringing in my ears to get a decent heartrate.

About a hundred beats a minute—a little slow, all things considered.

"What is it?" she asks.

I pop off the stethoscope, consider what to tell and what not to tell, what might worry her unnecessarily and what might calm her down, which is what she really needs right now. Then I remember she can likely see all this written in my own smoke.

"A hundred beats a minute. A little slow. But nothing to be concerned with."

She shakes her head. "I knew it."

My knees pop as I stand. "Honey, fetal heartbeat can fluctuate. Why don't you take a hot shower, and then we can get some rest. Tomorrow, she'll be *floofing* all over the place."

That gets a small smile and a nod. I lean back and leverage her up, and she goes into the bedroom. I hear the shower hiss on.

Then I sit down myself and listen to the hammering of my own heart. I stay that way, in the dark, while she showers and dresses. I hardly move.

I tripped going down the stairs the other day. Not thinking, I missed the last step and fell onto my knees and dropped a coffee cup, which shattered all over the place. Once I was down, I waited there, quietly and carefully, while I did a rapid self-assessment. Did I tear anything? Break anything? Or did I dodge that bullet? For a few terrible moments, I felt like the pain was looking for me, but if I stayed quiet, it might pass me by. I got lucky. Just a bruised knee.

But that waiting, that's how I feel now, with my family. We tripped, and the pain is looking for us. Something terrible is swimming circles underneath us as we try to tread water. But maybe, if we're quiet, if we can get to sleep and pass the night or the week or the month, maybe it will move on.

Caroline must sense it, too, because we smile at each other as we each go about our regular bedtime routine, but we do it very slowly and don't say a word as we slide in next to each other. The rain outside is loud when we shut off the lights, but its drone offers no peace. It's too easy to imagine something out there, searching.

I'M NOT sure how or when I eventually fell asleep, but when I wake up, Caroline isn't next to me, and I hear quiet crying in the bathroom.

My stomach drops.

I glance at the clock—just past midnight. Outside, the rain continues unabated. Three crows sit in a row on the cracked concrete porch, just underneath the roofline. They're facing out, toward the storm, but when I get up, one glances back at me sidelong. None of them are Chaco, but I still get a feeling it's trying to tell me something.

Maybe *"Sorry, friend, but I think you've been found."*

I knock quietly on the door. "Honey?"

"You can come in," she says, her voice breaking.

I don't want to. I really don't want to. But I have to, of course. And I do.

She's sitting on the toilet, holding a piece of toilet paper in one hand, and on it is a thin streak of red.

"Is this blood?" she asks. "I've been staring at it so long I don't trust myself."

If only words could will a different outcome. But I've been in this business long enough to know blood is blood. And I nod.

"How long have you been in here?" I ask. "Is that the extent of the bleeding?"

"I just had to pee. Nothing bad. Normal wipe. But this came back."

I lean back on the counter and hope it doesn't look too much like I'm having to prop myself up. "Any cramping?"

She shakes her head. "I mean, I feel sick, but I think it's nervous-tummy sick."

"Any more blood in the bowl?"

She shrugs. "Maybe a little. It's not, like, red water or anything."

"So just the little bit, then."

It could be anything, just like the quieting of the mist could be anything. But soon enough, the *anything*s start to add up to *something*.

"I think we should get you to the team at ABQ General," I say. "Start the drive. Just in case."

I try to keep my voice as professional as I can, but something about me admitting we might have a problem flips a switch for her. She goes pale.

"You think I'm losing her," she says.

"I don't think anything. I just want us in the best position to face whatever comes, and that's at a fully-staffed OB floor with your doctor on call."

I help her up and glance into the bowl—maybe a faint redness, maybe not. A small drop here or there would get diluted, but unfortunately, regarding gestational bleeding, the difference between *nothing* and *a tiny bit* is significant. In other words, that little streak of red is not something that can be unsaid. It screams.

"Well, I know you're thinking *something*," she says, shrugging one of four sundresses that still fit her over her head.

What I'm thinking is how beautiful she looks, even when she's sad. It's a special kind of beauty, sad beauty, because it's linked directly to her heart, which is linked directly to our baby. And it's all there, everything I love in that look. She's sad because this really matters.

I give her a big hug, side-by-side with her tummy. "I'm thinking we're going to get to the hospital and put everyone's mind at ease. That's what you need right now. Otherwise, you're going to go into one of your spirals."

She snorts. "A little late for that. My brain feels like it's in a tornado right now."

You and me both, I think. But I don't get to say that. She gets to say that. What I need to do is get her out to the car and figure out how we're going to get to Albuquerque in this storm.

I also need to get the voice of my father out of my head because he keeps repeating, *"There's no cure for middle age,"* in that voice he had whenever his patients would ask why they can't stop gaining weight or why their back no longer cooperates or why it takes so long to rehab the knee or, in the case of lot of those Catholic Southee families he served in his day that got started with it a little late, why all of a sudden it's so hard to have kids.

"It's all a patch job after forty," he always said.

I throw on a button-up and try to sweep my mind clear. That was my father, the old-school bitter-pill-is-best type of doctor who helped a hell of a lot of people but wasn't exactly invited to a lot of weddings—or baby showers, for that matter. I am me. Time to create a new narrative.

I grab the keys, and Caroline is already at the door, her prepacked hospital birth bag in hand. I manage a smile that I hope she can feel. She packed that bag a month ago. I remember she spent most of the afternoon listing out what would go in it.

Better early than never, I guess.

As I'm helping her into her coat, a pair of headlights sweeps through the front window. Grant is likely coming in late, which is good, because he should be told what's happening. Cell service has always been spotty here, and this storm is wreaking havoc on what little coverage we have. He'll want to know where his old truck has gone too.

When I open the door, Sani Yokana is standing on the porch, hat in hand, dripping water from the faded brim onto the cracked concrete. For a moment, we all just look at each other. He seems as surprised as we are.

I turn toward Caroline. "Did you call the police?"

She shakes her head. Sani looks from me to her to the bag, and if he doesn't catch the whole of the story, he's close enough.

"I see I caught you in the middle of something," he says.

I clear my throat, "Yeah, it's not exactly a great time, Chief—"

"I'm spotting," Caroline says. "We're going to ABQ General to make sure everything is okay with the baby."

Sani nods then purses his lips. "You won't get to ABQ tonight. This damn storm kicked loose a rockslide on the 491 near Newcomb."

"Then we'll take the long way round," I say.

Sani wipes his brow. His white hair is plastered to his head, and his faded denim shirt is soaked through at the shoulders. He looks tired, looks his age. "Farmington is all washed out. We got scattered reports of two and three feet of standing water in the towns out that way."

Caroline hangs her head. I'm suddenly feeling very hot. Right out that door, behind the chief, is hundreds of miles of open desert in every direction, but this rain has somehow made it feel like we're all boxed in. And the box is damp. This is what happens when someone can neither *fight* nor *flight* their way out of a threat.

"What about the clinic?" Sani asks.

I almost dismiss the thought outright, but a look from Caroline makes me reconsider. It's definitely not ideal, but it's at least a clean hospital bed, and it will have the right monitoring equipment and a generator and satellite coverage. We would have a good shot at a consistent line of contact with her ABQ medical team.

"It's a lot better than sitting here spiraling," Caroline says in a small voice.

"Okay, CHC it is." I step outside and turn to lock the door then pause. "Sorry, Chief. What was it you're here for, anyway? It's pretty late for a coffee."

Sani watches the motionless crows under the eaves, lost in thought for a moment before he puts his hat back on. "It can wait. Come on—I'll light the way."

5

KAI BODREY

I count ten spots where the roof is dripping water onto all the shit in the shop out front, along with another three here in the back of the trading post. Turns out a rickety old shack on top of Crooked Snake Pass isn't a great place to weather out a storm. Surprise, surprise.

I shoulda known this place wouldn't hold up to a big rain. Dad was a bootlegger, not a builder. Mom could barely walk, much less make home improvements, and my idiot brother spent more time in jail than he did here. And now he's gone. And I hate how often I look out back, waiting for him to come fire up that damn truck of his.

So I guess it's not really *our* shit anymore getting soaked up front. It's *my* shit, like it or not. And I don't like it. As if abandoning me wasn't enough, Hos left me with all this trash—rusted shovels, copper wire, bunches of dirty rope, a whole mess of construction vests. Most of it was salvaged or stolen. All of it is a front for the bootleg booze. Sure, we sell a few packs of cigs here and there, the ones my worthless cousins don't smoke up, but other than that, all this shit is basically here so that on the off chance one of Sani Yokana's boys stop by—the cops that can't be bought off—it looks like we're running some sort of legitimate business.

All I ever tried to do was keep the family low profile enough that nobody got arrested and keep the books balanced enough that nobody went hungry. Hos handled all the other stuff along with a network of sleazebag distant relatives. I'm sure Hos never gave a second thought as to what would happen to all this stuff once he and I split for the promised land with Dark Sky. Why would he? He was always really good at abandoning stuff—top notch at that.

Is, I tell myself. *He is real good at abandoning stuff.*

Or maybe I'm the one that's real good at abandoning stuff. I was the one that walked back out of the portal and left him with Dark Sky, after all. And I still can't really say why except that when I saw Grant was willing to sacrifice everything for us up on Knifepoint—for me—I just didn't feel much like going anymore.

I spend a lot of sleepless nights up here, wondering who really abandoned whom. But none of it changes the fact that I'm still here. And since I'm here, I still gotta eat, and I still gotta buy gas for the generator to keep the lights on. That means I still gotta sling liquor, no matter how dirty it makes me feel, at least until I can figure out what to do with my life.

I scoot a little closer to the electric heater and try to keep my laptop from getting dripped on. I have two tabs open. One is researching grants and scholarships at UNM, while the other is researching Dark Sky, the air spirit people, who the hell this Black Bear might be, and anything else that might get me an inch closer to figuring out where the Arroyo went. And to be honest, I'm hitting mental roadblocks on both fronts. Then I lost cell coverage, which basically bricked the thing.

I shut the laptop and slide it under the coffee table. A fat drop of water splats on my head for the umpteenth time. I should patch the roof. The longer I let this place go to seed, the less it feels like where I "live" and more like a place where I "exist." And that's not good because while Grant would give me anything I asked for within his power—he'd even give me his bed in the A-frame if I asked and do something dumb and noble like sleep in his truck—I'm still not ready to tie my life up with his. A girl has to have a room of her own first where she can make that decision from a place of peace.

That's what I'll do. I'll start cleaning this dump up. I was always the one doing it back then, and even though it feels like a different world, it was only a handful of months ago. I can do it again.

I make my way out to the shop out front and shrug on one of the stolen construction vests for good measure. It falls down to midthigh, and I could fit two of myself in it, but people are always saying success starts with how you dress. I'm snickering to myself now, which I suppose is a helluva lot better than moping in front of a computer screen, when I hear a banging at the front door.

I freeze.

More banging.

"We're closed!" I yell loud enough to get heard over the rain and the genny and damn near anything else.

"Open up, Kai. I walked half a mile in this shit, and I need a drink."

I look at the leaky roof and blow out a breath, hands on hips. I recognize that voice. It's Dunk Hoskie. I guess I could call him family—kin by clan, at any rate, but on the real shallow end of the clan pool. He and a couple other distant cousins live in the backcountry, manning the stills. I don't know why they didn't go with Dark Sky. Either Hos forgot to tell 'em, or they were too drunk and slept through it. Neither would surprise me.

I wipe whatever start to a smile I had right off my face and head to the front door, check the janky peephole, which is essentially a patched-up shot from a .30, then open the door.

Dunk's standing there with a sack full of something that clinks when he lifts it. "Next shipment. They need to sit for a bit, and another cheesecloth strain wouldn't kill 'em."

He pushes past me into the store, shakes himself like a dog, and sets the sack behind the counter. "So what's been going on 'round here?" he asks, craning his neck to look back through to the house.

"Rain. That's what's going on 'round here," I say, tossing it back in that same awkward lilt. I walk behind the register and pick up the sack. In an instant, I can tell it's too light by far.

When I look up, he's watching me carefully in a way that actually makes me grateful for this crappy vest covering my chest. Dunk always looked at me too long. Hos said so. But Hos isn't here right now. And neither is Grant, which leaves me. But that's okay. 'Just me' is a place I'm pretty familiar with.

Hos always said the best defense is a good offense.

I dump the sack out onto the floor. The jars roll all over the place. Almost all of them are empty, and the ones that aren't are clearly water. Dunk and his dumbass friends can't make liquor anywhere near that clear.

"The fuck is this, Dunk?"

He's moving over to the hideaway under the shovels. We have a lot of hideaways in the store. Used to be we would move the jars from place to place—or rather, I would move them from place to place—in case somebody saw something and said something.

And right about now, I'm starting to feel really stupid for all the things I've done to keep this place putting out poison. Funny how an idiot like Dunk can really throw your failures in your face.

He pulls up a hanging slat under the shovels. Good guess—too good. I wonder if he's been up here while I'm out at Grant's. I don't check jars like I used to cause I hate everything about these goddamn jars and always have, and without my brother breathing down my neck about inventory, I happily let it slip my mind.

Dunk picks up a jar and blows some dust off and pops the top. He takes a swig and puckers up, shaking his head like he's on a teacup ride.

"That's better," he says, standing and stretching.

My mind is already way ahead of the rest of me, sizing him up and figuring out options. He's not that tall, maybe half a foot taller than me, but he's fat. My mind is funny like this, patient, allowing me to come to the decision about these garbage men in my life in my own time while preparing me for the inevitable. I wonder how many generations of Bodrey women had to suffer to give me this type of foresight.

I'll mourn for them some other time—unless you call what I'm doing right now mourning. Which there's a good argument for.

"I can't sell jars full of creek water. Get the fuck out."

"Where do you keep the money, Kai?" he asks, and I

realize he's already glassy-eyed. If any booze was in that bag of his, he drank it on the walk over.

"Are you *robbing* me?" I ask, honestly shocked.

I thought he would drink up the place, maybe, or try to get handsy. *But robbing me?* Hos ain't even been gone for a year, and already clan means nothing to this clown.

"My still needs repairing. I'm just taking some cash to get some supplies, okay?" he says, looking me up and down.

"Get out of here."

"Where's the *money*, Kai?"

He steps toward me, lurching, really, and sort of in slow motion. He's counting on the pure shock of the thing to work. He's counting on the fact that he's a man and I'm a woman. And the worst part is he's doing it like it's worked before. Maybe on other women. But other women ain't me.

I reach over the counter and grab what I've got stashed. Not a gun. I'm not trying to be one of those Diné who kill Diné. I don't want that mark. What I've got is better. A woman I've come to admire taught me all about it.

I bring out a big monkey wrench. We got no need for public restrooms here, but I like to call it my toilet wrench anyway.

He scoffs. The big man who hides in the desert brewing poison and jackin' off actually *scoffs* at the woman holding this entire operation together by tooth and nail. *Unbelievable.* But he doesn't scoff for long.

I know where to swing that would keep him from ever walking in here again, but then I would have to figure out how to get him the hell out. So I sweep slow below the ankle, taking his feet right out from under him.

Dunk falls hard on one hip and dumps a whole jar of booze all over his face. He starts screaming, but I don't think it's from the wrench hit. Trash booze in the eyes can't feel too good.

I square up like I'm at the plate. "I'm gonna let you up, Dunk. And if you make a move anywhere but out that door, I'm swinging at your head next."

He backs up, pushing himself to standing. "Dumb bitch," he says.

Ah yes. *Dumb bitch.* The last gasp of trash like him. If he only knew what I've been called in the back of this house, by my own family. Coming from him, it means nothing. And if it gives him back enough face to get him the hell out of here, all's the same.

He limps his way backward, stumbling out the door. "You gonna throw me out when a storm's comin'?" he asks, as though he wasn't one monkey wrench away from robbing me and worse.

"Storm's already here, Dunk. So you better start runnin'."

He limps into a trot. I follow him out and watch him the whole way. He takes the path down the canyon out back. His still is beyond the flat where Dark Sky held his ceremony what feels like a lifetime ago. Nothing's out there now but torrential darkness. Part of me wonders if Dunk'll actually make it. Walking canyons in rain like this isn't smart, especially at night. But I bet he does. Flash floods will kill better men and somehow let roaches like him linger.

I try to hate them, Hos and Mom and the rest of the Arroyo people who all left. Dunk, too. I try to hate all of them, but I can't. Hate has always been hard for me to come by. But I can be angry. And for now, I hold on to that anger. Even though it makes me feel dirty.

I walk out into the rain, toss off my vest, and let the water run down my hair and wash over my face. If you can't beat the storm, might as well join the storm.

When I open my eyes again, I find myself looking at a big puddle underneath the rock overhang on the hillside. A bunch of sparrows are low to the ground beneath a bush. I only see them because the kerosene glistens off water on their feathers.

"Rough night for all of us, I guess."

One of the sparrows grabs a twig and tosses it into the puddle—a decent toss, too, practiced. Its two buddies watch it, and I watch right along with them.

"What are you up to?"

Three little sparrow heads tick in time with the movement of the stick, watching it until it's square in the middle of the puddle, bobbing and twitching with the downpour. Something tugs on it. A little flash of pink in the harsh throw of the kerosene light. That's what they were waiting for: a worm going for anything dry.

The sparrow that threw the stick darts out and catches the worm and wades back out to the mud, where all three have a little picnic under the brush. With one bad swell, this rain could sweep any of those birds away in an instant, but they don't seem to care. They got a system. They know what's in the puddles.

I've been with Grant and Chaco long enough to understand some creatures aren't all they seem. And I've been Diné my whole life, which means I know the old stories. One of my favorites, when Hos would let me down to the Arroyo, was when the twins would talk about the big flood, which was this one time when Coyote stole the kids of Big Water Creature, and Big Water Creature got all pissed off and brought on this crazy flood. The twins were teaching some lesson about stealing from one another and how bad it was, but when I was a little girl, all I wanted to hear about was how all the little animals banded together to get through.

That's about as fairy-tale princess as I get. I do have a bit of that side to me, despite what people around here might think. It doesn't quite square with the whole boot-legging, toilet-wrench-swinging side, but it's true. Squir-rels and birds came together to help. Even the weasels chipped in, which I wasn't so hot on as a little kid, but these days, I can get down with a weasel if it's a helpful weasel. These animals, they looked for safety, built this little house of branches and mud, and with the help of the breath of the gods, they made it through.

"Is that what you are?" I ask the sparrows, feeling a bit loopy. "Are you messengers? Can you tell me what the hell I'm supposed to do with this place? And maybe with my life, too, while you're at it?"

The sparrow tosses another stick, but a big clap of thunder scares the crap out of me, and I scuttle back under the porch. My vest is still floating out there like a strange jellyfish in the muddy water.

I rub the water from my face. This rain is messing with me, getting me talking to wildlife.

The lights are giving me a headache, so I go inside my leaky excuse for a home and shut off all the lanterns, and once it's totally dark, I go back outside to the porch and just listen.

Without the hiss of the kerosene, I hear the water in a different way. Something is gathering out there, low and sure, like a lion rumbling up to a roar.

The sparrows are still there at that puddle. I get this crazy feeling that they're watching me.

"This rain ain't stoppin', is it?"

Now they shuffle into the bush, one after the other. Like they needed me to see them one last time. From somewhere even deeper, I hear the slow, steady crush of larger animals picking their way through the scraggy dark. I think I catch the spiraling glint of a ram's horn somewhere back there. Then others. He's leading a family of bighorn sheep down from where they usually hang out on the upper slopes and bluffs. He sees me but has no time for me.

Smart.

I think I'm gonna have to make a decision here pretty soon about how much I'm willing to stick around for this place in the face of what's coming. About how I want people to think of me once I'm gone.

I'm no medicine man. I'm no chief—no warrior or holy man or singer. I'm none of that. I'm a bootlegger's daughter, a booze slinger, and the sister of an ex-con. I'm a Bodrey. And around here, that doesn't make you much. But just now, I think I had a moment with some birds, and I did kick a scumbag out of the shop earlier, so I'm going to keep focusing on what I'm doin' instead of what I did, on what I am instead of what I was born into.

I'm no stranger to storms. I've lived in and out of storms all my life, both the kind that rain and the kind that don't. I know how hard these storms can can hit and how long they can last, and I know this rain is more than it seems. It ain't gonna stop unless someone makes it stop.

Maybe that someone is me.

6

———

CAROLINE ADAMS

We follow Sani Yokana in Grant's truck, Owen at the wheel. The chief drives a boxy SUV that looks older than me, and the stick-on light he slapped on the hood makes the whole operation look a little janky, but he's getting the job done. He paves the way and honks us through when he needs to.

The streets are a mess. It's past midnight, but cars are stalled out everywhere, and those that aren't stalled are bumper to bumper, thinking about chancing these big puddles. Actually, we've gone way past puddle territory. These are more like little lakes.

Sani rolls down his window and warns off the line of traffic trying to caulk the wagons and chance the water. His car is what Grant calls "lifted," just like Grant's truck, so we can follow through the water, slowly, big toothy tires frothing up what the rain already set boiling. I can see Sani on his radio, probably calling in help for this swamped parking lot, if there is any. People are already crawling out onto hoods and roofs.

Owen rolls down his own window and slows near a beat-up sedan that looks like it couldn't hack it over fifty miles per hour on a highway, much less pushing through three feet of standing water.

"Hop in the back!" he yells. And they do.

We roll forward then stop once more for another couple to hop in the back. It's slow going, and I can tell by the way Owen taps his thumbs that he'd like nothing more than to mow through all this like a speedboat.

"Not sure this place can take much more rain," I say.

Owen nods, but I wasn't really talking to him. I was talking to her—force of habit.

The only answer I get is more of the dreadful feeling that I'm leaking down there. It started lightly as soon as I sat down in the car, but it's harder and harder to ignore.

I fight down the nausea creeping up from my stomach to my heart. I try to focus on the craziness I see through the windows, at the water world the Rez has become. Better to dwell on the disaster outside than the one that might be happening inside.

I take a deep breath once we're clear of the washout and the tires grip dirt I can actually see.

Owen opens the back window of Grant's truck and leans back. "Where were you going?" he asks, and I know he's thinking about how he can safely offload them as soon as possible so that we can get back to our regularly scheduled trainwreck.

"CHC!" says the man, his hand a brim over his eyes against the rain. Two kids huddle next to him, all blank stares and slack faces, that way you get when you're so drenched that it doesn't matter what else falls on you.

Owen looks at me. Something rings a bell, some

manual the IHS gave us that I read during our mandatory compliance training and promptly filed away in that spot under the bed where I keep all manuals I will never read again. It's right next to my triple-highlighted nursing school textbooks and the blow-up exercise ball. It said something about the CHC being on high ground.

Owen taps the steering wheel like that might keep that vein at his temple from popping. I try not to move. If I do, I might feel more wetness. I think I'm having some traumatic core memory flashbacks because it's been a long while since anything was wet down there without me planning for it, and I'm not having a good time with it.

Sani's SUV catches ground under a slurry of water and jumps forward, but he holds it steady. Grant's truck carves through the puddle afterward. Our boy would be proud to see how well this thing holds up—then terrified to see the state his parents are in. So maybe it's best he doesn't know yet.

We pass the Quik-N-Go where the Smoker used to set up shop. The halogen lights still blaze, but the little box that served as a convenience mart is dark, and the corner is empty. Something tells me that if things had turned out different, the Smoker would be working that corner hard during the storm, hocking his jars of poultice and his rocks and his herbs, maybe doing some sort of end-of-days discount—probably finding a way to smoke too. I can almost see him there in the mirage that the rain makes, shifting this way and that under the lights.

Then we're at the CHC.

And so is everyone else, apparently.

"Ohhh, that's right," I say. "It's a storm shelter. I highlighted that."

"Why didn't I know that?" Owen asks.

"Because you've never had to. Because we've never gone swimming like this before."

Sani's honks are basically ignored at the loading zone. Cars are parked all over the place. Hazards blink. Some people emerge from the dark wearing trash bags, while others are just sopping wet. Eventually, we throw the truck into park.

Owen looks at me. "Can you walk?"

"Sure," I say, already hating how it comes out.

And Owen knows it. But he also knows how to get the thing done, like any good doctor. When it comes to matters of the body and the weird stuff that can come out of it, it's best not to dwell—best just to do what needs to be done.

He's up and out and at my door, and all of a sudden, we're walking through a downpour that feels less like rain and more like a cold shower. Owen has his entire lanky frame over me like a fretting giraffe, which is just adorable enough to get me through the parking lot and through the doors without a grimace. The little things are what do it for me.

The front room is washed in frantic spirit smoke that looks rough and brown to my eyes, like the color of a spooked desert hare. People line the waiting room and stand by the baseboard heaters, drying out, watching the storm, and helping each other where they can. Others pass bowls of food and jugs of water. A thermos of coffee drains its way around a circle of folks I recognize from Boxes. Others pass our flimsy little wax cups around, steaming with what looks like the last of the office tea.

Dee sees Owen from behind the check-in desk and stands. "Thank God. I was about to call..." Then she sees me and the way Owen is holding my arm and the way I'm holding my tummy, and her face falls. "What are *you* doing back here?" she asks.

"Baby trouble," I say, right at one of those weird moments when the buzz in the room drops, and now I'm getting a lot of looks.

"We need a bed, Dee," Owen says, low. "And we need one of the fetal monitoring sets brought in. The good one."

"Oh shit," Dee says, waggling her bedazzled nails, eyes wide. "Is this happening?"

"I certainly hope not," I say, trying to smile. It doesn't work, but I figure if I at least try to smile, that'll get me a few steps up from the weepy frown I feel creeping in.

Dee scoots around the corner as quickly as I've ever seen, already reaching for her two-way phone. "This way," she says. "It's mostly displaced families in the patient rooms on the ground floor. I'll have Nascha clear out the back corner. It's the quietest."

"Dee, I feel terrible moving a family. I can take one of the smaller ones on the second floor."

"Uh-huh," Dee says in that way I recognize from intake, when she's already decided what to do with the admit and is barely listening to whatever they have to say about it. It's a front desk skill.

"What are you even doing here?" I ask her. "It's way too late."

"I got water running down the walls in my apartment," she says. "I evacuated here, same as the rest. Didn't have anywhere to sit out front, so I just stepped behind the desk again, and here we are."

"Thank you," I say quietly.

"Uh-huh."

Nascha, one of our very best nursing assistants, is

gently but firmly ushering five people from the corner room, back left. I expect them to be annoyed, but instead, the grandmother squeezes my arm and mutters what I'm pretty sure is a little prayer as she passes, herding two little kids, who skip away.

Inside, Nascha is stripping the bed and remaking it in what looks like one impossibly fluid stroke. She lifts the mattress and wipes the headboard, clears the trays, and wipes the equipment.

"I hear we're having baby troubles," she says in that flat, slow way of hers that says she's seen it and everything else before. "Up you go."

Being on this side of things is so surreal that I just stand there, blinking for a second.

"Come on, Ms. Adams. Up you go. Don't make me lift you," she says, lips a thin smile. She's half Mexican and half Navajo and got the strongest parts of both. Her arms rival Joey's, and she's got about six inches on me. She could lift me up and set me right down even with my extra poundage. I've seen her do stuff like that before.

I kick off my shoes and step up to lie on the bed. Nascha starts undressing me, and the whole sensation is so odd that I start nervous talking. "I thought you clocked out for the week."

"I never left," she said. "Saw the way things were going at the end of the shift. Knew we were in for a long night."

The good monitor is wheeled in by another CNA, a girl named Izzy, who's always been pretty quiet but looks down at me now and smiles. She stickies up the pads while Nascha lubes my stomach with jelly. Once things are affixed, Izzy pats my hand and heads out.

"Alright," Nascha says. "The doctor should be in

shortly—oh, shit, that's right. He's already here. Hey, Dr. O, should I send in Dr. Sadler too?"

Owen and Dee have been speaking low in the corner, and he looks up. "Thanks, Nascha. I can take it from here."

Nascha puts a hand on my knee. She nods and says everything'll be okay, and for a couple of seconds after she leaves, I still believe her until I realize I say that all the time to people when I have very little confidence of *anything* being okay, much less *everything*. And Dee and Owen are talking way too low for my liking.

I clear my throat. "What is it, Owen? I'm right here. It's me we're talking about."

Owen trails off.

Dee clips her phone back onto her belt. "I'll be up front if any of y'all need me," she says.

Just the two of us now. Owen comes to the side of the bed and sits down on that little black roller stool that's in every hospital room in the country. "Sorry. Force of habit. I was asking about the status of the blood bank in case we need to do a rapid transfusion. You're B positive, right?"

I swallow. I'd been all worried about the baby. Me bleeding out wasn't a concern until now. Maybe there really is something to all that doctor opacity junk that drives the rest of us nuts.

"Yeah, '*beee positive*,'" I say, all hokey. It's an old floor joke, but I'm trying not to let my voice crack.

"You comfortable?" Owen asks.

"No."

His smile looks a lot more real than mine feels. His smoke tells me everything is a mess in his head and heart too, and he knows it, but I guess he's better at faking it. "Good," he says. "Dee tells me satellite is spotty, but we're gonna try to get the ABQ team online, see what they say we should do here."

"I'm pretty sure there's more blood."

His demeanor cracks as his smoke roils. "You want me to clean it up?" he asks.

"Maybe just take a look?"

He eases off my underwear and holds them up—a streak, that's all. I've had worse when my period lingers longer than it should. But it's still devastating.

He slips a disposable pad underneath me and covers me up again. "Fetal heartrate is still steady, if on the slow side. We've got enough blood for you if it's the beginnings of a placental abruption..." He stops himself. "Well, let's just say we've got enough. Dee says there are a ton of people here but only a handful of actual patients, so you've got good cover."

He sounds like he's talking himself down as much as trying to do the same for me.

I grab his hand, and he comes back to himself a little. "Thank you," I say.

"I'm gonna hook into the system and get the ABQ team online. I can read out vitals over the phone. We'll get through this. Can't rain forever, right?"

A streak of lightning lights up the window with a flashbulb clarity that stuns us both. The clap of thunder that follows makes me flinch in his hands.

"We'll get through this. So long as—"

The lights sputter.

I stare up at the halogen. "Don't you dare."

More sputtering.

"Don't do it," I say. "Don't you dare do it."

The lights steady.

Owen unclenches my hand. "See? We're gonna be just—"

Everything dies at once. No lights. No cameras. No action. The room is plunged into darkness, and all the machines flatline. Several terrible seconds pass with the readouts showing my worst nightmare before the backup batteries kick in and the vitals find themselves again.

The same can't be said for the lights or the computers.

"You've gotta be kidding me," Owen says, getting on his phone. "Dee? What's going on?"

"Power outage," she says flatly.

"I can see that. What about the backup generator?"

The two-way radios hiss out but catch again. "Das is working on it."

That would be Dasan, our seventy-year-old handyman. He sleeps in a boarding house set off the main building. I'm pretty sure he was here before the main building.

Owen clicks the radio off and takes a deep breath. He looks at the fetal monitor printout. We both watch tiny heartbeats for a while.

"Do you know how long these batteries last?" he asks me.

"No idea."

"Are you okay if I go see what Das is dealing with?"

I'm sort of okay with it but also sort of desperate to be with him, not alone with my quiet child and my bleeding.

But I know others often need Owen. He's mine, but he's also not mine in times like these.

"Yeah," I say. "I'm not going anywhere."

"I'll be right back," he says. "We'll get ABQ on and talk this out. Don't worry."

He and I have a moment where we're actively fooling each other and know it. We both know we're not getting

ABQ online in this storm. And we both know that even if we did, my OB squad couldn't do anything except sit and watch these numbers with me, telling me to hang in there. The bottom line is that we aren't getting out, and they aren't getting in.

It's just us here, come hell or high water.

7

OWEN BENNET

I close the door to Caroline's room and turn around to find the CHC in a surreal hush. Every device without a battery is dead. The only light is coming from the green glow of the monitoring units in the rooms and the postapocalyptic blinking of the exit signs. The backup generator really should have kicked on by now.

I click over to Das's frequency on the radio and press the call button. "Das, it's Owen. What's your status?"

The darkness hushes conversations. The people lining the halls and crowding the waiting room speak in whispers. The pop and crackle of my radio startles me.

"Out back," Das says, his rock-tumbler voice a growl over the comm. "We got a problem."

I press the phone to my chest to mute him, but sound carries, and a low murmur is already rolling down the hallway.

I click the radio back on. "Alright, stay there. I'm coming."

Everyone is looking at me, even Dee. It takes me a lot longer than I care to admit to come to the realization that they're waiting for me to say something, like I'm the one in charge. This is ridiculous because I take charge of patients, not situations or institutions. Someone like Sani should say something, but Sani is looking at me the same way.

I clear my throat and almost say, *"Nobody panic,"* but thankfully bite it off because that's a sure recipe for panic. "Everybody just sit tight. We're working on the lights."

Sani joins me as we make our way through the waiting room and through the doors to the back. I push open the exit, and the pounding sound of the rain engulfs us. Only now, standing by the delivery bay, do I realize I have no idea where the generator is.

Sani pops a small flashlight off his belt and snaps it on. I fumble with my phone to do the same. "Dasan?" I yell, surprised at how much force I have to put behind it to make myself heard over the rain.

"Over here!" he yells, and I see a bobbing flashlight.

Sani and I run across the parking lot, but by the time I duck into an outbuilding, I'm soaked all over again. Das has his headlamp on and is on his knees with a power drill, pulling five-inch-long screws from the casing of some part of a very dead-looking industrial generator.

"It's not even manual firing," he says.

"Smells like it's fried," I say, waving a hand through the smoke in the air.

"Oh, somethin's fried, alright," he says, making his creaky way to his feet again. "Here, give me a hand with this."

Together, the three of us pull the case free, exposing a mess of shimmering wires and belts inside. And dark water.

Still not entirely sure what I'm seeing, I lean in until

Sani scares the hell out of me by stomping his boot right by my head. I feel a wet splash of water that I realize isn't water even as Sani pulls me up by the back of my collar.

"You bit?" he asks.

"Bit?" I wipe at my face, and my hand comes away smeared with blood.

"You'd know it," he says.

I look at my sticky fingers. Blood but not my blood, which means—

"It's a whole shittin' nest of the little monsters," Das says.

He pans his light over the guts of the machine, and I see the shimmering wires aren't wires at all. The backup generator is a snake den. Sani smashed the one that almost got me, but a couple of others are dead as well, including bits of a bigger one that looks shredded.

"The main belt must have sucked that one in when it fired up," Das says. "We haven't fired the starter shot for this backup genny for years. No tellin' how long they've been here."

"Rattlesnakes," Sani grumbles and says something in Navajo that sounds like a warding.

Das repeats it. I'm not the warding type, but I do know that it seems like these slithering bastards show up at the worst times around here.

"Can you fix it?" I ask.

"The starter?" Das asks. "Yeah, I can fix the starter. So long as we can get rid of the snakes."

"How do you get rid of a den of rattlesnakes?" I ask.

Das holds his hands out from under the shelter and rubs them clean of grit in the downpour. "Normally, I'd say fire. But then you'd burn the whole thing up."

"There's no backup generator for the backup, is there?" I ask.

Das shakes his head.

"Yeah, let's hold off on the fire," I add.

Sani has been awfully quiet since we stepped outside. He's staring at these snakes like they might start talking to us, which isn't exactly inspiring confidence. "Doc, you got a second?" he asks.

Everything has gone so wrong so quickly that I forgot this man showed up at my front door at midnight with something on his mind.

"Yeah, sure," I say. *What else am I gonna do? Sit and slowly panic with Caroline? Get myself snakebit trying to play mechanic?*

"Can you still pull medical records in the dark?"

I think for a minute. Even if my brick of a laptop still has juice, I think we're out of luck connecting to the IHS server. "Depends," I say. "Local?"

Sani nods. "Very local."

"Active patient?"

Sani sucks at his teeth. "Not sure. Definitely a past patient."

"In that case, maybe we have the paper file in the records room." I turn to Das and hold out my hands, helpless. "Are you good with... all this... if we run down a record?"

Das shrugs. "Fine by me. I'll keep an eye on 'em. Look for another belt and a miracle."

Sani slaps my back in a way that I think is meant to be encouraging, and we both walk back into the hush of the darkened hospital. He follows me as I cut through empty offices, taking the back way so that I don't have to try to give an update I don't really have to all the people out front.

Finding the right key takes me a minute, but eventually, Sani lights the way, and we're in the records room. We've been retiring the paper records in lieu of a digital database that would bring us up to where the rest of the medical world was ten years ago, but it's slow going. I haven't been in here in quite a while. Judging by the dusty smell, nobody else has either.

"Who are we looking for?"

"A man named Oka Chalk," Sani says, his voice strangely even.

Somewhere in the back of my mind, something stirs. The name is familiar, but not in a good way. I pull out the drawers until I find CH then flip through the files. "How do I know that name?" I ask, but Sani doesn't answer. A quick glance shows he's watching me carefully.

There it is, Oka Chalk. I pull the file, which is pretty thin. Sani shines his light over my shoulder as I open it. One look at his picture brings the details back to me. He had that gaunt, windburned face but those young, haunted eyes. And I had a sleepless night drinking bourbon, with crows taking flight from that big tree out front of my apartment. A silent explosion of black, careening toward my window before cutting upward. I remember flipping through Oka Chalk's file while I waited for Ben's diagnosis, a diagnosis I already knew.

I read the file through numb lips. "Says here he was an Arroyo man who died over a decade ago. Asphyxiated on his own vomit in the back of a place called Sancho's. NNPD asked for a toxicology report that came back inconclusive."

Sani rubs at his lined face and mutters something in

Navajo that sounds a lot like that warding he and Das gave the snakes. In the low light, his distant gaze isn't too different from this faded polaroid of Oka Chalk. He takes it from my hands.

"Picture checks out with what we got at the station. I remember him. We picked him up more than a few times for public intoxication. About the only place he spent more time than the bottom of the bottle was the Wapati dime slots. But I'm gettin' old these days and thought I'd double check."

"Why?" I ask. "Next of kin come around or something? Says here there were no known relations."

Sani lets out a big breath through his nose then glances at the door like he wants to make sure we're still alone in here. "There's a man at Wapati Casino right now on a big run. He's way up. Enough that the pit boss called in people who called in people who called in me."

"The casino is open?" The thought of someone gambling during this mess is so foreign to me that I nearly laugh.

"Casino never closes," Sani says, his face grim. "And this guy cleaning up says he's Oka Chalk."

I hold up the folder, which says Oka Chalk is very much dead. "That's ridiculous. Must be a relative."

Sani lights up the polaroid again. "Same faded gold jacket and everything."

"A twin, then."

"Oka Chalk didn't have a twin. He never had anybody, as far as the Navajo Nation is aware."

I drop the file back in and slide the drawer shut. I suddenly want to be out of this room, out of this hospital, out of this rain. "I can tell you one thing, if I could come back from the dead, I sure as hell wouldn't come back to Wapati Casino and play the nickel slots."

"I get it, Doctor Bennet," Sani says. "I'm pretty sure it's not Oka Chalk—"

"*Pretty* sure? Oka Chalk is dead, Sani—"

"But all the same, I was hoping you could come in and see for yourself."

This time, I do laugh. It's a little high and a touch unhinged. "What, you want me to take his vitals?"

"Might not be a bad idea, all things considered," Sani says, shaking his head as if he can't believe what he's saying himself, which gives me hope that between the two of us, we might make up one sane person.

"But no," Sani says, taking off his hat and swiping at the brim for water long gone. "The reason I'm here is that he's asking for you."

That feeling returns, the one where I get this urge to duck low to avoid being seen. It's so strong that I almost tell Sani to quiet down, as if his words are fishing lines for something dark and deep I don't want baited.

"That's ridiculous," I whisper. "I saw Oka Chalk a few times here for blood pressure issues years and years ago. That's it. I never knew the man." I step up to Sani and speak very low and slow. "Plus, there's the fact that he's *dead,* Sani."

In the hollow light of my cell phone, the bags under his eyes look like they're getting deeper by the minute, but Sani holds my shoulder with one hand and my gaze with his own. "Well, if he didn't know you so well then, he sure knows you now. He said something about you grabbing a crow and coming on by."

I hold his gaze as long as I can, taking in the words before I drop my head. I feel like I could just drop my whole body. Very few people know that I'm one of the Circle that carries crow totems, and Oka Chalk isn't—*wasn't* one of them. He died well before I came across mine.

Seven months of sweet stability—physical and meta-physical—is getting undone in one night. A decade of love poured into an empty spot between Caroline and me—a spot we didn't even know we had until we did—where a little girl is supposed to be happily growing, is now all up in the air.

I should know better, should be acutely aware of how quickly things can change here on the Rez. Someone can be a walking, breathing sum of all their many years one moment and a slowly cooling sack of meat the next. I've seen it countless times, and I used to let it wash right off, but the more I fall in love with the future of my family, the more horrified I am with that truth.

And now, on the same day my wife is bleeding, a dead man is asking about the crow totem in my pocket.

"You got any idea what he's talking about?" Sani asks in that same flat voice.

I pinch the bridge of my nose to try to stem the headache I feel building brick by brick behind my eyes, and I say, "I just might."

8

───────

THE WALKER

I haven't forgotten the Arroyo. I refuse to forget. I know forgetting is a problem of mine, one that's getting worse. But I make sure the Arroyo is at the top of my dusty mind, even if that means I'm doing nothing but remembering those people I've lost. I recite their names, down a list, as long as I can go when I'm between escorting other souls.

I've been so many places. I am so many places right now, even as we speak. But if I even get the slightest whisper of someone I recognize from the lost Arroyo folks thrumming through the great rope on which I walk, I'm there in an instant.

I never find them. All I find is water—water everywhere.

I step into a dammed-up branch of the upper Yangtze river in China, where the birds and the beavers work tirelessly, but I swear I hear the whispering of the Yazzie boys. They smoked so much you could hear their "whisper" a mile away. But no, it's just a beaver swimming hard against the current. A quick glance tells me no human soul is around for miles.

Next is Lake Baikal in Russia. I stand on the crumbling lip of a sandstone cliff and watch a bone-white eagle dive into the deep blue. Probably, I flushed her when I came through. That happens with eagles. I have enough time to see her come up with a fat grayling fish before I get another tug. No humans are here either—might as well go.

At Loch Lomand in Scotland, where the forest meets the freshwater, I walk out of a thick grove of trees to find a red deer dipping her head for a drink. This time, the birds don't sense me, but she does. She even looks up and scans the stretch where I stand, almost seeing me.

It's always almost.

This deer is closer to the thin side than most. Her haunches quiver like it wants to bolt, but she holds her ground, and my guess is she doesn't quite know why. Some animals are drawn to me like that. I step closer, expecting her to bolt, but instead she walks farther into the water, toward a big rock where she rubs her side free of a couple ticks. They fall into the freezing water and float down like little ruby beads.

"Just cleaning yourself, huh?"

I'm still talking to the animals. If anything, it's gotten worse.

The deer flinches again, looks everywhere but at me. Which is an animal way of acknowledging me.

These creatures are getting more and more bold. *Strange.*

But I don't have time for strange. I don't have time for much of anything. If I chase a lead and it ends up a dead end, I gotta bounce. Between looking for the lost ones and my day job, holding everything together is hard. And that's even with all the mental PT I've been doing: running down the list of names of my people. Holding tightly to the memories of the things I loved in life, the things that make me Ben Dejooli, the things that keep me from becoming Black Bear, a man who held my position just long enough to go crazy. Instead of floating the river of souls to his own peace, he decided to stay—forever.

That's what I don't want. The trick is staying sharp enough to know when to walk away.

The mental PT is working, for now. But the longer I hold it together, the more I realize I can't hold it together forever. And I sure as shit need to exit stage left before I go Black Bear crazy.

When I was going through the NNPD Academy training, we were put in a simulated ops scenario in a rundown section of shipping containers on the far north of Boxes. Nothing crazy—my class of recruits was just trying to get from one end of a rusty metal yard to the other without getting spotted by the vets, who had these big flashlights and were having a great time giving us hell. I remember a couple of the big boys got spotted right away. I, on the other hand, am small and quick. This was supposed to be my thing. And it was until I tore my ankle all to hell on a tire somewhere in the dark and had to be helped out like a little limping fawn.

I rehabbed that ankle for months, but every now and then, if I turned on it wrong, I still winced, right up until the day I died. Hell, even dead, I still wince sometimes. Phantom pain is a real bitch—never really leaves you.

The point is that we're not meant to be held together forever. Every part of us is just looking for a chance to break apart, whether it's an ankle or a brain or a soul.

Keeping it together takes work. For most people, that work stops when they step through the veil, but not for me.

Nobody is meant to do what I do for long. And whenever I feel myself start to lose time, it's another reminder that, sometime soon, my time oughta be up, before I overstay my welcome and become, well, become some sort of monster.

Every time I escort a new soul, I give myself a little checklist. A little tip I learned from Caroline.

I am Ben Dejooli.

I come from Chaco Rez.

I am known to Joey.

I am known to Caroline, Owen, and Grant.

I am Death, and I am Diné both.

I will not become Black Bear.

I'm back on the soul map, pacing, listening to the stories knitting themselves into the great rope, and I hear a very distinct sound. I recognize it because it's the sound Chaco always makes when he crosses planes—a zip like someone took a razor to the thin skin of sky that envelops the living world and slit it like a pickpocket.

But Chaco is a young thing still finding his razor-sharp wings. He can't cross like he used to—not yet—which means this is something else.

I find the thread that still thrums with the sound, but it's tricky. It's there and gone, like it's a run in the stitching. As soon as I trace it with my finger, it zips away from me, and when it goes, it leaves a spot in the rope that seems loose, like a snagged bit of fabric.

I grab that spot, hold it, and open it, and I step into Wapati Casino.

For a second, I just stand there, looking around like a cab dropped me off at the wrong house. I even swipe the soul map open again and check my coordinates because Wapati isn't supposed to be here. Wapati is the Rez, and I know where all the threads that make up the Rez are. I make it my business to know because my sanity hinges on it.

But this is Wapati Casino, all right. *Figures.* If someplace in Chaco Rez were ever to come loose and get thin and weird, makes sense it would be here. On the one hand, it's the last place anyone would look for any sort of spiritual meaning. On the other, it means a lot to our people, like it or not.

And I never liked Wapati. A lot of Navajo have what you might call a difficult relationship with Rez casinos. They help fund the place. They're the reason we get the handouts we get. but they're poison too. Especially for those of us with certain proclivities to addiction, which speaking from experience running the beat, is a lot of us. I can't tell you how many times Danny and I would pass the busloads of tourists walking through the glitzy front doors of this place only to go around back and find drunk natives by the truck docks, wiped out, looking for someone to spot 'em.

Casinos aren't great places for addicts, and the Rez has a lot of addicts. People say it's gambling or booze that hit the Navajo hard, but that's only part of the story. Addiction is what happens when you're lonely, and my people are getting more and more alone in this world by the day.

This place has been muddying waters on the Rez for

generations, and now it's muddying the soul map too, which makes me like it even less.

The storm didn't spare Wapati, either. The roof is leaking in a dozen places, and buckets dot the dizzying casino carpet. But the lights are on, and the old radio hits from when I was a kid are still playing through the tinny speakers. To kill a casino takes a lot.

Wapati is usually a popular late-night spot, but only a handful of people are gaming. Most are clustered near the front doors, watching the rain. I get the sense nobody really wants to be here tonight—except for one guy sitting at a blackjack table, laughing like he owns the place.

A sparse crowd has gathered around him, and normally, I'd gloss over some drunk gambler, but Owen is in that crowd. Sani Yokana is there, too, and Sani is not a gambler, which means this is police business. Both of them look uneasy, like they're sitting through a terrible wedding speech, and the drunk is the one talking.

The man has his back to me, and I've seen that gold track jacket he's wearing before. It's an old comp this place used to give years and years ago. Funny story—this guy, Oka Chalk, way back when had a dirty jacket just like that. We called him the Gambler, and in a way, he kicked off this whole wild ride when I found him dead at Sancho's...

And it's him.

The Gambler is here. Now. I don't want to believe it, but I'd know that face anywhere. It's Oka Chalk, but it can't be because this guy is alive enough to be splashing the felt with chips and telling the dealer to hit on a twenty like a fool. He's alive enough to laugh like an idiot when he gets twenty-one and doubles a fat stack, alive enough that his booming laugh echoes through the dripping halls of this place.

"Come on, Mr. Doctor," he says, "take a seat. It is more fun to play than it is to stare."

Owen watches him like he's a lit firework. He wets his lips before he speaks. "I left all my, uh, gambling money at home, I'm afraid."

"Nonsense. You can gamble with so much more than money. Please. Sit."

Oka Chalk never talked like that. This man sounds foreign, old-timey, like the words we use are distant relatives to what he's used to. Owen glances at Sani, who shrugs his eyebrows in a why-the-hell-not way. Owen pulls out the chair and slowly sits.

"I haven't played blackjack in years," Owen says. "What are the rules? Hit on seventeen? Stay?"

The Gambler waves his words away. "Forget blackjack. I like simple. One-on-one. Let us play what you call 'war.' One card each. High card wins. Ace beats all."

The dealer is a wide-eyed Navajo woman with a neat little arrowhead-shaped name tag that reads Val. She looks at the pit boss, who looks at Sani. The only person who doesn't look visibly uncomfortable here is the Gambler.

"So," he says, "what do you stake?"

"Stake?" Owen asks. "You mean bet? Like I said, I have nothing—"

"How about that crow in your pocket?" the Gambler says.

Owen's grip on the table goes white-knuckle. I find my own hands clenching into fists.

The Gambler seems to be enjoying this. "I like totems. Have one of my own. See?" He reaches into the side pocket of his tattered jacket and pulls out a little bear cut from a jet-black rock, maybe obsidian. When he sets it down on the felt, it makes the whole room feel heavier. If I had any blood left, it would be pooling at my feet right now.

The Gambler taps the black-bear totem. "I think he would like a friend."

Owen shakes his head. "I don't gamble with my totem."

"Everything has a price," the Gambler says, cocking his head strangely, listening.

He looks over his shoulder, right at me—not around me like the birds and the squirrels, not through me like everyone I know, right at me. And he nods. It's an acknowledgement that I've been waiting for so long to feel, but it's all wrong. I always pictured finally being seen in this place as a homecoming with friends. Instead, this is some strange creature, and his eyes are lit up with madness.

Owen clears his throat. "Like I said, there's no price—"

The Gambler turns back to Owen. "I hear you are having some power troubles at the hospital, yes, Mr. Doctor?"

Sani steps up. "If you know anything about that, if you can help, you better do it, or you'll end up sleepin' this off in a cell."

The Gambler clicks his chips. "I do know. And I can help." He peers up at Owen. "If you put that crow of yours on the table," he says, grinning.

It's all there: the Gambler's jacket, the Gambler's scruff, his thin, lanky hair, the missing teeth and hollow cheeks. All there. It even has echoes of the Gambler's soul thread, but this isn't the Gambler. This thing's thread is slippery, like something brought up from the bottom of a bucket of old rainwater. When I try to grab it, it disappears like a snake down a hole.

The table goes quiet, and a change comes over Owen. I can see some terrible sorrow just being kept at bay in his thread. He looks like he's hit rock bottom for the day, maybe the month—maybe the year. Only one thing could do that —one person, actually. Something is wrong with Caroline.

I haven't felt that pull, though. The veil is quiet for now. At least on the Rez. So we've got that going for us.

I know—my bar is low these days.

"Fine," Owen says, squaring up to the Gambler in his seat and plopping his totem bag on the table. "Deal 'em."

Poor, wide-eyed Val still looks at the pit boss, who still looks at Sani. But this time, Sani defers, and eventually, the pit boss nods. The cards whir in the shuffle machine until a set are spat out.

"Face up," Owen says.

The Gambler answers with a grin.

Val deals Owen a seven. Not great for high card, but not awful.

She deals the Gambler a seven too.

"Well, well," says the Gambler, as if he expected it. "Neck to neck, you and me. Means the game goes on."

The cards whir. Owen gets a nine.

The Gambler gets a nine too.

Owen narrows his eyes. He feels it too. The Gambler is toying with him somehow, making a show of it.

"One more, face down, or the totem goes back in my pocket," Owen says.

The Gambler shrugs. Owen gets his card and takes a peek under one corner. I can see it's a ten and have to keep myself from cheering. Val pulls the Gambler's card, but the Gambler doesn't touch it. Just threads his grubby hands behind his greasy hair.

"I want the next one," he says.

A decent crowd has formed—only show in town, after all—and they all chatter. You can't pass on a card. That's not how it works. But the Gambler's face splits into that terrible grin again, and I realize he likes this moment. He wants to be showered with attention, wants all eyes on their game.

Eventually, Owen speaks up. "Doesn't seem right."

"It ain't right," Sani says with that very unamused growl I know so well from whenever I screwed up on the beat, which meant extra paperwork for him. "Take your totem back, Dr. Bennet. I'm taking this fella to the station either way."

The Gambler ignores him. He stares straight into Owen and winks. He knows Owen is in a hard spot, searching for any glimmer of hope, and I hate to think why.

"Give him his card, Val," Owen says. Then he adds, "Please."

Val deals the Gambler the next card, face down. He looks Owen in the eye as he flips it over. The table quiets. The air is heavy.

It's another nine.

Owen wins. He lets out a heavy breath through his nose that comes out more like a snort. He grabs his totem and looks at it anew then pockets it with a strange reticence. Part of me wonders if the reason he staked it is because he doesn't feel like he deserves it in the first place. I wonder if, somewhere inside, he *wanted* to lose it. And all the baggage that comes with it.

"I guess I lose," the Gambler says even though he doesn't seem at all put out. "And fair is fair."

"So help us. I don't know if maybe you work with snakes—"

"It's done," the Gambler says, slapping the felt and standing up. He turns around on the uneven heels of his taped-up shoes and strolls through the crowd.

"Wait a second," Owen says, stumbling as he stands. "Hey, you said you could help us!"

The crowd parts for the Gambler, but I don't, and when he gets to me, he pauses.

"Care to play cards, dead man?"

"Who are you?" I ask.

The crowd falls murmuring again. They can't see me, but what they can see is a crazy drifter talking to air—air that feels bad, that makes the fillings in their teeth ache.

Owen, however, knows I'm here.

The Gambler holds his hands out wide. "I am just a man who likes games of chance. But I have been around for a long, long time. And in that time, I have won many things. Boons from people. Boons from holy spirits. Even boons from gods. I keep them all up here." He taps his temple, and his chapped lips curl into a lunatic's smile.

I make it a point not to gamble with madmen.

"I'll pass."

The Gambler turns around to the table crowd. "The dead man says he will pass. Which is what they all say, dead or alive. At first." He turns back to me. "Until they find out I have something that they want bad enough to play."

He pats me on the shoulder. This crazy son of a bitch actually pats me on the shoulder. And I can *feel* it.

Then, in a blink, he's striding past me. Sani calls out to

him, and the pit boss tries to push through the crowd to catch him, but the Gambler is already walking down the banks of slot machines, slapping them as he goes, before that razor zip sounds again and he's gone.

I can't stop staring at the spot on my shoulder.

The crowd tries to follow him, nervous at first, but then, once they can't find him, the chatter rises—people trying to make sense of things that can't be made sense of. Sani even calls in to the police station, like he might actually be able to drum up a few warm bodies to track down a dead man.

Only Owen keeps his head. Only Owen thinks to reach over the table and flip that first card, the one the Gambler passed on.

When he sees it, he sits back down again.

It's the ace of spades.

The Gambler would have won, and something tells me that madman knew it.

I know I should feel like we dodged a bullet. Owen has his crow. Everyone walked away alive, after all. But somehow, I feel like we got hit right in the gut instead.

9

______

CAROLINE ADAMS

I have to pee, but I'm terrified to. Nascha left me a radio and explicit instructions to call her if I needed anything, but I've put off the peeing for too long now, so it's either swing my heft off the bed and waddle myself, or call Nascha, and by the time she gets here, she'll be changing the bedding—again.

So off I go, herd-of-turtles style. I roll the monitoring equipment alongside myself like some sort of wizard's staff, slow and steady. The floor tiles are freezing. The power's been off for over an hour now, and the dampness from the constant rain feels like it's seeping through the soaked bricks of the walls. The whole place feels like a cellar.

The backside of my hospital gown is already flapping wide open, so sitting down is easy. Getting up might be another problem, but that's a problem for future Caroline.

The monitor gives the bathroom a green glow. Without so much as a shampoo bottle to read, I'm forced to face head-on the fact that the baby's heart rate is now in the nineties more than the hundreds, on average.

She's slowing down.

I place my elbows on my belly and my head in my hands and try not to cry. "What's happening in there, baby girl?" I ask. Her smoke is so still, fog-on-a-morning-lake still. I try to stir it with my finger, but it doesn't register my presence at all.

We were getting along so well. We had a really good thing going.

I wipe my eyes and clear my throat. The pee part is done. Now comes the terrifying part. It's not a matter of if there will be blood. It's a matter of how much. I tell myself that, sort of as a way of prepping my brain to face disaster. And as I'm talking myself into a barrel of low expectations, I hear machinery clicking on. Somewhere, a motor starts to cycle, and a breath of musty air from the vent tickles my face.

"He did it," I tell her, smiling through watery eyes. "Your dad did it."

I don't know how, but I know he did. He left, saying he had to, and now here we are with the halogens stirring themselves alive. That's what Owen does. He berates himself all the way to the plate then hits a home run. He's the only one who can't see it's going to happen. And maybe that's why I love him.

The fetal monitor is beeping, which gives me a minor heart attack until I realize it's a battery warning.

"I guess I gotta plug you in," I say. That's my way of giving myself some motivation to stand up and see what's to be seen.

I grab the old-folks bar—we used to call it the Oh Shit Bar back at ABQ General—and I move to stand. My back is killing me. I can't tell what's nerves or what's cramps anymore, but the halogens are blazing now, and not seeing the blood would be impossible. It's bright red and dripping like legs of wine down the bowl.

I feel like I'm going to throw up.

I slug my way across the cold floor again. I lean back on the bed and heave my way prone. The monitor is beeping about its low battery still, but I don't care. I keep my eye on those high nineties. Now mid-nineties.

The lights are on now, but the room still feels dark. *Where did I put that phone?* It's somewhere here, probably underneath me. I'm a whale of a princess trying to sleep on a pea. I wriggle to my right to free the poor thing and finally press the button to call Nascha, and that's when I see Chaco.

He's outside the window, in the pouring rain, profile flush with the window, his eyes on me.

He's still but not statue still, just calm. In an instant, my heart rate calms as well. I know because I'm hooked up to a monitor myself. We lock eyes, my puffy wet ones to his unblinking black ones, and he dips his head just a bit. It's like a hello.

I know Grant is having some trouble coming to grips with new Chaco. Owen and Ben too. They want the things old Chaco had: a main line tapped into endless knowledge, the ability to zip to and fro, an ace in the hole.

Don't get me wrong—the love they all have for this bird runs deep and always will, especially for Grant. But this bird is different. He's new. I mean he's old, and he has flavors of the Chaco we knew, but he's also a new thing. Like when you don't see a friend for years and years, but then you meet them for dinner and come face-to-face with someone you know that is also someone you don't. But they're still your friend.

I love the way he speaks his mind. He can't hold back

because he doesn't even really know what holding back means. He just calls it like he sees it. He's like a kid in that way—pure. That makes sense because he's only been here for seven months and change. He and my baby girl, both.

Nascha comes in and knows instantly that I've been up without her. She gives me a look that would put the most crotchety Catholic school nun to shame.

"I had to go," I say, but it's lame, and she knows it.

She also knows I'm basically falling apart in every way, so her tough-girl act evaporates almost as soon as it arrives.

She really is the best.

"There's too much blood," I say, my voice getting shaky. The truth of it stings. But I've always felt that if you can get the bad truths out there in the air and let them dry for a second, that makes the next steps easier. "We need to get our options together."

Nascha looks in the bathroom, and when she comes back, her face is that same calm mask. But we've worked together for years, which is why I know she was already thinking of options. She's probably been weighing options since she saw me waddle my butt in here.

We're not a baby unit by name, but on the Rez, we get a lot of people coming in with baby problems. I've even helped delivered a few myself. We have the supplies. But babies can be delivered in bedrooms and bathrooms and alleyways if the mom is healthy and the baby is healthy. That isn't the case here, and Nascha knows it as well as I do.

"I'll talk to Dee and Dr. Sadler," she says. "Dr. Bennet is on his way back."

That perks me up a bit. I need Owen.

Nascha turns to go, but something occurs to me.

"Hey, Nascha, it's so stuffy in here. Can you crack that top window, by chance?"

She walks around the bed and pops the top window without looking. At the door again, she stops and turns. "Caroline"—I realize in this instant that she's never called me anything other than *Ms. Adams*—"we might not have the ABQ team here, but we can make this work."

"I know, Nascha," I say—it's what I have to say. I even make myself nod.

She lowers the newly blazing lights to a dimness that feels a bit like a cheap hotel. "Try to get some rest," she says as she closes the door softly behind herself.

For a minute or so, I sit in the low light of the room, listening to the rain until I hear the small sound of little talons working their way inside. The sound makes more of those darn tears start leaking, then I'm full-on crying because of how delicate he's trying to be as he flops his way onto the bed. He climbs up my tummy with claws held back, fumbling all over the place.

"Hi, Chaco," I say, unsure of the rules about touching. I've tried before, and he kind of squirmed away, like the kid he is. But not this time. I hold a finger out and feel the smooth bill of his beak slide against it. "How'd you know to come here?"

I know I won't get an answer, but I could probably figure it out. Grant sent him to check on me.

Or maybe Ben did.

Chaco slides down the top side of my tummy and lands in the crook of my arm. He's still wet from the storm, but I don't care. He's warm. And he's listening.

"I don't think I'm doing so good," I say.

He cocks his bird head, listening to me.

"She won't talk to me."

The tears are streaming again. Clearly, another one of those pregnancy superpowers is endless tears.

Chaco bobs up and down slowly. Then he leans into my stomach, right above my hip, where these old hospital gowns have glaring gaps, and he presses his little bird head to my bare skin, and we both still.

A conversation is happening. I can't make it out, and the smoke still doesn't stir, but I get the sense of some small movement very deep below in the world Chaco walks, the thin places. This is no cheap talk. This is all business, child to child.

"Can you hear her?" I ask in a whisper.

His little head is basically a pinch of black fluff that I can hardly feel against my stomach. It's a whisper of pressure at best. But the look he gives me when he stands straight again tells me enough.

Sort of.

Not great. But not a 'no,' either.

"Tell her I love her. Tell her to hold on."

Chaco hops up onto my tummy and puts his head against my chest, right above my heart.

"What are you saying?" I ask. "Are you consoling me or telling me to sack up?"

Chaco snaps his beak softly. He's talking to me, but I can't hear.

I put my finger onto his beak, and he stops. "I need help, Chaco. I need all the help I can get. They're getting a plan together here. But I think she needs more. She needs help from your side too."

The look Chaco gives me says, *Are you sure you understand what you're asking?* but I feel like I'm dripping again, and I've never meant anything in my life more than I do right now.

"We don't have a lot of time," I say.

This seems lost on the bird, the concept of time in general, which I usually find wonderfully refreshing. But this time, I'm serious, and he gets that. He hops from my arm to my nightstand like a bird on a mission, almost knocking the cheap light over as he pumps his way awkwardly to the ratty chair then flutters up to the windowsill again.

He looks down at me from the window, and I don't need to speak crow to know he's telling me to hold on— just like Owen did, just like Nascha and Dee and everyone else here did.

And I'll hold on. I know I can hold on. I've done it before, and I'll do it again.

It's her I don't know about.

10

KAI BODREY

My cell is cutting in and out, and normally, I would say that doesn't mean much 'cause it's a shitty phone, but right now, I know better. This storm is all sorts of wrong. It's sticking around more like oil than water. I can't get it off my body, off my house, out of my head.

"Grant, pick up."

The phone clicks and crackles. I do that thing where you hold it up to the ceiling like that'll work. Unsurprisingly, it doesn't. Cell service is a fickle bitch here on a good day. I'm not sure what I expected.

I toss the phone onto a stack of old jeans in a corner. Water is an inch deep on the downslope side of the shop by now, and I hear it running underneath the floorboards. Even though the night is pitch-black outside, I know the water is coming from the mesa up top, the high point. We're next in line.

All the secondhand crap I pulled together to make us look legit out front is soaked. Some of it's already floating away. The stolen construction vests I never picked off the floor are twitching. A few ratty gloves in the corner are fluttering.

Next'll come the spools of wire then the rusty old hand tools, trowels and rakes and all that. Soon enough, I'll be floating in here right along with these stale-ass packs of cigarettes. All of us'll bob along like little paper boats until I slide down the canyon with the rest of the trash.

So what, I guess I just jump ship? Give it all up? I was born here, for whatever that's worth—and not *here* as in the Rez. I mean *here* as in that damn room in the back where my mom slept until she walked out of this world. And speaking of sleeping, I slept in that room across the little strip of wood from mom's room for almost twenty years.

Just because they're empty now doesn't mean I want them washed away forever.

I slosh my way around the counter and make my way to the flashlights. I know one of those big bastards is in here somewhere, one with the pack battery. One of the shepherds traded it for more bathtub booze than anyone should ever drink. But that's my family legacy in a nutshell: trading light for darkness—open twenty-four hours a day.

There it is. I flick it on, and it blazes. At least something works.

I make my way outside. I know how this place sounds, even in heavy rain, and something out there doesn't sound right.

The water hits so hard that I'm blinking a mile a minute just to see. Standing at the edge of the canyon makes me dizzy. The rain is coming down from the sky but also pouring in from all sides of the mesa. The big flashlight makes the water look dark red, like the desert opened up its veins. I shine down into the canyon. The rain eats a lot of the light, but I can see enough to know this is exactly the kind of place every one of those flash flood PSAs told all us poor Indian kids not to get near.

I hear a rising roar in the background, low enough that I shut off the flashlight and really listen to make sure my ears aren't playing tricks on me.

Rain finds its way into my poncho somehow, through some rip or just blunt force, like typical male rain would, but still I stay. A rustling from behind snaps me out of this weird hypnotic daze. A family of weasels emerges from the thick brush, their fur speckled brown. They look at me carefully, their ghostly eyes somehow picking up a pinch of light.

I didn't even know we had weasels in this country, but a lot of things that live high up are getting flushed out by the rain. The lead weasel stands on his back legs, balances on his long dark tail and flops his paws at me.

"What?" I ask.

Another stands, baring his razor fine teeth, which is a lot less cute.

"You really gonna come at me?" I ask, but as I'm backing up, I realize he has something in his mouth.

The weasels flop back to the ground one by one, and the toothy guy spits out a pebble. They look at me for another minute with their ghost eyes then turn one by one and slink down the path again. I creep up to the pebble they left behind and tap it with my toe. When it doesn't do anything weird on me, I pick it up. It's flat and wet and very much an ordinary pebble, not counting that a weasel gave it to me. Still, I know when the spirit world is trying to tell me something, even if I have no idea what it may be, so I pocket the pebble and keep listening.

I know Ben Dejooli is looking for the Arroyo, using his powers to cast a net as far as he can. I know Joey is as well, with his crow totem and all that can do. Everyone is looking far and wide. But I can't shake this feeling that the people we've lost are close, much closer than everyone thinks. And the way I keep getting all these weird signs from the animals makes me think the Rez is trying to tell me so.

I shake myself off like a dog and start back toward the trading post, but my conscience gets the best of me, and I turn back around. For the hell of it, I flash the *report in* pattern Hos always used to get a status update from Dunk's moonshine cabin on the far side of the valley. He should still be able to see it. It's the only blinking light for miles. Dunk is half as smart as a bag of rocks, and he tried to assault me, and I hate myself for giving in to whatever told me to make sure he's alive, but I already did it.

I wait.

I flash the pattern again. *C'mon, dumbass.*

Dunk's the kind of guy that needs to be told face-to-face when to evacuate. And even then, it probably won't work.

I flash the pattern once more, and this time, I catch a little reflection across the way, right about where his cabin is—or should be. What the light catches looks like a piece of metal siding surfing whitewater rapids, the type of shit you'd see floating down a big river like the Rio Grande.

More corrugated metal gets tossed around. I can't be sure, but I think I see some color, like a cheap lawn chair or something.

I can count the number of manmade structures out

here on one hand. My guess is that's Dunk's cabin. And if Dunk and his dumbass friends didn't get out of this valley about an hour ago, they're probably gone.

I know I should care, but it's hard. I got bigger issues. If Dunk got washed out, that means the whole upper plateau is washed out. That's how these canyons work. They're like dominos. One spills over into the next, along down the line, and every time one of them busts, it rains hell down on the next one with double the strength.

Everything in this country is connected: earth, sky, water, storm. When one part gets beat up, we'd better expect to feel it somewhere else. And at the end of it all, the last domino in the line is the Arroyo.

That sound I hear is dominos falling.

The trading post is done for. We're on the downslope of the mesa. The canyon can't eat all the water, and when it gets full, the quickest exit is right through the shop and on down the dirt road to town. Just ask the weasels—they know the way.

I think my time on this shithole outpost at the end of the world is done. But since everything will be gone if morning ever comes, I need to do some things first.

My brother is a disappointment in many ways, but thug tendencies aside, he did manage to get himself a pretty wicked truck. I'm not your stereotypical truck girl by any means, but the way Grant loves his is so damn adorable that it sort of rubbed off on me. So yeah, I know Hos has a nice truck. I mean, it's almost certainly stolen. If I was to take it off Navajo land, I'd probably get chucked into jail at the first red light. And Grant tells me that Hos beat it to hell during my dark time, when all I felt was a need to get out of this place and leave the gas stove on with a candle burning. But I'm *kinda sorta* on the other side of that, and Grant is really good at fixing up trucks. So the only net positive thing we ended up with after that whole disaster on Knifepoint is the souped-up monster parked out front, on its ninth and most powerful life.

It's an extended bed because of course it is. That means I can fit a lot of flood-fighting shit in there.

I climb into the cab and fire up the engine, and the way it roars against the rain makes me smile. The lights rip out into the rainy darkness like they're personally insulted by it. When I throw it into reverse, it washes the whole desert in red.

Trucks like this are crutches for small dicks. Everyone knows that. But now that I'm here behind the wheel of this thing, I kinda get the appeal—the way it switches you from defense to offense with the turn of a key.

I back right up to the front porch and hop out. Water has already swollen the front door so that I have to shoulder it open, and I think something cracks in the frame, but I don't care anymore. I wade in and start grabbing things: shovels, flashlights, canvas sacks for sand, ponchos, flares, rubber boots, and the last of the energy drinks. I make trip after trip, chucking anything that might have a use down at the Arroyo into the bed of the truck, things for bailing out and things for drying out, because I think we're going to need both.

I dig through all the vests to find the loose floorboard, but it's already underneath three inches of standing water, and I can't pull it up. I stomp it and start cussing, and before I know it, I'm crying and not really sure why except that I don't want any of that dirty booze money, but without it, I literally don't have a dollar to my name.

I walk away and come back. I walk away again and come back again.

Hos's voice is coming from somewhere in the back of my brain: *"Don't be stupid. Dirty money spends. It ain't gonna do anyone a damn bit of good floating away."*

And now, I'm talking back. "Easy for you to say. You never gave a shit about how many lives that poison destroyed. Never gave a shit about anyone but yourself."

"That's not true. I cared about you."

I stomp some more, knowing it's doing nothing but making a mess, but I gotta do something. "Shut up! Don't you dare start with that shit. Just 'cause you're gone doesn't mean I have to forgive you."

I hate that what I'm remembering less and less was the way he groomed me into a criminal enterprise specifically designed to prey on our own people, and what I'm remembering more and more is the way he was the only one that brought home food after Dad died, the only one that paid for Mom's pain pills, the only one that tried to find a way out of this mess our family found itself in. It was the wrong way, but it was a way.

I hate that I keep remembering how he wanted us side by side. The plan was to leave together, but then I came to my senses.

"You asshole," I say, but I can barely hear my own voice and somehow end up sitting on the floor with my boots crossed in what they all used to call Indian style, not even caring about the water because I can't get any more soaked, and I've got my head in my hands.

"Take the money. Think of it as an asshole tax. For putting up with me."

I push myself to standing and stomp my way back to the front, where I grab a crowbar from behind the counter. I stomp back to the floorboard and stand wide, raise the tool up wrath-of-God style, and start hacking. After the fourth smash, it catches in the slot between boards. I flip to the other side and pull. The board comes up with a splinter and a pop. The space is already full of water, but the box is in there. I pull it out and shake it off and take it outside. Before I can think not to, I toss it into the passenger's seat next to the little canvas bag that contains all my own worldly possessions, mostly the handful of outfits I can still stand and my computer. Packing up took me all of ten minutes.

I do one last wade around. I think I can push the generator across the floor and into the bed of the truck as well. I bet Grant could tape together some sort of jury-rigged water pump. A good genny is a terrible thing to waste.

That means it's time to do what I've been dreading.

I sniff and wipe my eyes, which basically does nothing but shift water around on my face, then I flick the generator off. The little lights I ran from an extension cord all die a second later, and with the lanterns already off, the whole building goes truly black.

You can hate a place but still find it hard to walk away from. Some memories are so strong they haunt the halls of our lives like ghosts. I feel like parts of my spirit are still walking around in there, same with Mom and Hos.

But the water doesn't care about memories, good or bad. The water doesn't care about ghosts. And the water is coming.

I push the generator across the floor. It rolls easily, cutting a wake across the porch until I thunk it down onto the truck bed. The cab scrapes, and the shocks squeak, but I don't hear anything break.

I throw a tarp over it all and slam the tailgate closed. Once I'm behind the wheel, I try not to look at the gaping hole that our little front door has become, but I have to say goodbye, if only with my eyes. This trading post has been here for generations. And up until about yesterday, I thought it would stand until the sky fell down around it, like just because it's always been here means it always will. But the truth is, standing ain't ever guaranteed. Standing requires fighting. It requires work.

I'm all that's left of my family, and the trading post isn't where I want to make my stand. The floodwater is coming for the Arroyo, and the Arroyo has things actually worth saving.

11

GRANT ROMER

As soon as I hear the *whoosh pop* of Dad comin' back to the Arroyo, I push myself off the wall underneath the twins' lean-to. I've been helpin' set up a perimeter of sandbags to keep their double-wide from drowning and my mind from spinnin' out after what Chaco told me about Mom—and what Dad didn't tell me about Mom.

My bird has been perched between the twins, starin' at the fire along with 'em. He looks up at me on the move and says, "Don't be angry. He's not steady."

"Don't tell me what to feel," I shoot back, which probably would have gotten a switchblade reply from the old Chaco, but this new one doesn't really know how I can sometimes pop off, and he looks a little hurt, which makes me feel even more angry.

Chaco's right, though. Dad landed a little unsteady in the soupy dirt outside the twins' trailer, and he's still getting his feet under himself when he sees me. But I break right in.

"What do you mean, she's bleeding? She's in the damn

hospital? And I have to hear this from Chaco? Are we gonna lose the baby? Is she...?" I find my throat all gummed up and betraying me. "Are we gonna lose her?"

I'm right up in his face, and seeing how fallen it is is killing me—how *sad*. Dad doesn't get sad. He gets a little lost every now and then, and sometimes he gets as cynical as hell, but he doesn't get *sad*. And now I'm pressin' him for some dumb reason, and he's lettin' me because he knows I'm angry.

Then he grabs me and holds me in a hug because he knows I'm not angry at him, not really. What I'm angry at is something we can't push back against. What I'm angry at is just about everythin' that's hit me for basically a year straight. Matter of fact, the only thing I *ain't* angry at in this whole Rez at this moment is the little girl Mom is growing, and now I'm told the world is doing its best to ruin that too.

I'm bigger than Dad, but Dad's taller than me, so when he's half hugging, half crushin' me to him, I'm against his chest, hat tipped up against one of his dress shirts, which is all soaked to shit—cold cotton that's warm beneath. I have a hazy memory of hugging him on a bloody street in Santa Fe, which I know should scare me, but right now, it's reminding me that we're both still alive, him and me. We're still breathing. So whatever is going on with Mom, she's got a shot. She always will as long as we're still breathing.

I step back, and the rain pours between us. Chaco flutters out and lands on me. He looks at me warily, and when he sees the anger has left me, he steps in under my hat and presses against my neck.

"Is it bad?" I ask Dad.

He brushes cold rainwater up through what's left of

his hair, which tells me all I really need to know. "It's not good."

Joey steps in, "The baby? Or Caroline?"

Dad nods to all the above. "She's a geriatric pregnancy, and she's bleeding. The baby's heart rate is slowing. She should be on a high-risk OB floor in Albuquerque, but..." He holds out his hands palms up to the rain, and for a moment, he looks a bit like a soaked scarecrow when he yells, "But clearly that's not happening!"

Something else is going on here, more than Mom and the baby. Dad looks spooked.

"We should speak near the fire," Joey says, scanning the darkness with narrowed eyes. "Careful yelling into the rain in the dark. Something might answer."

We long since stopped trying to convince the twins to leave their fire. Instead, we built a makeshift hogan in the backyard. It's nothing fancy, just a bunch of stretched tarps crisscrossing from the double-wide to the fence line. It doesn't keep all the rain out, doesn't even really keep most of it out, but it keeps enough out that the firepit still burns. That's good because when it was guttering earlier, I swear I heard another thing fall into the canyon out there in the dark.

Maria stands and offers Dad her seat, saying she's going to go put on some more tea.

Dad shakes his head. "I only came for a minute. I have to get back to her soon. There's not much I can do for her, medically speaking, but I can be there for her. So she doesn't have to go through this alone."

Tsosi holds out his gnarled fingers and slowly lowers his hand, speaking slowly. Joey translates.

"He says you came here for a reason. And you should sit. Get tea. He says you look weak."

Dad wrings his hands, but he sits. "Can't argue with that," he mutters. "I... I had a strange encounter. I thought maybe the twins or Joey might be able to... shed some light on it."

Tsasa holds up a finger to pause then grabs the biggest log at his side. He tosses it onto the fire and waits—finger up to hold the quiet—until he starts to see the flames lap up the wood. Then he nods at Dad to continue.

"The power went out at the hospital. Did Chaco tell you that?" Dad asks.

I nod. I've told them what Chaco told me: that Mom needs help, that she asked for the kind of help Tsosi and Tsasa might give, the kind the Arroyo might give.

If that's what Dad is here to ask, then he's gonna get the same answer they gave me. The strength the twins have is tied to the Arroyo, and the Arroyo is slipping away. It's all they can do just to keep the fire burning.

"It was snakes," Dad says. "A den of rattlesnakes infested the backup generator, ripped up the belts and gears."

Tsosi throws some sage into the fire. He's been keeping a stash dry against his body.

"Needless to say, we don't exactly have the people or the tools at the CHC to get rid of a den of rattlesnakes without setting fire to the whole generator, so we're kind of at the end of our rope, when Sani Yokana says there's this guy at Wapati Casino asking for me. About my crow totem. A man you may know." Dad puts his hands on his knees like he's bracing himself for what he's about to say. "Oka Chalk."

The twins look at each other. A sideways gust of wind flaps the canvas at the far end by the fence, and the fire suddenly pops with enough force that I nearly jump.

"The Gambler is dead," Joey says, crossing his arms. "The names of the dead should not be spoken here."

"Well, he didn't look so dead sitting on a pile of chips up at Wapati. And he didn't look so dead when he asked me to gamble against him. My totem for turning the lights back on at the CHC."

The thought of gambling a turquoise crow—one of a handful in the known world—makes me sick. "But you didn't, right?" I ask. "You phased out here, so you didn't."

Owen looks into the fire.

"You *did*?"

This is Owen Bennet we're talkin' about here—Mr. Scientific Method. He still looks shocked every time he uses his crow. I'm pretty sure he gets close to convincing himself the thin place and what's beyond it are all somethin' he dreamed up, right up until the time he has to go there again. And again.

If Dad is getting this reckless, things with Mom are real bad. Chaco said when he tried to listen for the baby, he could barely hear her, like she was hiding.

"I gambled it. And I won. And then the lights came back on at the clinic. Our handyman tells me the snakes just... left. One by one, out into the rain. He got in there with a new belt and replaced the plugs or whatever, and it fired right up."

The rain howls through the lull that falls over us.

"You think the Gambler did it?" I ask, and I can hear the disbelief in my own voice.

Dad rubs his face with the crook of his elbow. "I don't know. He was talking about having boons from gods and all sorts of nonsense, but he had a totem of his own." Owen glances over at Chaco. "A black bear."

Chaco chirrups low. He doesn't like that one bit, and I

don't blame him. He burned up in the sky over a black-bear totem. These floodwaters are dredging up all sorts of shit.

"My question is, if it isn't Oka Ch... If it isn't the Gambler, then who is it? And how did they turn the lights on at my clinic?"

I see another question on his mind too, one he and I and all of us are helpless to hide but too afraid to ask, which is *Can he help Caroline?*

Chaco says to me, "This Gambler, he is the reason the child hides."

Dad sees me look the bird's way and speaks up. "What's Chaco saying?" he asks, and the desperation in his voice is painful.

Chaco speaks to me, urgently now. "Tell Owen and everyone else to stay away from this Gambler, no matter what he offers."

In the short time we've had with my bird returned to us, I don't think I've ever heard him as sure as he is now. I feel like he's channeling the old Chaco, the one who knows his shit. That terrifies me.

I clear my throat. "When Chaco went to Mom, he listened for the little girl. He could barely hear her. He said she was hiding."

"She's not *hiding*," Dad says. "She's *dying*. And she could take Caroline with her."

I stand and walk over to him. He doesn't even look up, only into the fire, lost, as water drips from his nose.

"Hey," I say, snapping at him with one hand. "Don't be like this. Not you. You're supposed to be the one that grounds this crew, the one that can deal with this medical shit."

"I thought so too," he says, his eyes swimming. "Until it happened to me."

Chaco is there again, a soft weight on my shoulder, which settles me a bit. It's like finding a river stone in your pocket, which was the point. The bird can sense when I'm about to push too far.

Maria comes back with a mug of tea that steams like a locomotive in the damp cold of the late night. She presses it into Dad's hands in that way she has that don't take no for an answer. He sips and closes his eyes, seeming grateful to have somethin' to do with his hands.

Joey speaks up from where he stands just at the edge of the rain. He's been watchin' the dark beyond, but I know he's been listenin' as well. Joey can be a lot of places at once.

"The Diné believe no child is safe until they laugh," he says.

The elder twins nod. Tsosi speaks a string of pretty difficult Navajo I only catch half of, but Joey translates.

"He says it is known that to be born is a battle. But children understand this, and they have strength of their own for it. So take heart. When a child first laughs, it is their way of saying the battle is won."

The tea seems to be helping. Dad's hands have stopped shaking, at least. I wish I could say the same.

"Maria?" I ask. "Any chance you got some more of that brew in there somewhere?"

She looks at me with that unspoken understanding that makes me feel at home here and heads in again. I see her fussing with the pot through the bright windows. All around us is dark, sheeting rain, but these windows and this fire stand like the last house in the world.

"The Gambler is known to our people," Tsasa says.

"He is not who he seems. He only borrows that face. But he borrows it for a reason. He has gambled for many lifetimes of men. And he always wins. Do not stake with him lightly."

Owen looks at me, waiting. Joey lets me lead with this one, which I appreciate.

"I know what you're thinking, Dad. You're looking for anything, any tiny tree root you can grab while we're all falling down the damn mountain. But this ain't it. Chaco says stay away. The twins say this Gambler always wins."

Dad sips the tea and stares into nothing. "But I won," he says.

"He let you," Joey says. "Now, you must consider why he would do that."

Dad mulls this over. "And what about the black-bear totem?"

Joey looks at the elder twins, who pause their own side conversation to speak. "He could be another Chief of Black Bear, like Dark Sky. Or perhaps he is the Athabascan himself. Either way, the Gambler, the rain, the child-in-hiding—these things are connected," Tsosi says.

"We will look to the story of the people," Tsasa adds.

They fall back into their quiet muttering. I can't make it out—it seems like a language all its own, both Diné and also that secret language of twins. I imagine they're pulling things up from way back in the stacks of their minds, correcting each other, retelling tales told to them by people long dead who heard them told by people even more dead.

Joey puts a hand on Dad's arm. "They do not yet know the significance of the black-bear totem. The twins need time to think on things."

Dad stands as Joey's hand falls from him. "Time, huh? Well, that's a problem, then, because we're fresh out."

He sets his cup carefully at the edge of the firepit and warms his hands for a moment before he says, "I'm going back to the hospital. I'll prepare however I can."

"I'll come too," I say.

He shakes his head. "Even if you could get there, you'd just be standing around waiting, listening to beeps that drive you crazy. I'll deal with the medical realities. You're better at the... other realities than me. I think you can help best here."

I grip his hand and pull him into a hug, but Joey beats me to it. Even Chaco flutters in and lands on his shoulder. He's soaked through, shuddering, and feels as thin as I've ever seen him. This rain that chips away at the Rez is chippin' away at his soul too. I know because it's startin' to get through to mine as well.

Dad takes in a big breath then steps softly away into the rain. He gives me one last look. "You're not a kid anymore, Grant, so I you deserve the white-coat truth, face-to-face. The outlook both for your mother and for the baby is grim. She needs all the help she can get, and fast."

In the time it takes for his words to get flattened by the rain between us, he reaches into his pocket and pops out of existence.

12

THE WALKER

I've spent some time trying to trace back this Gambler's thread, but it's damn near impossible. He flits in and out of the living world and the thin place. He even walks beyond the veil. Following him on the soul map is like trying to track a rabbit in a blizzard. His thread will break entirely then pick up its loopy stitching somewhere else down the rope.

He took Oka Chalk's look on purpose. I know he feels connected to Wapati, if for no other reason than he smells the games like a shark smells blood in the water. So Wapati is where I wait for him. I can already sense him close. It's only a matter of time until he sidles up to the tables again.

Staying present here in the casino is hard. I have to split my mind in hundreds of ways to allow for it while still doing the day job the veil requires. It's risky, especially given my history. But I'll be damned if I let this thing just waltz all over my Rez without keeping at least some part of my attention on it.

Wapati opened its conference rooms and hallways to

refugees from the storm, and a lot of them are there. People are soaked head to toe, carrying trash bags full of whatever they could grab. They weave in and out of tables and chairs, drunk with exhaustion, throwing sleeping bags into corners or just collapsing under coats. More than a few of them sit at the slots, smoking cigarettes and mindlessly spinning the wheels.

It's a depressing scene, even for a fallout shelter. Something about all the dinging bells and glitter and lights flashing on people who live in the rundown IHS apartments across the tracks or in the rough outer neighborhoods like Boxes—it grates on me. Tourists can lose more in a couple hands of blackjack here than these folks will make in a week.

The Gambler walks among them. He's been in and out. I see him moving through the makeshift cots and sad forts made of conference chairs. He walks like he's on a campaign trail. A few people talk to him, and whatever answers he gives look canned and grinned through. He counts these displaced folks like he's counting his chips at the table.

Someone hits a decent win on the slots behind me, and the sound snaps the Gambler's head around like a hungry cat hearing a can opener. His eyes grow wide, and he licks his lips. Seeing this kind of inhuman hunger on the face of Oka Chalk is strange. I don't know how he's done it. Maybe he scratched out some remnant of Oka Chalk's soul from where it's supposed to be sewn up in the great rope. Maybe he knows some sort of magic I don't. Either way, the poor old man's skin isn't meant for this creature. It doesn't fit quite right. He looks stretched thin.

The Gambler walks toward the casino floor, where the lights still blaze and the machines still ding and ring, leaving the homeless to their corners. The Rez council might let a power outage hit the old CHC, but they'd never let it hit this place. I bet Wapati has backups for days.

He sees me, which seems very strange, but he does, and he walks up to me. I tense, not quite sure what I'm waiting for. He pauses and smiles that thin smile. Opening his arms wide, he looks up at the big display hanging in the main room: a trio of warriors frozen midride, thundering after a glittering bull elk. Wapati is Cree for elk. I always wondered why a Navajo reservation would name their casino after a Cree word. Danny Ninepoint, in his typical gruff way, said probably because nobody cares what it's called, only what it is.

What the Gambler sees up there—the glittering hunt —is the kind of shit that hasn't happened here for a hundred years, the idealized textbook shit, the stuff only a handful of Navajo here have any direct memory of.

It's the way-back version of us, and the Gambler loves it. Which tells me maybe he's from the way back himself.

I follow him as he threads across the casino floor. He doesn't seem to like what he sees at the tables: mostly uneasy people, no real action, dealers checking their watches, people flinching at the thunder.

He makes a turn toward the slots. "Join me," he says. "I can teach you to walk the worlds with your own two feet. I know the ways."

I keep pace directly behind him, an old cop trick to make folks nervous. "You count those poor people soaking the hallways and floors back there like you own them."

The Gambler runs his hands along the little swivel chairs in front of each slot machine like he's walking through a field of flowers. "That is because I do," he says simply. "They are mine."

Just when I'm about to get a lot more into that, he stops, and I run into him. It's been a while since I ran into anyone with weight. But not this guy—he's solid. If he really is dead, the veil has forgotten him somehow. I have a kneejerk reaction to apologize, and it comes out before I can bite it back.

The Gambler says, "I remember running into many things like that. When you get your body back in the living world, you are like a child. But you would be surprised how fast it comes back."

"What comes back?"

He holds his hands out. "Life, of course. And I can make you feel alive again."

I stare at him, trying to piece that one together until he shoos me back. My mind is racing, not computing, so I back up. He follows me until he finds the chair he's looking for. He slaps the worn red pleather in front of a run-of-the-mill slot machine. Nothing special—just three spinning wheels.

"She is the one," he says. "Sit down, Walker. We will talk."

I can do nothing but sit. My chair feels like an echo of a chair, but his squeaks. When he moves, the pleather crunches. That's real.

He props one ratty foot up on the machine. He's wearing taped-up old sneakers with about a thousand miles on them. He checks his pockets, pulling them inside out, then pats his breast pocket and stops. He pops open the cheap burnished button on the ancient gold comp jacket and pulls out a nickel. "We are in luck," he says.

"You had twenty grand in chips on the table last night," I say.

"Hmm?" he asks, distracted. "Twenty grand?" He says it like he doesn't know what it means. He purses his chapped lips and seems to think for a moment before waving me off. Either he forgot, or he doesn't care.

"Watch this," he says. He puts the nickel in, flutters his fingers, and pulls the arm of the slot machine.

The symbols spin by, some bullshit Indian stuff: arrowheads, tipis, buffalo, tomahawks.

He plucks out that bear totem again, sets it on the little lip above the buttons, and gives it a spin too. It flips onto its back and flashes like black glass in the lights.

The symbols lock one reel at a time, but I already know what's gonna happen.

Jackpot.

It's a nickel jackpot, but it's still a jackpot: twenty-five hundred bucks.

The Gambler slaps the machine on its side like an old friend. "Every time," he says. "When I gamble, I win."

I think of the people down the escalator, the people he said he won—people from Boxes, from the station apartments across the tracks. He won them, just like he won the people from the Arroyo. I don't know how, but I know it's true. These people are under his power now.

The Gambler watches the coins spill like water onto the carpet, and when he looks up again, I can see he knows I know.

He is Black Bear, the Athabascan, the madman that was the Walker. He's the one who died but never left.

"What were you expecting?" he asks, puffing up the lapels of his grungy jacket and nodding at the frozen display of the hunt hanging above us. "A painted warrior in a loincloth? Or maybe a farmer? Corn in both hands?" He laughs, and the sound clicks in his throat.

"You brought the rain. This is you," I say. "All of this mess is because of you."

He lets the coins from the machine spill out over his hands like water. "No. No, no." He nods downstairs before shaking his head in disgust. "This did not happen on my watch, Walker. I did not put our people in this place."

I'm not about to get lectured on the plight of our people by a filthy thief. I stand and grab him. I pick him up from his seat and pull him up to eye level. "You stole them. You stole the people of the Arroyo."

He smiles up at me. "That is where you are wrong. I did not *steal* them. I *won* them."

I think about shaking him, think about slamming my fist into him like I told myself I'd do if I ever found this son of a bitch. But he found me. And slamming my fist into people never got me anything but trouble back when I was alive—and the few times I've done it dead. Plus, I think he's telling the truth about winning. Something else is going on here. My guess is if I want to get anything out of him, it's gonna take more than a fist.

I drop him back into his seat, and he spins around and around like a child, splashing coins each time he comes full circle.

"What do you mean you won them?" I ask.

The Gambler holds out a finger against the machine and stops the chair from spinning. "I walk this... What do you call it? This *reservation*? I walk this patch of desert that has been *reserved* for us by strangers—foreign people who know nothing of what we were. And I find many, many people who want out."

He stands and brushes himself off then drags his feet

through the coins. "Many of them will do anything for a chance at something better, something more. They stake themselves, and I take them. But really, it is they who are winning in the end because they will help build our new land, our new world. One where *we* do the reserving."

He walks right under a leaky spot in the roof and lets a thin stream of falling crud water pour over his head for a second, barking a lunatic laugh before stepping out and shaking like a dog. "*Tó Neinilii*, now... He likes to gamble," he says, smoothing wet wisps of yellowed hair over his bony skull. "He loses many times. But he cannot stay away from my games."

Tó Neinilii is the rain god. The elder twins always said when a big rain came, it was because Tó Neinilii lost a bet.

"You good friends with the rain god?" I ask, trying to keep my head.

"I would not say *good*. No. We are gambling friends. Even though I take so, so much from him." He holds up a hand to the thin stream. "So much it sometimes overflows."

He walks up to me, dripping wet and not caring. He comes up to my shoulder, but when he touches me with a finger to the chest, the real force behind it pushes me back a step. "Is that why you are here, Walker? Do you want to stake something as well? I have many boons to win, some that may be of great interest to you. After all, I once stood where you now stand, before I turned the tables."

He's reading me, looking for tells. It's an old gambler's trick, but it's also a cop trick. And I play my cards close to my chest.

"Where are they?" I ask. "The Arroyo people you think you own."

He cocks an eyebrow. I want to know about the

Arroyo. Of course I do. But I think he also knows what I'm not telling him, that I want to know how he does what he does, how he can walk worlds and touch people and feel things.

He smiles a flakey, chapped smile that I'm pretty sure is nothing like the real Oka Chalk's smile.

"The Arroyo was yesterday's game. I'm here for the rest of the... *reservation*." He says the word like it's dirt on his tongue. "The people here cry out. I am a just god. I will give them their peace."

"Wait a second. You're a god?"

He turns and walks down the hall, feeling out the slots machines again. "Finally, you understand."

Now, I'm not gonna stand here and tell anybody what can and can't exist in this world. Hell, I'm finding new things every day, and in these parts, a lot of them track back to the Diné Bahane', our origin story. Gods, holy people, spirits, ghosts—we got it all. But I'm wracking my brain, and as far as I can remember, none of them come looking like this thing in front of me.

"I don't buy it."

This stills him, and he turns slowly. "You do not *buy* it?" He shakes his head and looks toward some invisible sky. "He says he does not buy it. *Him*."

He slams a hand against the side of another slot machine, and the wheels spin until each clicks in quick succession to hit another jackpot. Coins rain down, and he spreads them with his filthy shoes. "If you could speak to them, our people would tell you of what I have won." He picks up a Wapati coin and flicks it back toward the escalators, where more and more refugees are pouring inside to escape the flood. "I have won their hearts. I have won their souls. Everywhere it rains is mine. And when the flood comes, I will take my winnings to their new home."

"Is that why you came here?" I ask. "To steal from people when they're down? What do you really want?"

He looks like what he *wants* is to slap me. I want him to slap me, too, because I'm about ready to see how far this newfound connection between us goes. I clench my fists, but he holds off, and so do I. For now.

"A new world needs new people," he says.

By now, we've got a bit of a crowd. The coins are spilling everywhere, but he's eying the people with open hunger, not the money.

"People never change," he says. "They will gamble even when they almost always lose. Do you know why? Because they will do anything for a chance to see what it is like on my side of the sky."

He pushes his finger into my chest again, and I swat at it, but this time, my hand passes through. I try to push him, but I can't feel him. Neat trick, that. To be real when and where you want. I wonder who—or what—he had to do to win that power. He looks at my grasping hand with pity. I know he can see how sick with envy I am.

The Gambler tosses the black bear into the air and catches it with a *thwap* before pocketing it again. I feel that pop of pressure that comes when the worlds get razored. The cut he makes is clean and practiced.

He steps into the slit he's made in the air, but he's looking back over his shoulder. He wants me to try to swipe at him again, wants to watch my face drain a bit more when I touch nothing.

"You are right, though," he says. "I am here for something more than the reservation—some*one* more. A truly special boon."

"You leave my people alone."

"They are *our* people, Walker." he says. "And *they* come to *me*. You know this is true."

Then he walks through. The zip folds in, leaving nothing but stale casino air and the ceaseless ringing of bells. The floor managers are already holding folks off at the aisle. Two slot machines spitting out everything they've got into empty space makes a tempting sight if you're broke, like almost everybody in here right now.

I don't know exactly who he wants, but I've got an idea. It all comes together: Owen's desperation at the tables. Caroline strangely absent. Like she's hiding. Or something is wrong. But Black Bear and Dark Sky have been attacking us for the better part of a year, and since then, the only thing that's really changed, that he could really want...

He wants the child.

The thought makes me sick. I need air like I haven't since I was alive—not the soul map air, either, but Rez air, high-and-dry desert air that clears the lungs. I look around for a way out of this damn casino, but I feel like even if I could find the door, this whole place is almost underwater already. Black Bear said whatever the water touches is his. I start picturing where the rain is falling, start looking for it on the soul map, start going down rabbit holes. Not even caring that my mind is drifting apart again. Only looking for anything I can do to help in a world I can't touch.

～

WHEN I COME TO, I'm still standing here in this same row of slots, which is never a good thing. I've lost time again.

The coins have been all swept up or stolen away, but the roof is still leaking. Which means it's still storming. So it can't have been that long. Not days. Hopefully just hours.

I feel filthy. One thing that's underrated among the living is showers—having some actual good water rain down on you while you don't think. I took that shit for granted when I lived, just like everything else. Man, I could use one of those right now, one of those showers that kills the hot water for the whole building. You'd never get me out.

I'm pretty sure I'm perched on the lip of another rabbit hole, but then I sense the thread of someone I know, who is very near.

Sani Yokana paces the empty row of slots the same way he used to pace the desks at the station—and probably still does. Hands clasping his black hat behind his back, he looks at everything and at nothing. Finding something on the floor, he bends over slowly. I hear the creaks and cracks as he reaches between the folds of a seat cushion and pulls out another Wapati slot coin.

The chief grumbles.

I'm surprised at how old he looks. A year can flash by in the blink of an eye if I'm not careful, so I see all the slow wear and tear that afflicts my people piled on at once. It's in his slight stoop and the way his eyes—which always used to be narrowed to a knife's edge—are softer now.

"First the Arroyo, then the north tracks. Now Boxes."

He always did this back when I was on the beat. I'd come into his office, and he would be talking his way through a case out loud, speaking to nobody.

The chief sets the Wapati coin flat on the chair with a soft *thwap*. "The Gambler, the flood. They're connected somehow. But I got no help. I can't prove it. And I'm getting tired."

I know he can't see me, but I reach out to him anyway. "No, no, Chief, we're here. There are people still fighting. I know it looks bad, but that's how it goes at first. First, you fight to survive. Then you fight to win."

He takes in a big breath and wipes the dampness from his brow with a disgusted look on his face. "Ah, who the hell am I talking to anyway? I don't even know anymore."

He has a fallen look, that of a man on the twilight side, rolling the film back in his head, trying to see if he's made a difference with the time he's been given. I see this look a lot in my line of work, and in every case, every single person has. They just can't see the thread I can see. What they remember—what they *think* they've contributed to the great rope of humanity on which I walk—is only a grain of sand on top of the mountain they *actually* give, because what they *actually* give is impossible to see for anyone but me. It echoes beyond anything the living mind can comprehend. A Navajo should know this, but even we get caught up in the world of the seen sometimes. Even we forget.

The chief is taking the flood hard. He has more of himself wrapped up in this place than almost anyone. And he's wondering if this Gambler is something different. I can see it. A part of his thread still believes he saw Joey pop into existence in that evidence room all those years ago. A part of his soul has seen more than his eyes, and that part is asking for help from me.

"I'm right here, Chief. You're talking to me. And I hear you."

He can't hear me, of course, but maybe some small whisper of my words gets through—an echo crossing the line from can to can. Either way, he stands a little taller then pulls his comm and clicks it on. "Station, this is Yokana. Where are we at with those blankets? And the food kits?"

Station buzzes back that they're on their way, probably using the big trucks. The chief clears his throat and walks back to the main floor. He gets back to work helping people. He'll do it as long as he can.

And so will I.

13

CAROLINE ADAMS

Bed rest sucks. Now I get why all my patients are always on the lam when I give them strict orders to stay put. People aren't meant to be in beds all day, especially large people like myself.

Owen told me to stay put while he went to update Grant and the squad trying to keep the Arroyo from washing away, so that's what I'll do. I have this queasy vision of my baby girl on a little life raft in there while, all around her, my tummy sloshes. If I get up, it'll be like her going over Niagara Falls in a bucket.

"You don't wanna go over Niagara Falls, do you?" I ask her with my hands over my tummy.

Her smoke barely ripples. I'm already starting to forget her voice. Well, it was a voice to me, but to others, it might sound like a hum, just the start of a voice.

The more that hum quiets, the creepier the clinic gets. Rain is coming in sheets, like waves of water from the sky. There's cozy read-a-book-with-tea rain, then there's this. The drops drone when they hit the windows. The sound reminds me of glass pressed to cracking.

I could try the TV again. The live broadcast is long dead, but it does have some prerecorded nature stuff. I watched it for a bit earlier but was surprised how quickly I felt like I was in a psych ward, watching videos of baby deer and waterfalls on loop. Plus, baby deer—baby anything—hits a little too close to home.

She's *not* dying on me. I puff the air clean of the thought with my breath. I won't say it aloud. I don't even want to think it because I'm afraid she'll hear my thoughts, then she'll run with it. So instead, I call her my going-away baby. And what I say to myself is she's going away to get strong. Something is coming, a time when she will need all she has inside her little soul to make this whole "life" thing work.

And I can almost believe that.

I hear a strange *whoosh, pop* and thank God for the company. Owen is being all doctory about the heartbeats, I know. The last time he came in, he read the reels as though things might possibly have gotten better. His face is very measured in this place, but I know every twitch. I don't even need his smoke to tell me her life is a light switch slowly dimming. I can feel it myself. He likes to get me me ice chips and the little ice-cream cups from the freezer, the ones with the pull tabs and the balsawood spoons that you can taste just as much as the ice cream, it helps us go through the paces.

I heave myself onto my side and try to ignore my mind manifesting a sloshing sound. "Owen, if I have one more of those ice-cream cups, I'm going to be in a dairy situation nobody wants—"

An off step is all it takes to make me notice—the gait is wrong. The way it claps on the linoleum has too much shuffle. Owen never shuffles. He doesn't like the way it "worries at the heels of his shoes."

This isn't Owen.

"Joey?" I ask, trying for a conversational tone but failing miserably.

Joey doesn't make noise. I know this.

I feel a weight in my bladder that I now and forevermore will associate with blood.

"Who is it?" I ask.

I glance down at the smoke of my tummy just like I've been doing every thirty seconds for almost three days, and the perfect little circle of a pond has gone dry in an instant. The last bit of that beautiful yellow goes to ground like a rabbit darting into a hole.

It's him, this thing that makes my child hide. He's here, the one they call the Gambler.

The door is already cracked. He doesn't even have to fuss with the handle. All he does is push, and it slides open with a soft whoosh. My room is dark, but even in the shadows, I can see he's old. Or the body he's wearing is old, at least. I can tell in an instant he's wearing this face as a mask. It isn't real. But the color of his smoke is like nothing I've ever seen before. It has a patina, aged and cracked like really old porcelain that's somehow stronger than the day it was fired.

I hate that it's kind of pretty.

He dusts his hands of black dirt then pokes at a bouquet of wildflowers I got from a family down in Boxes that grows them in their windowsill.

"What do you want?" I ask, trying to work my way to sitting.

He looks around at the hospital room and nods like he's been here before, which tracks with what Ben told us.

If he really was the Walker once, he's probably been in millions of these.

His watery eyes fall on me. "It is not what *I* want—it is about what *you* want."

Her heartbeat slows. I pick up on the change instantly, both on the readout and in my soul. The machines say she's ticking in the eighties now.

"You need to get out of here now," I say, reaching for the call button. Nascha is somewhere out there, and I could use some Nascha right now.

He watches me press the call button like I'm some sort of science experiment. "These rooms never change," he says. "People attached to machines they hate. Then when they died and I came for them, all they wanted was to be attached to these machines again for a little longer. And for what? There is more to be done on my shores than in this prison cell."

I stop pushing the button. I don't think the button is working.

His face is pitted and pooled in shadows. His stained jacket glitters here and there in patches like fool's gold. He looks at my stomach, and I feel completely exposed.

"I can see her running away," he says.

I bunch more blanket over myself although I think what he sees goes far beyond anything I can cover up. "It's you she's running from. You're drenched in death. She's just trying to live."

I say all this before it occurs to me to ask where she's going. It just comes out because she has nobody else to stick up for her. He knows it, too. And he waits, smiling, for me to ask, to acknowledge that he has the upper hand, to bite off my pride.

Lucky for me, I have no pride. All my pride left me

when I started to bleed from inside and everyone waited outside the bathroom when I peed and people tiptoed around me and brought me chipped ice. When I pushed that button to get help changing the absorbent pads under my butt, pride went out the window. Hospital rooms are the great equalizers.

"Where is she going?" I ask.

"The river. But you knew that."

I feel the truth in his words. I think maybe I've always known that's where she's disappearing to.

He rummages around in the stained pocket of his jacket, and for a wild moment, I picture him pulling out that black-bear totem and calling in Dark Sky to pull all of us to wherever he dragged the Arroyo. I grip the arms of the bed and wince when more warm-then-cold wetness seeps from below.

Instead, he pulls out an oversized, grimy casino coin and thumbs it like a lucky charm, looking out the window. "Everything the rain touches on this reservation is mine now. I won it."

I snort, unable to help myself. Some people laugh in the face of death—I guess I snort. "I'm sure it was fair and square, too," I say.

He shows a flash of anger, real anger. But it's brief, and soon, the distracted madness takes over again. "I offered them things I have won, wonderful boons. They staked what they could. Their land. Themselves. Even I was surprised to see how desperate they were to play."

He flips the coin up and catches it, and in the weird glow of the machines, I see dust spin out from both sides, dust with that same patina of white.

He almost catches me looking.

"I think you and I both know there is a decision

coming for you, Caroline Adams," he says. "The way things are going for you—and for your child—both of you will meet the Walker soon. But I came to tell you there is another way."

He flicks the coin up again, end over end. It wobbles strangely with the weight of the dust. This time, after he catches it, he sets it flat on the tray table with a *thwap*.

"I know you still hold out hope that I might leave and she might live. Many others have thought the same." His voice takes on a mocking whisper. "*No*, they all say. *Not me —can't be me.*" He pushes the coin over with a slow scrape. "But it can. And it is. And when you are ready to bet what matters, all you have to do is tap that coin, and I will knock on your door.

He brushes the flowers again on the way out, and a handful of petals drop from the daisies. The lights flicker overhead along with his steps. I hear that strange *whoosh-pop* again, and he's gone.

My eyes track right away to the machines, and I eat up the numbers. Mine are through the roof, but that doesn't matter to me. Hers matter. I'd hoped that once he left, she might tick back up, but she doesn't. Her heartrate pattern is like a shallow staircase, little drops, one after the other. But if you combine enough little drops, you end up with one big drop.

The cold light from the hall leaks into the dark of the room and falls on the coin.

The windows are dripping water. If I took the Gambler at his word, that would mean he owns this place too. But I don't think he owns all that he says he owns, at least not yet. If he did, he'd have noticed the crow sitting there, right out of sight.

Chaco looks at me and then at the coin. He fluffs his

drenched wings and works them up for flight. He can't go very far and has to stop a lot, and my guess is the dry places to stop are few and far between.

I hold out a hand to him, and he slows his wings. He scrabbles up to the lip of the window and perches on the handle, watching me then watching the coin with that patented side-eye. He's coming more and more into himself every day.

I watch the coin too, and part of me expects it to scoot around. If it did, I think I would drop every last ounce of blood in me right out onto these diaper pads. But no, the dust the Gambler put on it has settled. Solidified. I think about the weird weight of it, about the way the Gambler seemed like he could control how it fell. He made it wobble like that. Luck had nothing to do with it.

"Chaco, can I ask you a pretty big favor?"

The bird doesn't immediately shiver out a no, which is a good sign because what I'm about to ask him, even old Chaco might have some trouble with.

"Can we keep all this to ourselves?" I ask. "Just for a bit. I have some thoughts I need to keep small."

Chaco side-eyes me this time, which I deserve. He and Grant are bonded, and he knows I'm asking him to keep a secret he may not even be able to keep.

"It's for her," I say, and my voice is very quiet, so quiet that I think he can't possibly hear, but somehow he does.

He nods. Then he turns and leaps outward in a burst of black, leaving me with this coin, the coin that wobbles a certain way—if you know what to look for, that is.

14

KAI BODREY

I'm going way too fast down Crooked Snake, but the water is going faster. I hook a right at the base only to find the BIA road looks like a whitewater rapid. Fish could literally jump out of this thing, and I wouldn't be surprised.

That's the bad news. The good news is Hos's truck don't care what's below it. The teeth on these tires grip like the biggest bitch of a girl you ever knew, with a fistful of your hair in her claws. I spew up mud against the side-walls, and when the tires catch, they turn everything behind me into boat wake.

Driving in a downpour is an optical illusion. Even with the blinding front beams of this monster, the water throws everything off just enough to make me feel like I'm sliding sideways. The spazzy back-and-forth of the wipers cuts the rain just enough that I second-guess everything I see.

The animals got me this far. I expect they'll keep me moving if I can listen right, but listening right is a real bitch in a downpour. Just when I think I see something, like a deer staring at me or maybe an actual honest-to-god fish out here on a washed out Indian Road, the truck hits some deep puddle hard and revs, and for a queasy couple of seconds, I'm floating.

The truck catches bottom again. The jolt yanks me hard right, and I throw the wheel left to recover, and in my mind, I can hear Hos laughing because he got that extra half foot of lift on this truck, and he wouldn't shut up about it, and I hated it because I wished he cared even half as much about me as that extra half foot, and here we are with that extra half foot of lift saving my ass.

I tap the roof. "No offense."

The elder twins say everything is listening, which might mean even big-ass trucks, and I need this big-ass truck to take me to the Arroyo pronto because everything just broke in the high country, and the Arroyo is about to pay for it.

The more I try to focus on not sliding off the road, the less sense everything makes. I turn on the radio and rip up the volume. I guess I'm hoping for a voice, any voice. The Rez underground radio would be perfect, but I'd take evac orders too. I'd take anything. All I get is static.

I slam a hand on the dash, aiming for whatever pricey piece-of-shit stereo my brother got put in this thing, and the cupholder kicks out, and inside is a picture of Mom. She looks mobile, so it's old, back from before the foot problems. She wears the only true Diné rug we ever owned, draped over her shoulders. She looks like an elder, like she could have been if things had worked out differently.

But that was before the diabetic neuropathy and the pills, and it's really best not to think of "could have." "Could have" gets people nowhere.

Something black flits across the windshield, maybe a bat or a crow. I slam the brakes, and the truck fishtails. Water sloshes all around me. I can smell it coming through the vents, all heated up by the engine block with that ozone taste like baked mud in the air.

I come to a stop before anything tips over, and when my heart stops hammering, I take a good look through the windshield and find I'm about ten feet from pitching off the side of the bank. Nothin' down there but bloated roadkill.

I gotta get it together. If I don't get down to the Arroyo, nobody knows what's coming. If nobody knows what's coming, it's all over. I can tell the elder twins about the animals. Maybe they'll help me—if we have time.

I slide mom's picture off. She doesn't need to see me freaking out. But another picture is behind hers, and that picture is of me. It's me as a freshman in high school, which was the first and last time I ever got a school picture, and I look like a scarecrow with pimples. But it's me.

My brother has a picture of me in his car next to Mom, in a place where nobody but he knew. My asshole brother has a picture of me, which means that in some tiny speck of his brain, he might, just maybe—

"Get driving, Kai."

His voice makes me jump, and I choke a bit on my own spit. I tuck the picture of Mom back in the spot behind the cupholder. But I roll down the window and toss the picture of me out into the storm.

"You don't get to do that," I tell him. I tell the rain. I tell nobody. "You don't get to do that now. Show me that you might have cared, now that I can't reach you. Fuck that. Absolutely not. I won't let you."

I expect some sort of snap back, something painful. But the silence is worse. So I get driving again.

CHACO REZ IS BASICALLY UNDERWATER. I come upon the North Tracks neighborhood around three in the morning. I've driven in and out of this part of town a thousand times, but this time, I don't recognize anything. I have to peer at mile markers and the few fluttering street signs to get my bearings. The outskirts never really had consistent electricity to begin with, but right now, all the duplexes and double-wides are dark. I only know when I cross the actual tracks because the truck rumbles.

Boxes is the same way. The shipping containers lowest to the ground are swamped. The ones stacked on top are at double capacity. Whatever light I see comes from gas lanterns and open fires, which isn't a good combination.

Someone waves at me, or maybe they're trying to flag me over. Either way, I can't stop. For one, I'm not a hundred percent sure I'd be able to start up again. But mostly, I have to get to the Arroyo. Once I know my people are safe, I'll come back.

Everywhere I look has been claimed by the rain. The street bubbles with trash, bushes, and branches, as well as clothes, toys, and other things I can't quite make out. I swerve to avoid what I then see is a stuffed bunny bobbing butt-side-up down the gutter.

I try to stay in the middle of the road and maintain momentum, but not being able to turn around or back up puts me in a weird part of town I don't recognize. I start to panic, checking the gas gauge and listening to the motor with my ear up to the vents as if I could hear what it sounded like or know what sound meant what. My sweaty palms slip on the steering wheel, and my panicked animal brain is wondering how I can back out of this and run to high ground again when I see flashing lights materialize out of the gloom ahead. A cop car is parked in the center of the road, and next to it, someone is waving a flare. The searing chemical purple gets brighter as I drive up until I have to look away.

The man holding it is Sani Yokana. He jams it upright in the trusses of an orange-and-white-striped roadblock, where it hisses angrily out at the rain, then he walks over to me. He's wearing an industrial poncho over his usual faded denim and still has his big black cowboy hat on. I roll down the window, and he angles his hat to direct the rain away.

"Kai Bodrey! I thought I recognized that truck. 'Bout the only one that could have made it in."

I'm not a huge fan of cops. From what I've seen first-hand walkin' in and out of the trading post, at least half of them are crooked. But I always thought Sani Yokana was alright, mostly because he knew how much the Bodreys butted heads with the NNPD but still tipped his hat to me every time he saw me in town. Hard to hold a grudge against a person who doesn't want to hold one against you.

Also, it's hard not to feel for a guy who looks as tired as Sani but is still standin' out in the rain, waving a flare for people.

"Can't get through this way," he says. "Main Street is two feet deep all the way back to the Welcome Center. Detour is over by Wapati." He looks out that way, and the wrinkles at the corner of his eyes catch shadows in the flare light, making him look cut from really old rock. "But it's tricky there too," he adds.

"This is Main Street?" I ask, trying to make sense of it. Sure enough, I think I see the sign for Manuelitos down the way, the outline of it, anyway—same with the other trading post, the "real" trading post that sells nonillegal shit. Apparently, I drove all the way around and found my way to the northeast side, which means I have a straight shot to the Arroyo if I can get through.

Yokana pockets his hands. The rain popping off the brim of his hat makes the felt look like it's boiling. "It is Main although you wouldn't know it to look at it. After all this, I wonder if it'll ever dry out again."

"I gotta get to the Arroyo, Chief."

He's still looking strangely out over the hood of the car toward Wapati, but he nods. "I figured as much. That's low country. We're trying to get everyone out of there to higher ground. I got two officers doing the same on the other end of this street."

I wipe my brow. "The only people left at the Arroyo aren't going anywhere, and you know it."

Yokana looks back at the flare, which is sputtering. He pats his poncho until he finds another. He reaches under the plastic and pulls it out.

I keep pressing. "Flatrock Canyon is flooded out. If the trading post ain't gone, it's on its way. The bootleg camps north are floating down right now in little pieces."

Yokana winces, but I can't tell if that's because of what I'm saying or just because he's old and it's cold and wet and late. Old bones ache in the damp. Mom taught me as much.

I keep pressing. It's what Bodreys do. "If Flatrock falls,

it spills into Kanosha then down to Antler and Little Antler..."

Yokana takes his hat off and wipes his brow as if that could possibly do anything. "On and on," he says. "I know."

"There's a wall of water headed to the Arroyo. I don't know how much time we have," I say.

"Not enough. That's for damn sure," he says. He lifts the canvas covering the truck bed and looks in. After readjusting a few things and setting the canvas down again, he checks the tires and looks at me through lidded eyes of dark brown. "You know, I always rooted for Hosteen."

"Yeah, well, that makes one of us."

"Don't get me wrong—that boy gave me more hell than any ten of the most troubled Arroyo boys combined. I had every opportunity to ship him downriver. Plenty of people on both sides of the Rez line said I should. But every time his file came across my desk... I just couldn't send him to some federal prison."

Yokana looks back at the black distance in the fading light of the flare, but I find his eyes with mine.

"Why?" I ask. "Why not?"

He takes a deep breath and crosses his arms over his barrel chest. The rain is falling off the back of his hat again. The flare sputters out completely, and only the lights of the truck are keeping the two of us afloat in the darkness.

"I have this memory of him as a little boy, maybe three. Four. Before your time. At one of the elder twins' Diné Bahane' campfires. I don't even remember the story the twins were telling, but I remember that boy scooting his way forward, through the big kids, all the way to the front of that fire. He always loved that fire."

Sani looks at me square. "Every time I looked at him—even after he was all grown and causing trouble—all I saw was that little boy, scooting, and I couldn't send that little boy to jail. Juvie, yes. But fed prison? No. And maybe that's part of the reason he's gone. Maybe I should have—"

I stop him right there. "The reason my brother is gone is because of decisions of his own, decisions no amount of jail time would have hammered out. He followed Dark Sky because of something in his blood."

Something in our *blood.*

"There is fire in your blood. That is for sure," Yokana says. He steps aside and slaps the hood. "You won't get to the Arroyo the straight way. Water scooped five feet out of the road. Take the access just before Manuelito's, and don't stop. Alleys are washed out the farther you get, but this thing oughta make it. If you stick to the left of the bootleg markers."

That's what we always called the "quiet way," the way the cops aren't supposed to know about. I can't help but grin. I wonder how long he knew, how many people he pulled over there. And then, when he had bigger fish to fry and fewer cops to work with, how often he had to watch as Dunk and his dumbass crew ran jars of booze up and down his town.

"They won't evacuate," Yokana says. He's talking about the crew at the Arroyo, but specifically the elder twins, and I realize after a second that there's the smallest note of pride in his voice. "So you tell 'em to hang on."

He walks away into the downpour and click-fires the new flare, which leaps to life. He holds it up and moves the barricade out of my way, then he waves me on through like this was nothing more than a DUI checkpoint at the border.

I watch him in my rearview, and he looks like something from a story, a purple outline in a cloak of black rain, getting smaller and smaller as the truck grinds on. Then I find the turn before Manuelito's, and he washes out of view along with everything else.

15

GRANT ROMER

The water has never been higher. First, we watched it drown a railroad spike that Joey says was hammered in to mark high water on a flood when he was young. Then, about twenty minutes ago, it passed a big piece of carved wood the elder twins say was dug into the canyon fifty or so years back. Now we're in uncharted territory, and somehow, all I can think of is where the hell my parents are.

I mean, I know where they are. I know where Mom is exactly, and I wouldn't have her here. Wouldn't have Dad here neither, because I'd rather he be with Mom. *But still... where the hell are they?*

I know the three of us are gettin' hammered at in different directions, fallin' apart in our own ways. This fallin' apart here at the Arroyo, the one I'm in the middle of, is important. But their falling apart at the CHC is important too. I guess I'm pissed that we got two fallin' aparts at the same time when either one would be enough for a lifetime.

"We don't get to choose when things happen," Chaco

says. He's been walking circles around the firepit, and I feel like I'm watching some ancient ritual. I don't even think he knows he's doing it. This little guy is so new in so many ways. Even his language hits different—not bad, just different.

"I can still be pissed," I say.

Chaco bobs up and down as he steps. "Yes. How you feel is still in your control."

He seems like he's thinking, working something out. He's been flying a lot. Practicing. He can't cut between planes yet, so I think he's throwing himself into flying through this world to make up for it, but he has to sit a spell each time. He tires out, and I got no idea where a thinning like him gets its energy from. So I let him be. He'd do the same for me.

The twins watch him, which seems to give them a bit of calm. Otherwise, they're askin' about firewood. I don't claim to know even a corner of their brain, but I'd say the more pressin' thing is the rising water. But they won't leave the firewood question alone.

"How many?" Tsosi asks.

"I told you, grandfather," Joey says gently. "Two logs."

Joey doesn't really get it either, this obsession with the fire, but something about it all makes him uncomfortable enough that he's scratching at his arms in a way I haven't seen for years.

The twins don't like the "two logs" answer. Maria comes to Tsasa and gets down in that linebacker stance and starts shooing, and even these timeless old boys know it's time to move farther under the lean-to. And just like that, everyone is plastered against the double-wide like we're in a lineup with nowhere else to run—except inside, of course, which the twins won't do.

The fire is weaker. All of us are weaker. I've been shoveling out mud from underneath water for hours, splitting shifts with Joey, trying to give this water somewhere to go that ain't right up our asses. But time is running out for shovelin'. The only thing that keeps me huckin' waterlogged mud is the fact that whatever Kai is dealing with up-country, closer to the heart of this evil storm, is probably way worse.

I know I should be worried for her. The CB is busted. The phones don't work for shit. But somehow, she's the one I'm worried about least, which is what Pap would have called a "small blessing."

A big gust of wet wind rolls in, and without thinkin', I try to cover the fire with my body, but Joey's already there. We look at each other surprised to find ourselves here, like we'd take a bullet for the flame. And I don't know why except that we've been fighting to keep this thing burning for almost three days now in a raging downpour, and it's startin' to get personal.

Now, what we're gonna do once those two logs are gone, I got no idea. I'm just hoping that, when it happens, the twins don't die. That's how much focus they got wrapped up in this thing.

"Why are you shoveling water in a flood?" Chaco asks, still circling the fire.

"Are you being a smart-ass?" I return.

"As soon as you toss the water out, it fills up again."

He's right, of course. And he don't mean nothin' by it. He's just curious.

"I guess because it's somethin' to do. Sometimes, when you see things going... going the way they're going, and you feel like it's all just happening to you—like you got nothin' to do with it, you're just the clay the world is beatin' on—it helps to do something. Anything. Even if on its face, it looks like doin' nothing."

Chaco circles a few more times as I huck a few more shovels full of black water, then he says, "That is what Owen is doing."

He says it matter-of-fact because he knows how I'm feeling about the two types of mess my family is in and how I'm pissed we aren't in it together. Times like this, I got no idea how the world has enough gunpowder to keep chucking cannonballs. But it does.

"It's not really the world," Chaco says. "It's the Black Bear."

"The Gambler," Tsosi says, loud and out of nowhere, somehow making all of us jump even in the white-noise drone of falling water. Both he and Tsasa have been talking all about the Gambler, but the Gambler they're talking about is the ancient one, the one from the Diné Bahane', whose name is Nááhwiilbiihi.

Tsosi grumbles in that way that says he's about to talk shop. "It is said that long ago..." he says, but then he trails off.

Tsasa picks up. "Long ago, the Diné gambled," he says.

Joey snorts. "Not much has changed, grandfather. Just head to Wapati. Spend enough, maybe they'll comp you the prime rib."

Tsasa turns toward him slowly, and Joey clears his throat and gets back to shoveling. The only two people on earth I've ever seen make Joey look like a kid are these two, and I gotta admit that I kinda love it.

Tsasa eye-slaps Joey for a bit longer then says. "White people think we put casinos on our lands to take their money, that we woke up one day and thought, *Ah! Casino! That is how we take back what was ours.*"

He shakes his head. "That is the white way of thinking. It's always about *them*. Our ways are because of *them*. No. Gambling runs deep in the Diné, but not the flashing lights and bells you know on top of the hill. The true games are simple... and much more powerful."

Tsasa clears his throat in that slow rumble the old folks have that reminds me of a rusty engine turning. "The Gambler knows this," he says, "which is why he has won most of our land."

Joey stops shoveling. Maria leans against the door, watching. I guess we ain't talking about old legends anymore.

"Nááhwiilbiihi has come to our home once more. And he wants more than coins and jewels this time."

This is the man my baby sister is running from, the man killing my mother. That means he's killing my father, too, and killing me.

"How can we beat him?" I ask. "How can we banish him?"

The brothers look up to me as one. The answer is obvious, of course.

"The same way we have since the sun and the moon walked the earth you stand upon," Tsasa says. "You play his game. And you win."

In the silence after his words, Tsasa takes our second-to-last log and tosses it onto the flame. The fire laps at it quickly, and we get a burst of quiet heat that beats back the cold of the rain, but not for long. Tsosi grips his brother's thin hand and squeezes it, muttering something about patience.

We wait like this, watching the fire die. The last log goes on, which gives us another breather, but the fire is starving, and soon enough, the crackling fades. The sucking sound of the water pouring into the Arroyo grows. It's like the canyon is one big whirlpool, eating away at the earth, taking it all down with it.

Joey snaps his head toward the front entrance. Moments later, I hear the engine and stand. I recognize the sound of it because I tuned it.

Hos's truck sweeps around the bend and throws a wake of water to its right that splashes out into the night. The tires spin then catch, and it lurches toward the gates. The wind tries to close the things, but the grill of the truck pops them back open like a boxer's jab. That's a Kai move if I ever saw one.

The storm seems to sense her cutting through it. Something gives in the darkness up the road. The sound is a low rockslide rumble, and a wall of water pours over what's left of the entrance to the Arroyo.

I scream for Kai as the truck gets a broadside. It's enough water to kick the back out, but Kai corrects, and the back tires catch again just in time to get a knockout.

It's like someone pulls a rug of rocks out from under the truck and tosses it right back on top of the thing. The driver's side window shatters, and I'm up running toward her with Chaco beating the wind at my back.

Mud piles up against the driver's side door then oozes inside. The tires spin and spin then stop. I wade through water that's knee deep to get to the truck, and I'm screaming her name until I see her climbing out the back window. She picks her way over a big tarp and stands tall.

"You alright?" I ask.

She yells something over the rain, and I'm not sure I hear her right.

"What?"

"The fire! Is the fire burning?"

I look back toward the twins' camp, where the glow is low, but it's still there. "Yeah, but we're out of wood. How did you know about…?"

Kai scrabbles underneath the tarp and comes up with a big bundle wrapped in a ratty blanket. "Take it!" she yells. "Quick!"

I wade up to the bed and take the bundle from her. "Are you sure you're alright?"

"It's the fire, Grant. The actual fire. Sani Yokana told me about how Hos used to scoot up to it—" She cuts herself off, waving away the words. "Just take it. I'll be close behind with the rest."

Chaco loops over us and boomerangs back. I make my way slowly. The last thing we need is me falling on my ass and soaking everything.

By the time I get back, the ratty blanket is already heavy with water. I set it carefully under the lean-to. Tsasa gets up and comes over to it, moving faster than I've ever seen him move. He chooses one, feels it, puts it down, and chooses another. He sets it carefully on the fire—no tossing this time—and everyone seems to hold their breath. Chaco lands on my shoulder.

"It's too wet," I say.

Without a strong base to beat back the occasional side gusts and rain, the coals are sputtering in the wind.

"Anybody got some lighter fluid?" I ask.

"That's not how it works," Joey says, coming up to it and getting on his knees, gently blowing air. "It has to be lit from the fire that came before it. I should have known."

I get down and work the other side slowly, carefully. But the fire doesn't catch. Chaco hops up and over the pit, pumping his wings to make a downdraft. He works and works, and if a bird could sweat, he would be drenched.

The color flares. The fire climbs its way back up one finger at a time. The log starts to sizzle.

The twins let out a breath as one. Then the rest of us do too. Joey puts the other wood in a tarp and the tarp near the pit to dry out. He wipes his hands on his jeans. Maria wipes her brow. We're all shaking, and none of us knows quite why.

Kai stomps her way over what's left of the fences, wearing big rubber rain boots and faded jeans soaked back to black. Most of her hair is in a wet braid, the rest is plastered to her forehead and neck in strands. She's hauling a hobo's bag of canvas tied to a shovel, and her chest is heaving under a baggy reflective vest. She looks part construction worker, part escaped convict, and I don't think I've ever been more attracted to her in my life.

As the piñon smoke washes over her, she closes her eyes and reaches a hand out toward the heat. "My canyon is flooded," she says, eyes closed, soaking in the warmth the way she does under a blanket on the couch. "Kenosha is probably gone by now too. Same with Antler. And all that water is coming for this fire."

"The water already has the Arroyo," I say. "Look. It's a sinkhole."

Kai looks at me in a way that tells me politely to shut up. "How long has this fire been burning?" she asks.

I look at our small little party, the last of the expedition. "All day," I say. "Kai, I thought you were gonna try to hold down the trading post even if it meant—"

"No, I mean how long has it *really* been burning?"

She's asking the elder twins, and they turn to each other in a conversation of their own, but Maria is the one who answers.

"As long as I can remember." she says. "And I can

remember a lot. The first time the twins brought me here, this fire was burning, and I was fourteen."

Tsasa reaches for her hand, and she gives it. Maria's eyes are on the rain, but she's looking into the past. "They gave me food, a home. All they asked was that I keep the coals burning. Add the hard wood at the end of the night. Cover the pit, but leave enough air to let the coals breathe. That was forty years ago."

Even Joey seems confused at that. "You're telling me this fire has burned for forty years straight?"

Tsosi says, "It has burned much longer than that."

Kai drops her payload out of the full force of the rain and stretches her neck this way and that. "I was in and out as a kid, but I can't remember a time this firepit was cold." She turns to Joey. "Can you?"

Joey stares into the fire for a long time before shaking his head.

She pulls the tarp a little tighter around the bundle of wood. "Think about it. Every story this part of the Rez knows started around this fire. As long as it burns, the Arroyo stands. If it dies..."

I can feel the truth of her words. I wasn't there for these Diné Bahane' talks I've heard so much about, but I've been in and out of the Arroyo a fair amount over the years, and every time I pass through those gates, the first thing I do is look for the glow of that fire, if it's night, or the thin line of smoke it makes, if it's day. I do it without thinking.

In a way, fire is like blood. It can pass on down the line. Each log it touches burns differently, but if the flame stays lit, a bit of the spark that started it remains deep inside. Fire can have history. And in this country, anything with history has power. The right people sparkin' the right history, keepin' the right flame lit, why, hell, that might just be enough power to keep a little island like ours alive.

The elder twins ease back in a way that tells me they've been heard. "You're right," I say, amazed.

"Of course I'm right. The animals told me," she adds, offhand. "Help me bring in the rest of this stuff. It's basically what's left of the trading post—"

I blink in the rain as she sets off. "What's this about the animals?"

She turns around and holds out her arms in the rain, "You ever see a bunch of sparrows tell you a flood's coming? Or a family of weasels give you a rock?"

"Uh. I can't say I have," I reply.

Kai starts unloading the tarp of all sorts of stuff: shovels, sandbags, flashlights. "It's the fire," she says. "It has to be protected. The animals know it, and so do I."

She freezes and snaps her head toward some sound I don't hear. I pan the dark expanse of the Arroyo right along with her, but if somethin' is out there, I can't see it. She goes back to unloading, handing me the remnants she's smuggled from the trading post.

"With the wood you brought, we can probably last out the rain—"

"Nope. It's like I said—Flatrock spilled over," Kai says, cutting me off. "It's already coming down the line."

"And I reckon we're at the end of the line."

Kai points with her shovel at the glowing pit. "The water is coming for that fire."

"The Gambler is coming for that fire," Joey says.

"Two sides of the same coin," Kai says. "We better start filling sandbags either way. If we can build a retaining wall around the yard, I got a generator and some gas. Maybe you can rig something up to pump out the water?"

I should tell her it ain't that easy, that we're missing a pump for one, but she's on fire right now, and I sorta love that she thinks I'm some sort of handyman wizard, so all I say is "Sure, I can try."

Joey looks at the shovels and bags and mud. We've got more shovels than hands. He's turning something over in his mind.

"We're gonna need help," he says.

Kai wraps her tarp up into that hobo bag again and slings it over her shoulder. "We're all we got, Joey,"

"Maybe not," Joey says. He carefully sets his shovel down and pulls out his totem pouch. "Do what you can. I will return as fast as I am able."

Before any of us can argue, he pops out of existence. I grunt. Two strong hands gone, but I gotta trust Joey, and we gotta make do. I pick up his shovel and grab as many sandbags as I can. "I bet there's still mud that ain't soaked to slurry a bit up the slope," I say, and I turn to go, but Kai stops me with a touch.

"The trading post is gone," she says quietly. "I got nothing now."

So that's what all this fire was for, to keep her moving so that she could put off facing the reality that just hit her. But that don't mean she's gotta let it hit her alone.

"That ain't true at all," I say. "'Cause you got me. And you always will."

She drops her tarp and grabs my face and kisses me hard enough that I almost slip on the mud. Her mouth is so warm. In all this rain, I forgot what warm feels like.

"Let's get to work," she says, her breath in my ear. She picks up her load again and wades back to the truck.

After a second, I find my feet and eventually pick up where I left off. I can feel Chaco's smile on my back.

"You're all over the place in your head," he says.

"Tell me about it," I say, giving him the side-eye this time as I trudge through the water up the hill toward dry sand.

All over the place is what happens when you're in love.

16

———

OWEN BENNET

Caroline is finally asleep. I'm on one of the clinic's remarkably uncomfortable pleather chairs next to her bed—no sleep for me tonight. I can't stop watching the fetal monitor for my daughter. I'm helpless as the heart rate drops and drops, about a beat an hour. Caroline is sleeping due to exhaustion. Her body shut itself down. But I don't have that shutoff button anymore.

I used to be able to sleep anywhere in these clinics, hospitals too. When I was a resident at Mass General, before I left all that insanity behind for ABQ, I could sleep in the cleaning closet if I had to. That's what happens when a person works fifteen hours a day. In my experience there are two types of exhaustion. One is aching bones, day-work weary, and after it's all done, the sleep comes easily. The other type is deeper. You might call it a weariness of the spirit, of the soul. It's every bit as bad, probably even worse, but it won't let you go. It holds your eyes open at night. Scares away sleep. Makes you consider every new disaster, every ungodly reality.

And the reality I must face is that soon, this little unborn girl will be nonviable.

Caroline and I have this policy of straight talk, but I couldn't tell her. I said, "The best thing you can do is sleep," when what I meant was, "The best thing you can do is sleep through this." If your body gives you the gift of blacking it out, please, God, take that. That is a gift a great many do not get.

Dad never thought I'd make a good doctor. He said medicine wasn't where I'd make my mark. The Bennet bloodline sneezed good doctors. Our bench was deep. I guess he thought I'd never stand out. He said I should try farming instead and even walked me through the soil and seasons with the caretakers we had at the Concord estate, which did nothing but piss me off and push me even more into the medical books. And when I actually ended up being a good doctor, I remember him saying, "But I bet you'd have been a *great* farmer."

Never a day in my life did I think I should've been a farmer—until today. Even in the early stages of Caroline's bleeding, I thought it was routine. Plenty of literature would back that up. Then she kept bleeding, and she bleeds now, in her sleep. And I realized that nobody is here to tell me "it's routine" or "plenty of literature will back up the idea that women in her risk profile come out just fine."

I'm the one that says that, but I know that if I were to say that now to someone else—some other woman in Caroline's place in this mess—it would be so that she could get some sleep before the inevitable happened.

Here are the realities I am not telling her, listed out the way she would:

1. Our unborn baby girl may already be brain
   dead from a lack of necessary oxygenated
   blood. Bleeding is often a lagging indicator.
2. I believe Caroline's placenta is slowly ripping
   apart from her uterus, and when she has to
   deliver our daughter vaginally, there is a good
   chance the placenta will completely tear out of
   her uterus, and she will bleed to death.
3. Heavy bleeding is an irritant to the uterus and
   can induce early labor, so whatever is going to
   happen will likely happen within hours.

These are the trench facts, the foxhole facts. This is
the shit keeping me awake even as this godawful rain
drones and the air is heavy enough to bury us. We are in a
very bad situation here. At ABQ, they would've had this
child out days ago. She would be in a warm incubator in
the NICU with all the high-flow oxygen necessary,
wearing cool sunglasses to block out the bilirubin lights,
and sleeping like a baby should.

I've walked other realities, other plains, but they've
always been hazy to me, cold, blurred. Not this one in my
mind—not the one where my baby girl is under bright
lights and taking baby breaths, and Caroline is in one of
those ratty old hospital wheelchairs, watching her, and
Grant is next to her, and I'm next to Grant, and the nurses
have given us some time, just the four of us.

I can see it. I can see this other reality more clearly
than any of the ones I've ever walked. But I feel like I'm
watching someone else's story, and it feels like it's slipping
away.

The Navajo love Caroline, and they know she's struggling here in this room. Food and fetishes and flowers are

piling up at the door. I take a short walk to stretch my legs every half an hour or so, and each time I get back, more gifts are here. The Navajo can sense in the air what I see in the charts, especially on a night like tonight, when the sky feels like it's pressing down on every plane of existence and the walls are very thin.

I know everything is meant well, these gifts, and they are given out of love for Caroline, perhaps the only person on the planet who would be surprised at how much everyone here loves her, but they feel too much like flowers on a grave to me.

In medicine, we talk about decisions a lot. The decision of what to prescribe. The decision of which incision to make. The decision that puts the pressure down on the knife that marks the start of surgery. The decision that calls the time of death. Doctors are often in these positions, for better and for worse. We mark the clear before and after. I certainly have. And now, I have to make one more decision, maybe the most important of my life.

I want so badly to kiss her goodbye, but that would wake her, and every good doctor knows sleep is the best medicine. So instead, I make sure the call button is close to her hand, and I slip out the door.

17

KAI BODREY

I didn't know a person could be freezing cold and sweating like an animal at the same time, but then again, I've never hauled dirt through a flood before. Grant found a patch of loose sand underneath a huge creosote bush that we could dig out and work into the sandbags. The drill is that he loads up the sandbags, I cinch them, and we both haul them to the yard. We've been doing it for hours now while Joey is off doing whatever it is he's doing with his crow totem.

We're building a wall bag by bag. It's a little wall, but it's a wall. I thunk my bag on top of the layer below and wipe grit and water and sweat from my face. Somehow in all this, the night became day although, with the sky the bruised black it is now, nobody would ever really know.

"How you holdin' up?" Grant asks, wiping his face with his soaked T-shirt. "We can take a break if you want."

"No, we can't," I reply. I keep looking at him as his body steams in the night.

"What?" he asks.

"Might as well just lose the shirt, hotshot," I say, only half kidding.

His teeth are bright white when he laughs. "Neither the time nor the place."

"The end of the world?" I ask. "Seems like the perfect place."

We trudge back uphill with new burlap. "It ain't the end yet," he says. "Not as long as that fire burns."

I hold a sandbag open, and he starts shoveling. We have to go deeper under the brush for usable dirt, stuff that isn't soaked scree already. We don't say what I know we're both thinking, that the water is rising a lot faster than we can fill these bags.

Grant stops shoveling midmotion and looks back toward the camp, where Chaco is squawking and hopping from bag to bag.

"Uh oh," Grant says. "Chaco says big water is coming."

"When?" I ask.

"Now," Grant says, tossing the shovel down and half sliding, half running back.

I'm right at his heels.

We get to the yard, and Chaco flops down, tracing his way along the waterline and flaring his wings out at the gloom. I hold out my hand. The rain is slowing. Grant looks up at the sky, blinking. The twins and Maria notice it too. Tsosi and Tsasa look at each other and share a grumble.

Rain has been falling so long that I forgot what nonrain was like. But I've been through enough flash floods to know that once the rain dies, the real shitshow begins.

The canyon bank at the far end of the Arroyo looks blurry, like it's vibrating. I can feel it under my feet and hear it too, like a big machine is rolling our way. But we all know what it is—water, dark water, sludgy with all the crap it picked up during its miles-long trek from the high ground. It slams itself around the bend, sloshing over the wall and taking out a big chunk of the bank along with it.

The Arroyo eats what it can, but the Arroyo has been eating junk for generations, and it's nearly full up. The floodwater is a big bite it won't be able to handle.

Grant is yelling something at me. I look down at the retaining wall, maybe three feet high and twenty feet long, wrapping around the firepit. I know in an instant it's nowhere near enough. Already, the first wash pushed out by that huge dump of water is skirting the sides of the canyon. Grant and I brace our backs against the wall as the water slaps against the sandbags and kicks up a gritty spume.

A few bags fall from the top, but it holds. The water regroups. I pick up the sandbags in a daze, ignoring the ache in my lower back, in my whole body, and plop them back up top. It's a dumb thing to do, kinda like sticking your finger in the busted dike, but I don't know how else to help. Grant does it too. We're both in the same boat, so to speak.

Come to think of it, a boat would be great right about now.

My lip trembles, and I don't know if I'm about to cry or laugh. I slap bags on bags. The Arroyo eats up the last of the first water wave, but more is coming. The ground rumbles again. The canyon is loading up to fire.

Now, I'm crying, but it's because I feel like an idiot. I don't know why I thought slopping together a crappy little sandbag wall might somehow save the heritage of my people. More bags fall, and now I'm stumbling back and forth, not sure where to go first. I plug up a hole with my hand, standing stupidly. Another bag falls. Somewhere, Grant is calling for me. The water slides around the wall, through the wall. A bag falls on my foot and opens up, dumping mud all over. I try to yank my boot out, and it comes off, and I slip on my ass. My hands sink into the earth, and part of me wonders if it wouldn't be easier if I just drowned right along with this place.

I'm lifted bodily from behind, and my other boot comes free with a sucking pop. Either I'm losing my mind, or someone is carrying me like I'm a sack of sand myself.

I'm set down carefully next to the fire. The ragged wall has been rebuilt. The water is already sloshing up against the sandbags and sluicing through the cracks, but the fire is still lit. I'm helped back to standing and turned around by two hands the size of dinner plates, and there in front of me is an enormous man in overalls and nothing else. He steps back respectfully and nods.

"You must be Ms. Kai," he says.

I think he says it, anyway. His big red beard is bobbing up and down with the words, so I'm pretty sure he's the one talking. This is no Arroyo man. He sounds like he walked right out of the deep swamps of the South.

"Apologies, ma'am. I hate to grab 'cause I ain't the grabbin' sort. But time is short." He takes a carefully folded handkerchief from his breast pocket and wipes daintily at his absolute unit of a forehead while he looks around, taking everything in. He checks the handkerchief as he refolds it, and I catch a flash of brilliant turquoise sewn into it before he tucks it into the front of his overalls like he's about to chow down on spaghetti.

For a terrible second, I think this is the Gambler, the one who brings the rain, and I wonder why the hell nobody told me he'd be so polite, but I recognize that crow. I've seen it before or something very close to it.

Joey swims into focus next to him. I never thought I would see someone make Joseph Flatwood look like a teenager, but here we are.

"He's with me," Joey says.

I let out a wet breath. "Well, thank the creator for that."

"The name's Big Hill, miss," the huge man says. "I'm with Injun... with Joey. We can talk it out hard later, but right now, we gotta get you and everythin' else on this here wet earth up toppa that double-wide."

A burst of water washes up against the retaining wall, and a good amount gets over. The twins are forced to stand slowly as spray hits the fire with a hiss that makes me wince. The air smokes up, and we all freeze for a moment.

Enough of the smoke clears to show that the fire still burns, but barely. The twins look at each other then Maria and us. With another spillover, it's done for.

"They won't leave without that fire," I say.

"That's what Ms. Zahara is here for," Big Hill says. "It's like I always say—the Circle never fights alone."

A tall black woman with a gleaming bald head pops into thin air in the remnants of the smoke. She gently covers her own crow inside a green leaf and slides it into a fold of her long robe. Brass bangles tink softly as she reaches into another fold behind her back and pulls out a small ceramic pot so deeply lacquered that it looks wet.

The roar rises again. We all turn back toward the bend, where the canyon now looks chipped, like someone dug out a huge chunk of the edge. It's vibrating again, getting blurry with the thunder of oncoming water.

The woman wraps her robe over one arm, just enough to keep the hem dry, as she approaches the twins. She looks down at them with a gentle smile, the first really radiant thing I've seen in what feels like years.

She opens the top of her pot. "May I?" she asks.

The twins look at each other then back at her. They nod as one.

Without a second's hesitation, she reaches into the heart of the fire and grasps the last white hot log there. She brings the pot over to the lip of the pit and shuttles it inside like she's ushering a songbird into a cage. She does this two more times, deliberating only for a moment over the choice of coals. Then she takes in an enormous breath and blows a thin stream of air into the pot before closing it up with a deft twist of her long fingers. She looks over at Joey and nods.

"Up we go," Joey says.

The earth shakes as water explodes around the canyon bend, leveling it like a sandcastle before the waves. Water goes up and over. Water rebounds. Water crashes into water. The wash skates easily over an Arroyo too swollen to blunt anything. I'm still staring at it rushing toward us when Big Hill picks me up and sets me on top of the double-wide like a doll on a shelf. Zahara is already seated here, robes arranged in a perfect circle around her. Next up are the elder twins then Maria and Grant. The twins settle next to Zahara, the three of them around the pot. She encourages them to each lay a hand on it, and she does as well. The twins start a chant I can't make out. Zahara looks like she's humming her own song.

The water rises fast, gobbles up the firepit in a puff of smoke, and tosses all the chairs and tables. It's up to Big Hill's knees and Joey's waist, but they stay on the ground.

"Get up!" Grant yells. "Joey! What the hell are you two doing?"

Joey looks up at us and holds out a hand, fingers spread wide. "You make sure the fire stands. My redneck friend and I will make sure the roof you sit upon stands. Won't we, Big Hill?"

"Hell yeah, brother. Injun Joe and Big Hill. Just like old times," he says, rolling up his sleeves.

They force themselves through the water and around to the back of the trailer, where they space out to both sides. I look from the wall of oncoming water back to where the two men stand braced against the outer wall of the double-wide, and I gotta say the math doesn't add up.

Grant knows it too. "Joey, if it does take the trailer down, it's coming down on top of you!"

Joey takes his totem pouch out and loosens the top. I can feel the weight of the wall of water coming like the rushing suck of a train ripping past. Chaco launches from Grant's shoulder to the pot, where he settles like he's nesting an egg. And really, that's what it is. It's our nest egg. All of it is in one basket on top of a double-wide in the face of a five-foot wall of filthy water. Grant screams to hold on. Big Hill and Joey pop out of existence—either that, or they're already swept away—and I can't get a solid grip on anything, so I drop to my belly instead.

Joey and Big Hill pop back with a strange other-worldly momentum that settles against the back of the trailer just as the water hits us. It's seamless, like a dance.

The trailer lurches underneath us, sliding as one piece, and I close my eyes and wait to feel that helpless sensation of weightlessness before we flip end over end, pieces of us flying in all directions—the last of the Arroyo scattered.

But the slide slows. As quickly as it creeps up, that sensation of helplessness fades. I open my eyes. Joey and Big Hill are straining against the back of the trailer with all they've got, dug in against the push of the flood. They're cutting trenches with their heels and gritting their teeth.

Both men give ground, but the giving is less and less. We back up against that creosote bush, and they pace it slower, slower, until we stop, still standing upright.

Big Hill and Joey pop out of sight, and suddenly, they're on the front side of the trailer, facing the flooded canyon. Big Hill braces his back against the wall, his head up near the roofline where we crouch, all of us still aboard.

Joey grabs sandbags and tosses them under the front and sides, bracing wherever he can. Big Hill grunts and drops the front end one inch then another. He staggers forward, the strength of a mountain spent.

The trailer settles. None of us dares move. I don't even want to turn my head.

The water sucks back out, but the trailer stays put.

"Did we win?" asks Big Hill.

Grant taps my shoulder and points toward where Chaco sits, fluffed still, on top of the pot that holds the Arroyo together.

I look around at this wasteland of water. It doesn't look like us winning, but we've got fire burning and hearts beating. I'll take it.

"Not sure about winning," I say, "but we sure ain't lost yet."

18

THE WALKER

When I arrive at the Arroyo, I think I've made some sort of mistake. I felt a thing dying here, felt a twinge in the strings of this place, so I dropped all the other work and stumbled my way here, and now, I'm looking at a lake where the Arroyo used to be.

"What the hell is this?" I ask, as if all this flat water might answer. This is no fresh-sprung high-desert lake, here today, gone tomorrow. This is a watery tomb.

Chaco barks out three little high-pitched caws, and I spin around to find him with a handful of people on top of a block of metal in the water on the far side. I orient myself to the horizon and realize the block of metal is a trailer, the twins' trailer.

"Where the hell did the Arroyo go, bird?" I ask.

"You're looking at it," he calls back.

I walk across the water toward them. And no, I cannot walk on water. Even dead, I sink into the muck like everyone else. I don't make any impression on the living world, but enough mud is here that it crosses all realms, and pretty soon, I'm wading through muck in my own plane too. At one point, I even hit some sort of junk pothole and drop down to my waist. I get nothing more than a sensation of wetness, an echo, but it's still enough to make me cuss a lot.

Grant pans the space between us. His eyes pass over me, but he's used to talking to air when Chaco says I'm around. "Hey, Ben," he says. "Come on up."

I climb from the water up to what's left of the stairs then use old flower boxes to hike to the top of the roof, and there I find one of the strangest scenes I've ever come across in the land of the living. The elder twins are with a woman I recognize from the Circle, hunched over a little pot. Chaco picks up a sprig of sage from a pile next to him and walks it over. Tsosi pulls the top off, and Chaco plops the sprig in. He looks terrible, like a wet black sponge. They all look pretty terrible.

The smell of the smoke hits me, and I'm blasted back into memories over memories: the elder twins reciting from the *Diné Bahane'*, Joey and me sitting as close as we dared to the pretty girls, pretending not to listen to all their whispering gossip, watching the sparks mix with the stars. It's like a pure shot of the Arroyo.

"Is that all that's left of the—"

"Yep," Chaco says. "The storm nearly took it, but it's burning."

"I'm sorry," I say. It's all I can say these days. "I should have been here. I was looking for our people. But I get lost sometimes—"

"I know," Chaco says. "You keep saying that. Do you really think you can be everywhere?"

"I know I can't," I say, looking away at the water.

"If you can't, then why do you think you should? You'll only make yourself suffer."

For some reason, the only answer I have to that is my eyes watering, so I sit down on top of the double-wide with my ragtag group of friends, adrift on an inland sea. I rub at my face and look out on what's become of the place I used to call home.

Chaco peers at me, curious. "Everyone has a part to play in what is coming, Walker. You can't take it all on by yourself."

"You're pretty smart for seven months old," I say.

"I'm timeless," he replies, matter-of-fact.

"Yeah. Well. Seven months going on timeless."

For a while, we sit together, the living and the dead and the thinning. We've hit what I call a calm pocket. Sometimes, stretches of time pass when nobody on this earth dies. It's rare, but it happens, and sometimes, it can even last a minute or more. Eight billion people on this planet and counting, and they're dying faster than they're being born, these days. But calm pockets happen. And when they do and I get a second to breathe, it's like seeing a deer before the deer sees you. I know it won't last long, and I almost don't want to move in case I scare it away.

"There have been many floods in the history of the Diné," Tsasa says, his voice a soundtrack to the quiet. The twins never miss a chance to teach. "But the first flood was the greatest."

Chaco feeds the fire with sage and twigs. Every sound is amplified: the soft slide of the lid of the pot, the tiny clicks of Chaco's claws. A flock of sparrows dives at air bubbles popping on the surface of the water, the breath of the Arroyo trapped beneath. A crow walks along the back of an overturned lawn chair bobbing in the water.

Another perches on a Tupperware bowl spinning in slow circles. They watch the water carefully, heads turned to the side.

"Long ago, our people were split by a river, man and woman each to a side. And during that time, we longed for each other. When the pain of our longing grew too strong, some of our people tried to swim to one another, only to be swept away. Lost.

"It is said that three women, a mother and her two daughters, sought to cross the river. The mother made it to be with the men of her clan, but the daughters were swept away—taken by Big Water Creature—and dragged down below."

More sparrows dive. A flock of crows is gathering on the shore, probably from the family that used to perch on the fence now long gone. One by one, they arrive, flaring down from the trees and stepping carefully through the mud.

The crow on the chair looks my way, just like the squirrel did.

"The men jumped in the river to look for the daughters but could not find them. Until they listened. And when they listened hard enough, the gods told them to follow the footsteps to the water's edge, where they had placed two bowls made of shell in the water and set them spinning."

One of the sparrows skims the water and pops a bubble with a snap of its tiny beak. I look back at the pot and find Chaco staring at me too. This whole place feels like it's looking at me, even the things that can't see me.

"Where the bowls spun, the water opened up. And the opening led to a large house underground that contained four rooms, each made of water. Dark waters to the east.

Blue waters to the south. Yellow waters to the west. And the north had waters of all colors."

Most of the crew is watching the pot or the twins, but Kai is watching the birds. The more I get to know Kai, the more I think she hears some of what I hear. Her eyes trace the sparrows as they cut low, wingtips slicing the water. I can see her mind working.

"The men checked each room. They found nothing to the east, south, or west. But in the many colors of the north, they found Big Water Creature. And next to him, they found the girls he had stolen, alongside two infant children of his own."

Stolen people. Big floods. Talking animals. I've heard this before, but it's never hit like it does now, now that we've lost our people and had our land flooded. And the animals seem to know things.

Tsosi takes a handful of wood chips from the crumbling log in his lap and holds his hand out to Chaco, who takes them piece by piece and places them in the pot. If I didn't know better, I might think they were brewing some sort of crazy potion, a big healing tea made from fire and smoke and stories.

"We do not know why Big Water Creature stole these children. But it is said that when the men demanded them back, he said nothing. Perhaps he was ashamed. Perhaps he wanted nothing more than to give his own children company. Perhaps he wanted to bring them together."

He shakes his head as if the pain of Big Water Creature was his own. "But it is known that the men were followed. Coyote also crept down to the house of four colors. And after the men took their daughters home, Coyote stole the children of Big Water Creature as well. So it was that he was left with nothing."

I know this next part. "Big Water Creature was angry," I say, watching the water, watching the birds. "And so he brought the flood."

"So he brought the flood," Tsasa says, right on cue.

He used to tell this one in early summer, when the rains would wash across the Rez. But those rains were usually soft, leaving nothing behind but blooms on the brush.

I expect more to the story. I think all of us do, but the twins are done. They settle in.

Kai isn't having it. "So that's it? The flood came? The end? Seriously?"

Maria pops an eyebrow, doing a gut check to see if Kai is showing disrespect, but she knows as well as I do that Kai is only trying to make sense of the story. Her sandal ain't coming out for that.

"That brings us to today," Tsasa says. "A story of theft on both sides. Loss on both sides. And what it brings."

"So what did they do? How did they get through the flood?"

After the twins look at one another and confer without speaking, Tsasa says, "They listened to the animals. And they were saved."

Kai stands and steps forward enough that Grant inches her way like he might have to pull her back from the edge. He sees what I see—she's not on this roof anymore. She's out there somewhere, listening like me or maybe hearing like me.

"They told me about the fire," she says, so quiet that even Grant has to lean in to hear. "It's like..." She takes another step forward, and this time, Grant does grab her. She lets him and even seems to lean back into him when he gently brings her back, but her eyes are still way out there.

"It's like I could reach out and grab him," she says, "grab them all."

We're not talking about animals anymore. We're talking about Hos. We're talking about the Arroyo folks.

I know this because I feel it too. The sparrows, the crows, all these small things that fly in the air and run along the ground—they've been trying to tell me the same thing for a while now. I just had to be up here to listen.

The crow flaps its wings out there in the middle of the water and sets the bowl spinning again, which seals the deal for me.

The answer is under the water.

Kai gets it too, but I know if she goes into that water, all she'll find is more water, then mud, then a floating graveyard of what used to be people's homes—nothing but wet trash with sharp edges.

Not me, though—I walk where others can't.

So I stand and look at this band of refugees who can't see me, then I start to climb down.

As my foot finds purchase on the flower box, Chaco says, "Good luck, Walker."

I feel like this storm hasn't passed, and everyone up here knows it. They aren't waiting for rescue—they're steeling themselves for what's coming.

"You too, bird," I say.

The water feels oily and saturating even when I can't truly get wet. I step down into it up to my waist. Some old hardwiring in the back of my brain shivers even though the cold is just an echo. I bet for any of the crew on top of the double-wide, this water would feel as cold as hell.

I start walking. Water rises up to my chest then my

neck. The crows are all eyes on me now. That's how I know I'm going in the right direction. I take a deep breath then walk under. I know that I have no lungs, no blood, and no real breath, either. But old habits die hard.

The water is murky and brackish. Weak light from the broken sky drifts through in fits and starts, little beams that seem to die halfway in. I walk through mud for twenty or so paces, dodging all sorts of things that would be a sure ringer for tetanus back in the day. Then I come to the drop-off.

I used to jump off this lip into snow, used to dare Joey to "count coup" by tagging up on the trashed-out cars at the base. But that was then. What I'm seeing now looks a lot deeper and a hell of a lot darker. For a Navajo kid who grew up, lived, and died in the same twenty-mile stretch of this desert, looking at deep water like this hits me in some fear zone I never knew I had. I feel it pulling at me, yawning bigger and bigger.

I look back, as though I could possibly go back, as though I could do anything on top of the double-wide other than talk with a bird and freak out the local wildlife. Still, jumping into black water takes a lot.

The broken daylight flickers in time, like it's passing through a lazy overhead fan. Above me, up on the surface and out over the middle of that blackness, the plastic bowl spins in slow circles.

"Alright," I say, and the words echo in my head if nowhere else. "I get it. I get it."

I push off and tread water through the darkness until I'm right underneath the bowl, and when I get there, I take one last look up. The crow looks down at me, ticking its head to keep me in view as it spins.

I give it a little salute, go stick straight, and start dropping.

On the way down, I catch glimpses of the canyon I know—the junked cars with windows long broken out, the piles of tires, old metal cabinets, rods and pipes more rust now than metal. They appear in wavy snapshots, like a dream.

The floor of the canyon is here, somewhere. If the junker cars are here, they must be resting on something. But I keep going. I pass the floor and pass the water itself, like I'm dropping through an hourglass. I even feel the pinch of the center where the stream gets very thin, then I'm inverted and climbing—not floating but stepping. The darkness fades, and I find I'm climbing a twisty staircase up through a tunnel of wet mud. The walls are damp, and everything smells like deep earth where the leaves have been rotting for years.

A light shines above. After a few more steps, the wet mud turns into dry mud then sand. Now, the walls look dug out, crisscrossed with scrapes and gouges. I'm tracing a hand along one when someone comes around a blind corner and shoulders right into me. I start to mutter an apology before I realize I felt it. I felt the shoulder hitting me.

And the shoulder belongs to someone I know, Maria Bodaway. She lost her three grandkids to bad dope. I remember walking them through the veil, and I remember her walking through the break at Knifepoint with her hands clasped behind her back.

I've found her, which means I might have found all of them.

"Grandmother?" I ask, rubbing my shoulder.

She's gotta be almost eighty. I should have bowled her

over when we ran into one another, but I was the one that got pushed back.

Her back is toward me, her face inches from the sand wall where she's stopped. She holds a big bowl made of shell in her twitchy hands.

"Maria?" I ask again. "Maria Bodaway?"

She swipes the bowl at the wall fast, like a snake strike, and gouges a big melon ball of sand out all at once. She turns back up the path, toward the dim yellow light, all without ever looking my way.

I put my hand on her bony shoulder. "Hey, Maria—"

She turns around slowly and steps up close to me at the same time. Her face is slack, mouth sagging, but her eyes are wide open and milky white, swirling with smoke I recognize. It's the poison that drips from the tendrils of Jacob Dark Sky. I stagger back against the wall. She steps closer, her white eyes searching all over, but she can't see me. Her mouth moves as if she's mumbling, but no sound comes out.

"What did he do to you?" I whisper.

She brushes the shoulder where I touched her against her slack cheek before turning away and trudging back up the stairs. I move after her but nearly get shoulder checked again, this time by Yas Hathali, her cousin and another of the lost. He stops feet from me, turns toward the wall, and gouges out another big chunk of sand. His white eyes have the desperate glow of a stunned deer as he turns back up the cave path, both hands under his bowl.

I follow them up, passing others going down along the way. It's a witchy mining operation of some sort. But what they're digging for, or why, I have no idea. All I know is they can't really see me. I'm not sure they can do anything but dig.

The yellow light gets brighter, and with it the sound of water grows, slow water, a lot of it. I run a hand along the sand wall, and it feels real—no echoes here.

I come up from the ground in what looks like a big horse barn made of twisty driftwood. The walls are half done, at best. The roof is maybe a third covered. Everywhere, the Arroyo people I've been trying to find for the better part of a year are at work, patching walls here or laying thatch there. Old people—people that shouldn't really be walking—are somehow carrying logs. Folks that had trouble standing are somehow on top of wooden ladders patching the roof with thatch.

Every eye is white, and nobody speaks. The silence is deafening, which makes the roll of the river sound like one long peal of distant thunder.

I know where I am. Only one place on all the planes of existence feels as real to me as the living world did, but I still gotta see it to believe it.

I walk right through a big unfinished hole in the sun-bleached driftwood wall, and there, about a stone's throw away, is the river of souls.

The river has no true current. Souls float like wish lanterns on the water, glowing globes on missions of their own, passing around and beside one another. Some bump here and there with little pulses of light. The only rule to the river is that down one side—the right side, to my eyes—things move toward order. Going toward the left side means moving toward chaos.

I've been to the chaos side and wouldn't recommend it—unless, of course, you're into that sort of thing. And as I can plainly see, plenty of souls are. It's way more of a fifty-fifty split than you might think, which makes sense in the great balance. I used to think chaos meant bad. But the longer I've been at this job, the more I've come to see that good and bad are not so easy as right and left.

The last time I was here, I passed through the veil that keeps the balance, the veil that exists because rules govern coming here, and the first rule is that people come dead. The second rule is that people don't come again.

"I can teach you to walk the worlds with your own two feet. I know the ways."

The words of the Gambler—of Black Bear—come to me in a soft recall that's so real that I look around expecting to find the man-god-thing in his ratty gold jacket standing behind me, whispering in my ear.

"I can teach you to feel alive again."

This is his house, Black Bear's. This is where Jacob Dark Sky took the Arroyo. He promised them a new home, but he's forcing them to build it first. And my guess is he's forcing them to build it for him.

Now that I'm outside, looking in, I have a hard time seeing the structure. It shifts like a mirage, moving with the sand. It blends in, and I realize that the reason the veil hasn't crushed this place into sand by now is that the veil can't find it, just like I couldn't find it.

Someone is shuffling down the sand to the shore up ahead. An old man wearing a family rug over his shoulders, heirloom weave, a prized possession on the side of the living. He drags an oxygen tank behind himself on a little cart that cuts two mouse-trail divots behind him.

I set off after him, and when I get close enough, I recognize Shilah Yazzie. He and his dad both crossed through at Knifepoint without a second thought. When

I'm about twenty feet from him, Shilah turns toward me. I expect to see white eyes, but instead I see soft brown.

"Ben Dejooli..." he says. "I remember you." It's a sentence of two parts with a big wheeze between. His nasal cannula isn't even attached right. It hangs off his ears by some ratty duct tape. I don't think he realizes he still has it on. He seems to be just carrying the whole rig because that's what he and his dad have done for years.

I wait for some follow-up questions, like maybe why I'm here when I've been dead for years or why he finds himself on a shore at the end of the world. But I get none of that. Instead, he looks back out at the river and continues limping toward the water.

"You don't want to go there," I say. "That's for the dead."

He nods and takes another shuffling step.

"Shilah, I'm serious. That river is a one-way ticket."

He narrows his eyes at me then waves me off in that grumpy-old-man way before taking another few steps. His swollen feet are almost at the water's edge.

"Where's your dad, Shilah?" I ask.

He nods toward the river. "He was one of the first to go in. I tried to stop him just like you're trying to stop me. But those were early days."

A low, sad cry floats our way from somewhere in the house. The sound sends spiders up my spine, but Shilah looks back stoically. I get the sense that's not the first cry he's heard from that place.

He drops the oxygen tank and steps forward. The water around his bloated toes starts to glow, and everything the water touches fades.

This shore is supposed to be a place of calm, a place of choice where the newly dead decide which side of the river they want to float along. Say what you will about the merits of order versus chaos, one thing is for sure: this isn't a place for crying. If you get here, it usually means the crying part is done.

"He's coming around again," Shilah says and shuffles in up to his knees. His legs turn into light, and he sighs. Before I get a chance to say a word, he dunks himself, lookin' right at me the whole time. And just like the countless souls that walked into these waters before him, his body dissolves before centering itself once more as a globe of light. His soul bobs about a bit before edging toward the side of order. Hopefully, he's following his dad.

Shilah knew what he was doing. His look was unflinching. Now, the question is what could drive a living man to walk willingly into this river in the first place.

I walk past the oxygen tank, flat on its side like a tipped robot. Already, the sands shift around the metal, burying it, as if they know how out of place it is here. I track back the little rivulets cut by the wheels of the cart. Shilah came from the far side of the big barn.

I keep my distance as I circle the place. Two men are gathered just inside one of the unfinished walls on the side opposite the river. One of them, I recognize instantly. His ratty red Cleveland Indians jersey stands out like blood on the sand. He's poking his head out from a break in the wood that resembles a door.

It's the Smoker.

He takes off running, which is something I don't think I've ever seen the Smoker do. It's desperate and sloppy, and he doesn't get far because a big guy with sand-stained jeans and a ripped up T-shirt comes out after him and closes real fast, fast enough to grab the Smoker and chuck him to the sand like one of those birds that drops fish on the rocks to stun them. I can hear the thud of the earth.

Hosteen Bodrey.

All I can do is shake my head. Even in the world of the dead, this guy still starts shit. But at least these two don't look milky-eyed. They move like their own brains are controlling things.

"Hey!" I say, surprising myself. I don't have a lot past *Hey*, but it sort of just jumped out of my mouth. The Smoker wasn't exactly my buddy back up top, but he and I always abided by each other.

Both men flinch low and freeze in that beaten-dog reflex I've seen too many times before on the beat. They can hear me, at least. Hos is the first to find me. The Smoker does too, but he seems more interested in the river than anything.

"Who the hell are you?" Hos asks, eyeing me up and down as I approach. "You didn't come across with us."

So he can see me too. Well, that's something, at least. I'm pretty sure he sees me as I see myself here—pale, probably a little sick lookin', dressed in an all-black NNPD getup that's starting to fade at the collar and fray at the cuffs.

The Smoker pushes himself standing, slapping his jersey free of sand. "Who fuckin' cares? He's another one of us caught in the fly trap. He'll walk into the river sooner or later, same as all of us. Even you. So you might as well save yourself the bloody hands and black memories and get it done with."

He turns back toward the river, and for a second, I think Hos might throw him down again, but instead of swinging a fist, he lays a hand on the Smoker's shoulder.

"Please," he says.

Wonders never cease. If I didn't know any better, I'd say Hos was pleading. The way it comes out makes me think his mouth doesn't quite know how to form the word, but it stills the Smoker.

"Please," Hos says again, stronger this time. "You can't leave. If you go, others will go, and then…"

The Smoker shakes his head. "Nobody gives a shit what I do. Never have."

"I do," Hos says quickly. And he looks at me like I might call him on it or something. When all he gets from me is silence, he turns back to the Smoker. "I mean, look around you, we have our world. We have our land, and it's endless. Dark Sky says it stretches forever up and down the shore. Once we build this house, he'll give it all to us."

That's a lie. But Hos says it like he's trying hard to believe it. So I'm gonna let this play out.

The Smoker reaches behind his ear and finds nothing —phantom cig. Force of habit. He flutters his fingers instead. "You don't believe that shit, and you know it. We got conned, Hos. Just like we always been conned." He looks toward the river, and his face falls into a desperate hopelessness that hits me hard. "Ah, hell. I'd probably walk all the way up to that fuckin' river and then just stare at it, too scared to move. Just like I been too scared to do anything. And then I'd end up doing what I'm gonna do now: go back in, get to work, hope Dark Sky doesn't notice me. Pray whatever witch magic he uses to wipe our minds while we do his dirty work lasts forever this time."

When he walks past me, he slows, narrows his eyes, and scans me up and down. I think he almost recognizes me as that man that came to Oka Chalk's totem pile all those years ago. Or maybe he's just mean mugging the cop uniform. Either way, he moves on. Once he's off the shore and on the higher ground, he turns and says, "Just so you know, Hos. If things was switched, I wouldn't stop you from jumpin' in that river. Hell, I might even push."

Hos looks away, stung. The hardness in his eyes fades with each step the Smoker takes until we're alone and he looks more lost than angry. This version of Hos is the one I saw at Knifepoint, the one who realized he'd screwed up but thought he was in too deep to make it right.

Looks like whatever passes for karma here might've come knocking.

"You're him, aren't you?" Hos asks, still watching the barn.

"Depends," I say.

"The one Kai talked about back before..." He shakes his head like nothing matters, and I'm surprised to find he's turned and looking at the river the same way the Smoker was, hating it but longing for it. "When I die, will I ever get to see Kai again?"

"Hos, that river isn't for you. Not yet," I say.

He ignores me. "Just tell me. Will I ever get to see her? And, like, will she see me for me, or will she be pissed?"

"I don't quite know what happens to living souls in the river. It doesn't work on me like it works on you."

He rumbles up to me, and before I know what's happening, he's got a fistful of my uniform in one hand. "Just tell me. Will I see her again?"

I stare at his hand for a second before gripping it in mine and pulling it slowly away. He stares bullets at me for a minute until he sees something in my eyes, maybe a reflection of him, one he's not proud of. "If I had to guess, I'd say yeah, she'll see you for you, and yeah, she'll probably be more than a little pissed. And if that's not what you want her to see, maybe don't go into the damn river just yet."

I drop his arm, and he lets it fall.

"The way out is down, Hos. Down the tunnel all you are digging."

He shakes his head. "Inside that house, we're Dark Sky's. His smoke finds us, creeps into us. The rest is..." He pops his fingers in a little explosion near his temple. "I can't even remember what I'm doing. I only know it's manual labor because when I come around again, my hands are bloody and my muscles burn. All that time in between? It's black."

I swallow down a bit of gunk I feel rising in my throat. I knew Dark Sky was a con man, but I just thought he and Black Bear were collectors, hoarders of things and people. I never would have guessed he's a slave driver too.

"How did you get outside?" I ask.

"Dark Sky patrols the house in a slow circle. When he's not in the room you're in, his power fades a little. I think he does it on purpose, to fuck with our heads. Gives us a chance to..."

"He gives you the chance to kill yourself? How generous of him."

"A lot of people took him up on it. If he finds you outside, you work double. That's why, if you make the decision, you run fast and hard and don't look back."

The crying from inside is louder now. Awful sounds of sadness that come from around the corner in fits and starts, cut off almost as soon they begin. I imagine that cry comes in that moment when his smoke tentacles hits their eyes, but just before he takes over.

"He's coming," Hos says. "He'll take you too. If you can get out of here, do it. Tell Kai..."

He tries to find the words but ends up raking his fingers through his hair. Whatever he wants to say to her, he doesn't know how yet, and he hates it. So he scrambles back to the house, taking the long way around, opposite the clipped cries, keeping the structure between him and Dark Sky until he disappears around the corner.

That leaves just me, waiting on what's coming. I appreciate the sentiment from Hos. But I ain't going anywhere.

When Dark Sky sees me, he stops, and for a string of seconds, we just watch each other. He walks upright like a man, with arms and legs, but the longer I look, the more I can see how wrong it all is. His human face is blurred with squeezing pincers, fluttering mandibles, and waving sprigs of insect hair. His eyes flick everywhere at once, and his limbs bend in the wrong places. What at first I took to be a shimmering jacket is actually folded layers of veiny wings vibrating almost too fast to see.

There's a reason the gods told his people—the Air Spirit people—to clean themselves up and get looking right. His kind is a horror from way back.

"How did you find us, Walker?" he asks in that same deep voice he used to command the masses on the mesa at Flatrock. If he's shocked to see me, he doesn't show it. If anything, he sounds pleased.

I'm not about to tell this thing about the passage from the Arroyo. He may already know, but I need all the cards I can play. "Let's just say I listened hard enough. What is this place, anyway? A home for your master? I met him, you know, on the other side. Black Bear. He calls himself the Gambler now. Big fan of games."

Dark Sky smirks. Or I should say his jaws sort of unhinge in a way that looks smirky.

"He is not my master."

"Uh-huh."

"We will rule together, side by side."

"I bet. He tell you that?"

His smoke is on me in a flash, way faster than what I saw on the Rez or at Knifepoint. It whips from his eyes and catches me around the neck. Before I can even think, I'm yanked face-first to the sand. My nose crunches, and the pain is dagger bright. When I can breathe again, my first thought is that I should have remembered this place can actually hurt me.

His smoke moves over me, little fingers probing my face, and when they find my eyes, they push. The feeling is violating, like someone's finger in your mouth.

This is the point where the clipped screams come in. Dark Sky pushes, and the pain is migraine hot, but whatever it is that these things infect in the living to give him control, I ain't got it.

I stand slowly, and as I do, I rip the smoke from my face and drop it to the sand, where it melts away. "I'm not some poor grandmother you can swindle into doing your chores."

I rub my hands with sand and roll my shoulders. "You steal souls that aren't yours and think you're some great chief. But I reap souls. I bring them home. The Walker has been doing it since the first soul, and we will do it until the last. Your shitty party tricks don't work on me."

His whole head tips back, his antennae wave around, and he stares at me like a roach caught in the lights. I dig my feet into the sand to make a run at him and shove aside thoughts telling me I may not even be able to touch him, let alone tackle him. The only thing I'm sure of is that I gotta make some sort of stand right here because one, if I somehow lose him and this house—and get sucked back out—I probably won't find him again. And two, this is a war of attrition, and my people are losing, throwing themselves into the river one at a time. Soon enough, nobody will be left to bring home.

"I don't have to control you to rip you to pieces," he says with eerie calm. "It is said even Coyote was ripped to pieces, ground by pumice stone into powder and stuffed in a box."

I run back my dusty memory to the twins' fireside chats. That checks, but there's more to the story. "Coyote came back," I say. "That tricky little shit knit himself back together. Some things just don't go away easy. And I'm one of 'em."

"Coyote did heal himself. Eventually. But I bet the pain was horrendous. Can you imagine it? Growing sinew back string by string, sewing muscle, pumping clotted blood back through a crushed heart." His antennae swirl slowly. "But the difference between you and Coyote is Coyote *wanted* to come back. He had a place, a home, something of his own to fight for. Something he could actually touch."

He unfurls his wings and stretches his buggy legs to full height. In a span of seconds, he's half again my size. "Let's face it, Walker. You are no Coyote."

The smoke seeps from Dark Sky's face. His wings spread wide, and his steps hardly make a sound on the sand as he closes in.

19

———————

CAROLINE ADAMS

I've never been so tired of bed in my life. I'm cramping up, leaking, greasy, going crazy from the drone of the monitors. You'd think I'd be used to it by now—the beeping. But it's just as jarring on day four as it was on day one. I think about just ripping the wires off, but that would send out a code alert, and Nascha would come, and Nascha would not be happy.

Instead, I use the wires to gently pull the rolling chassis nearer and press Mute.

I don't need the beeps anymore or the monitors. I know how this story ends. A bleed this long doesn't end with a healthy baby girl. If she's not in trouble already, the birth will be the end of her and of me too.

The silence is like a blanket. The rain seems to have let up, but the sky is just as gray. Gray in the day, black in the night—gray, black, gray, black. It's too much. Chaco is on the windowsill outside, watching me, and I can tell he's not thrilled, to say the least. That makes two of us. But what's done is done.

"Don't look at me like that," I say. "You know it's what has to happen."

I'm oozing again. It's nonstop now, a slow bleed like a wounded animal. And that's the choice I have in front of me, the choice of a wounded animal. I can limp along, hoping for things to change while I get weaker, or I can take a chance at turning the tables while I still have a little bit left in the tank.

I think my little girl would agree. I almost ask her. My throat does that weird little jiggle like it's thinking about it but not sure what to say. Eventually, I chicken out. I'm not afraid she won't answer—she hasn't answered for days—it's more like I'm afraid I'll be speaking into an empty cave. I'm afraid it'll echo.

"You know what to do," I tell Chaco. "Whatever happens, you know what to do, right?"

Chaco fluffs up his feathers and sits there like an angry fuzzy. I told him I'm tapping that gross coin on my end table, and he is absolutely not a fan. Puffing up is his version of hiding under the covers. I get it. I've done more than my fair share of hiding under the covers. I'm a big fan of shutting the world out for a while. But I can't hide anymore, not if I ever want to see her.

"I'm serious, Chaco. You know what to do, right?"

Chaco deflates back to his sleek little bird self and leans his head against the glass. I feel a little bit like we're on two sides of a visiting room in prison—me and my tiny bird friend whom I have to tell it like it is on the inside.

He's a little creature, but he gets it. Maybe he gets it *because* he's a little creature, little like her. He turns and perches to jump, wings outstretched. I get one more side-eye, and holding that look right back at him takes a lot.

He's already getting pretty good at saying things without saying things.

Chaco jumps. I hear two or three wingbeats, dull through the glass, then I'm alone with my bleeding and my coin.

I've learned that when bedrest isn't going well, getting angry is really easy. I'll look for anything to be mad at because getting mad at the outside is easier than dealing with what's going on inside. In my case, finding a target—something to pour all my anger and my desperation and sadness on, something to hate—is not hard.

Black Bear. The Gambler. Whatever he calls himself. The man who was death for so long that it wafts off him like bad cologne. The one who *takes* things. He gambles for people like chips. He eats and eats and never stops to consider that one of the things he's eating might be my entire world.

It's *really* easy to hate when it's quiet and I'm alone and bleeding. This is supposed to be wonderful, having a kid. I'm supposed to have a baby shower with dumb games where Owen and Grant and all the boys try to make baby formula and wrap diapers on dolls and everyone laughs. I'm supposed to be taking cute little bump pictures, and my mom is supposed to be here, in from Arizona and pretending that she's not terribly uncomfortable on the Rez. Then, when the egg timer goes off, a few tough pushes amongst family before the epidural. A screaming pink bundle of joy—some sweaty pictures. *Sleep. New life. Tada! Rest up. Take maternity leave. Start new life together.*

That's what's supposed to be happening.

How stupid all of that sounds here, now. I feel cheated. *Everyone else sneezes out babies, so what the hell is wrong with me?* It doesn't have to define me, but growing a baby is supposed to be one of the things I do. I am a woman. It's built into me. *Why else did I have horrible cramps for, like, thirty years? What was all that crap for? We get to the big show, and all of a sudden, nothing works?* A little advanced warning would have been nice. Maybe I would've opted out of wild mood swings and night sweats as well, just checked No, Thank You there.

One little secret about how a lot of women get through all the crappy parts of being female is by holding fast to the belief that we're putting money away for a rainy day. One day, all this will be worth it. *And here I am at the bank, ready for my nest egg, and whoops! Sorry! Mismanaged funds! Systemic failure! Run on the bank!*

My ears start ringing, and I'm breathing too fast. If I hadn't muted it, my blood pressure monitor would probably be screaming at me.

Anger spirals are real. People can get too deep before they know where they are. If your brain starts using words like *supposed to be*, run the other way. The truth is there's no such thing as *supposed to be*. There's just what is.

I see Owen's bracelet, the woven one he got from the Navajo girl he helped through a really bad thyroid issue. Recognizing it takes me a minute because it's never been off his wrist, not in all the years I've known him. One time, it was fraying, and he took it to the Arroyo and had Maria stitch it strong again while he wore it. But here it is, whole, wrapped around the handle of my water jug. For me.

I take it up carefully, fold it in my fist, and hold it tight.

Owen was gone when I woke up. I know what's going on at the Arroyo. I know what it takes to keep a place like this together. I know I should call him before I tap that coin. *It's just that...*

He wouldn't let me do it. He would understand why I

want to, but he would do it himself first. He loves me too much.

I watch the windowsill for a while, hoping for Chaco even though I told him to go away. Just having him here was nice, his little black body like a fearless slice of night. I wonder how many times in my life I've said "go" when I really mean "stay."

I could drop down that rabbit hole all day, but I'm bleeding, and I don't have much time. So I tap the coin.

FOR A LONG WHILE, nothing happens, enough nothing that I end up tapping the coin a few more times like it's a busted flashlight. But just when I ease myself back into bed wondering what the heck to do next, the lights in the hall flicker. A couple of the really old halogens here buzz like pissed-off wasps, and the sound of them going in and out shakes me from my own thoughts.

The door was open a crack, but now it slides open more, slowly. And in walks the Gambler. He's wide-eyed and smiling and looks way too happy to be here. I sit up and try to look as normal as any girl can, who's been laid up in a bed for days.

The Gambler doesn't seem to care if I'm sitting or standing or lying down or dead. He looks at me like I'm the biggest trophy he's ever seen, like he wants to mount my head over the fireplace and sit back and drink scotch and talk about how he caught me.

And that's alright by me. That's what I'm hoping for.

"I want to place a bet," I say.

20

KAI BODREY

When you're stranded five bodies deep on top of a double-wide in a flood, it gets pretty tight pretty quick. We would have been seven, but Big Hill and Zahara have their crow tickets to the cosmic highway or whatever, and waiting around isn't their thing. They got their own shit to deal with. I get it. They're like Joey but for their own worlds, so it's probably for the best. Zahara gifted the pot to the twins, and Big Hill offered to stay for a bit, but having him up top here would be bad news, all splayed out like a bayou gator while the whole thing sinks into the mud under him.

Now is a time of waiting. I knew Zahara and Big Hill for only a couple of hours, but I missed them the second they left. The strength of this Circle is real. Grant says the crow totems find the people. I'm just glad they seem to find the right people.

I pull a pebble from my shoe and drop it off the side. It sinks for too long, not that I needed that to tell me we're in some shit here. The lawn chairs floating about a hundred yards out did that hours ago. So did the crows. Grant says the Walker was here but now is gone. And I think he went down, down, down.

Chaco took off to the hospital a while ago for an update, but in his absence, crows come one by one, like little black jets hooking the landing on our boxy aircraft carrier way out in the middle of nowhere. And they bring twigs—each of them, one twig. The Arroyo fire is safe for now, thanks to them.

Grant tells me Chaco said the Gambler has something on the Rain God. I don't know a whole hell of a lot about the Rain God, but I sure as shit know about gambling debts. I never went to Wapati, but most of the men in my family did, and it never worked out too great for them. I bet card games snare gods just like they snare people. Same shit, different world. One where the Gambler won the rain, so now he can call down the flood. And whatever it touches is his. I'm just hoping he doesn't know it ain't touching that pot.

The sky is a glary type of gray. The light is all flat. Grant is walking back and forth at the edge of the roof, squinting out into the distance, waiting for Chaco. He checks his phone and mutters, shaking his head. Service is spotty. He got one text out to Owen but hasn't heard a response.

"So, what, are we just supposed to wait up here all day?" he asks.

"Where you gonna go?" I fire back. "Trucks are swamped. And even if you could drive, you got no roads." But I know the waiting isn't really what's bothering him.

"Where is Dad?" he asks.

"I don't know, but clomping around up here isn't gonna bring him around any quicker."

He slides to sit next to me, boots hanging off the edge.

"He would be here if things were okay," he says, by which he means Caroline and the baby. "Hell, he's the one supposed to be *makin'* things okay. He's the damn doctor! What's he been doing this whole time? Everyone else threw their hat in. The Circle kept the fire lit. We did our part."

I put a hand on his shoulder and pull him around. "Hey, look at me. Get angry at the right things."

He takes his hat off and wipes his brow. "What?"

"You think Owen isn't doing everything he can for her? Really? He is. So get angry at the right things. Because I know it may look like our storm is over here, but this isn't the end, Grant. It's the eye. I know you can feel it too."

He takes a deep breath and puts his hat back on, and just as he's settling it, a little black speck appears on the horizon.

"Incoming," he says. His face goes distant, and I know he's already talking to Chaco. And not liking what he's hearing.

We stand to make room for a landing. "What is it?" I ask.

Chaco comes in low and does an awkward little scrape and roll on the metal until he bumps against Grant's boots. His feathers are all out of whack, and he's breathing like a spooked rabbit.

Grant picks him up and speaks with him, translating on the fly. "He's not making a ton of sense. Something about how Mom figured out his trick."

"Who?" I ask.

"The Gambler. He says... says he's so old that his smoke has weight. Says he uses it like grease. Marks the cards with it. Weights the dice with it. Moves the spinners and the slot wheels and pretty much tips the scales of any sort of game his way... Wait a second," he says, asking Chaco now. "How did she figure this out?" His face falls. "What do you mean she made a wager? What kind of wager?"

I eye the elder twins and find them already eyeing me back. Joey is too. The stories call Nááhwiilbiihi the Winner of People. And more and more of the stories are coming to life.

Grant walks to the edge of the roof and stands there, looking out at the water like he's at the bars of a cage. "Chaco doesn't know what kinda bet she made. Doesn't know if she won or lost. Mom told him to come straight here. She thinks if we know how this guy cheats, maybe we can find a way to beat him at his next game."

I open my arms to the mess all around us. "What more could he possibly want? He already has the Arroyo and the bell, and now the rest of the Rez too."

"Why don't you ask him yourself?" Joey says, standing, his voice a low growl. He points back up where the car path used to run toward the entrance.

The Gambler pushes open the gates, and the water ripples out before him. He walks our way slowly, picking a careful path where he doesn't sink. His footfalls make soft sucking sounds.

"Impossible," Maria says.

I admit it's an impressive sight. I'm sure he wants us to think he walks on water and not on the mud underneath. Maybe if he caught me on a down day and I was feeling desperate instead of pissed off, I'd believe it. But Caroline saw through him, and so do I. He's no god.

"He's a con man," I say. I think I mean to say it to myself, but it comes out. "A cheater."

Grant's hand trembles in mine, with anger and grief,

both. I know he's steeling himself to go toe-to-toe with this man, to somehow beat him with grit, guts, hustle, belief— to use his love for his family as armor to do whatever it takes.

Grant's been to hell and back since the bell fell to him. He's faced down monsters, chaos, wayward souls, all sorts of shit I wouldn't even know how to start dealing with, and the fact that he's still standing means his way works, at least most of the time. But one thing he hasn't had to deal with is cheaters.

Me, on the other hand, I had a family full of them. "Cheater" is kind of the word that comes to mind around here when someone says "Bodrey," and for good reason. My piece-of-shit brother and our worthless cousins and uncles have been cheating and conning their way up and down the bootleg highway for generations. They cheat strangers. They cheat friends. Shit, they even cheat each other.

I know cheaters. They talk tribe, talk loyalty and history and all that until they're blue in the face, then the second you turn around, they rob you blind.

Grant ain't been robbed blind yet. And as long as I stand next to him, he won't be, because I been robbed blind enough for the both of us. And I know that the only real way to beat a cheater is to cheat right back.

21

THE WALKER

Hitting Dark Sky is like swinging at a tree trunk. It doesn't hurt him any, but my hand feels shattered. I stumble back onto the sand and grit my teeth to keep from screaming in pain.

His smoke is relentless. It has this raking power, like steel wool ripped down your skin. And I'm out of shape—not physically, since that doesn't matter out here, but mentally. After years and years of feeling nothing but echoes, suddenly coming back to the real thing is like throwing open the shades on a room in my head that's been dark for a decade.

His smoke catches me around the neck again and squeezes. I know I don't breathe, but I still panic at the crackling sound my windpipe makes as it gets crushed. I rip the smoke off, toss it away, and instinctively grab at my throat.

He took a chunk of me with him, like skin under fingernails. No blood, but I can feel the raw grooves, and the pain hits just as hard.

Dark Sky extends a wing, and the tendril of smoke I

tossed shakes little bits of my neck on top of it like cheese gratings on a dinner plate. He ponders my skin while I fight to breathe through the pain. "I wonder what would happen to the living world if the Walker was shredded to pieces and stuffed in a box?" he asks. "Could you still labor as you do?" He brushes his wing clean. "Should we find out?"

His smoke thrashes my way again, and I barely dive clear before it cracks like a whip and kicks up a divot in the sand where I was just standing.

I got one rule I live by in a fight: keep moving, especially after you get hit. So I suck back the pain and scramble low to get behind him. I land a kick to his lower back like I'm trying to break down a door, but it breaks me down instead. My knee crunches, and I drop onto my ass. He has no give whatsoever.

He turns slowly. Everything about him is slow. I got my one rule, so I'm up and moving again. Even with a limp, I'm clearly faster, but fast doesn't matter much when I'm up against something with rotten roots that go this deep. He's anchored like a fire hydrant.

Bottom line is I'm gonna get my ass kicked up and down this shoreline unless I get a plan together. And since I have no idea what to do I do the only thing I can think of. I keep him talking.

"You wanna know how I got here?" I ask, turning circles as he comes around. Dodging smoke where I can and breaking it off when I can't, I try not to cry out in pain as I lose more bits of myself.

"I don't care, Walker," he says, pausing to straighten himself out. He gathers his smoke around his veiny wings, rolls his neck, and that's when I see the flash.

The bell.

He catches me looking, so I own it. "Looks heavy," I say.

The ground he unearths makes a ripping sound as he squares up with me. He uses the momentum to swing more thick smoke tendrils my way, and before I can roll, he's got me in his shredding grip again.

"It is my boon. Black Bear gave it to me as a spoil of war."

He picks it up off his slickened shell of a chest and holds it out on its lanyard. The silver has a heavy tarnish, like a wedding ring on a long-dead corpse.

"I know the weak run to the river. I feel it in the bell. It forms," Dark Sky says, holding it in his twisted hands. "How does it feel to know that with a shake of this little thing, I could end you forever?"

He wears it awkwardly. Like jewelry. But I know more about that thing than almost anyone, and I know it's not a jewel. It's no boon, either. It's a terrible burden.

"You would never do that," I say.

"Oh?" asks Dark Sky. "And why not?"

"Because then you'd have to do what I do," I hold out my black-veined arms and pull down at my frayed black collar to show where he cut me, to show the darkness within, which can never spill out. "You wouldn't live anymore, not even in the half-assed servant's way you do now. You'd be the Walker. And you'd serve the veil until you're too fucking crazy to remember who you are. And then, if you're lucky, some asshole like yourself rings that damn thing and puts you out of your misery before you end up like Black Bear, crazy as a rabid dog, sucking in everything he can to fill a hole that can't be filled."

Dark Sky snaps a smoke tendril around my cheek and yanks, nearly slamming me to the sand again. I stand my ground but lose a good bit of my jaw. The feeling is somehow empty and burning at the same time, a phantom limb on fire.

I dodge the next swipe, but barely.

"You're right, Walker. You know the story of our people as well as I do. There's a reason we don't speak of death. What you do is a curse."

I try to swipe open the soul map, but my hands spin up a fat lot of nothing. I'm out of service, way out of service. His laughter sounds like clicking deep in his throat.

Okay, rethink. Keep moving. I could take off down the bank of the river and run toward the side of order. If I get far enough away from this shifty place, maybe I can find the veil and get the hell out of here. I glance that way, but Dark Sky reads it.

"My smoke can fly faster than you can run, Walker. And if you're looking for the veil, you will not find it here. The veil has forgotten this place. We are invisible."

I take off toward the house. It's the only thing I can think to do. I'm losing parts of my face, and I don't want to be stuffed into a box. Maybe I can put a wall between us and buy some time to think.

Dark Sky just watches me, which even in my animal panic, I know is a big red flag, but I'm already clawing my way toward the house, and no better plan is coming to me. Dark Sky follows, but he's slow. He was slow to begin with, and the bell has made him slower. It might buy me a couple of minutes.

Shadows move in a gap in the driftwood ahead—a flash of red jersey, a tattered white T-shirt. Hos and the Smoker step out, so at least we're all in it together. Then I see how white their eyes are, and I realize in an instant that Dark Sky doesn't have to be fast, not if his people are fast for him.

I skid back like a horse at a cliff's edge, but it's too late. Dark Sky is inside them just like he was in Kai and Hos back on the living plane. Their speed and their strength isn't theirs. It's his.

The Smoker snatches me at an ankle, and Hos stuns me with an elbow to the temple. I go limp without wanting to, which is a terrible feeling. That disconnect between brain and body is something I haven't felt since the moment I first died.

The Smoker grips me under one armpit, and Hos takes the other. They rip me to standing and drag me back down the sand to where Dark Sky waits.

"Hos," I mumble. "It's me. We just talked about Kai, remember? Help me help her."

His white eyes twitch and skitter all over. Hos is in there. So's the Smoker. But they ain't driving. And they never will be as long as Dark Sky stands on these shores.

Dark Sky wraps his smoke around my waist and tears at it like a nine-tail whip. The pain is blinding, maddening. Sky is picks up the parts of me he's stripped away and puts them in a totem pouch at his hip.

"I want nothing of your position, Walker," he says, picking up right where we left off. "But what if I command one of my dying acolytes to ring the bell? They would do your job for me. Think what I could do then, how many I could bring into the fold for Black Bear. Our house would be overflowing."

He looks at Hos with a sickly type of grooming smile. "And I believe I've found the one."

Dark Sky is as much in thrall to Black Bear as the Arroyo people are to Dark Sky. Maybe the creature is some sort of boon himself, some long-forgotten stake of the gods, a prize pulled down from the shelf after a long night at the cosmic poker table. Or maybe he's just as crazy as Black Bear, a madman following a madman.

Either way, I know one thing is true. He's the pit bull at the end of Black Bear's chain. As long as Black Bear has his claws in the living world, Dark Sky is unbeatable. And if this is a war of attrition, I'm the one that's gonna end up in pieces.

22

OWEN BENNET

Dr. Sadler is telling me that the bleeding triggered the labor, and I'm standing here like some first year freezing up at his first code. It's just not processing. I was filling up my stained mug with burned coffee when Sadler found me, so that's what I continue to do. I pour black coffee and let his words settle over me. I nod and pretend I comprehend. Sadler's voice sounds like it's down a well, and mostly, I need to pour the coffee to keep doing something so that I don't keel over.

"Owen," Sadler says, gripping my arm.

I look down at it like it's neither his hand nor my arm.

"Her water broke," he says. His brow is beaded. I can smell the sweat coming off him. "It's happening."

My mind says, *This is the last night you'll ever see her alive,* before I can shut it up with a scalding sip of terrible coffee.

"Alright then," I say, sounding very much like Dr. Bennet on the outside when I feel like a schoolchild on the inside. "How do we approach this?"

Like I said, the curtain between patient and doctor is

very thin. It gets even thinner when family is involved, but pretenses must be made because without them, I will lose my mind.

Sadler talks to me the entire way back to Caroline's room. I register what he says, but most of my cognitive ability focuses solely on keeping myself walking.

"Nascha radioed as soon as the water broke, maybe ten minutes ago. First contraction was five minutes later. Could be real, could be a false flag. She's not super hydrated, and it could easily be a function of stress."

I look at my watch as if it means anything. Fifteen minutes ago, I was on break with my phone shut off at the insistence of the team. Funny how that works.

"Dilation?" I ask.

"Three centimeters."

That is nothing. She needs drugs to get more dilated.

"Can we help her along?"

Sadler shakes his head. "Anything we have would take too long."

No drugs, then. I should have been more prepared, but up until fifteen minutes ago, we were trying to keep this baby in at all costs. "What about an epidural?" I ask.

Sadler shakes his head again. I knew the answer before I asked, but I still felt like I had to ask. Even if we had an epidural set up, nobody here would dare, not even me. Those are long needles with little room for error, and nobody here is an anesthesiologist.

None of us is an OBGYN either. We all had our specialties at one point, but since then, we've been blunted to the mean. And even back in the day, none of us were labor and delivery. My specialty was oncology. Sadler was ear, nose, and throat or something, which would be great if Caroline had strep and wasn't in labor seven weeks premature with a potentially nonviable baby and a ruptured placenta.

"Blood?" I ask.

"She's B positive. We have some universal donor blood available, but not much. I've already prepped one bag and brought in the large-bore IV setup in case we need it."

That's not exactly what I mean although it tells me all I really need to know. If we're prepping with the large bore, it means there's blood.

We get to her door, and I hear Nascha's voice inside: "I know, *amiga*. I know. Try to breathe it out."

I pull Sadler aside the door before going in. A glance out of the window shows me that it's gray o'clock. These things always happen at when it's gray out.

"You've delivered a baby, right?" I ask.

"Yes," he says. "But not for a while, and not like this." He wipes sweaty hands on his khakis, which have the kind of stains you'd expect to see on a rotating physician who's been working for basically seventy-two hours straight during a natural disaster. "You?" he asks, with just enough hope to break my heart.

"Same. Nothing remotely this high risk." Sadler's face falls.

I realize he's very wrapped up in the outcome here, and with that realization comes another, greater: our friends, our coworkers, all care deeply. I'm not quite sure why that comes to me as a bit of a shock.

"We can do it," I say. "People deliver babies in taxi cabs, for God's sake. But it's the bleeding that worries me. Anything we might try to do to mitigate it could scar her womb forever."

We sit there for another second in the darkening hallway. Both of us have been at the CHC long enough—

worked together long enough—to cut the bullshit. A lot goes unspoken. We're as prepped as we can be with what we have, and we're probably better than your local cab driver. The moment strikes me as one where there is a clear before and a clear after, and no matter what happens, nothing will be the same after we go into that room.

I straighten my collar and go down one button. "Alright, let's go."

Even though I put on my best doctor face, as soon as Caroline sees me, she says, "That bad, huh?"

Her face is sweaty and pale to translucent, and whatever mask I had cracks like an eggshell. I should have known better.

She swipes weakly at hair stuck to her forehead. Her knees are up, and Nascha is there on the other end. In between is a mess of bloody sheets.

Nascha looks up at me and nods but looks away before I can get a read, which means it's not good.

Sadler rolls back her vitals, and I go to her side. With anyone else in the world, I would probably try to velvet hammer this. Draw it out and wait for more data. But I won't do that with her. She can sniff out that kind of thing like a bloodhound.

"It's not great, honey," I say, and the hitch in my throat feels like a pine cone. I try to cough it out, but she sees through that too.

"Don't worry," she says.

A sick laugh creeps up on me that makes me huff through my nose. "Just like that, huh?" I ask, trying to smile, trying to hold her hand without shaking. "Just switch that worry switch off? Why on earth didn't I think of that days ago?"

She reaches up and cups my jaw. Her hand feels light, devoid of all strength. Cold, too. A mannequin's hand.

"Don't worry," she says again.

Somewhere in the back of my mind, an alarm bell goes off. She's too sure. This is the same woman that worries if our low kitchen ceiling catches too much stove gas, the same woman who listed pros and cons of lock replacement when I lost our front door key for half a day.

"Dr. Bennet," Sadler says, snapping me back. "I think we better wash up."

Caroline looks at me the same way she did ten years ago when she handed in her notice at ABQ General and I asked if I could leave with her. The two of us were standing under an endless sky in the parking lot, the crows wheeling high above. She treats this like it's a beginning, and I don't understand. Nothing about this screams *beginning* to me. This has a very definitive *ending* feel.

I come very close to telling her how much I was willing to give up for even the smallest chance to keep her alive, how much I laid out on the line with the Gambler when I walked out on her while she slept. I still don't believe he has the power he says he has. But when the people I love are hanging in the balance, the amount of belief I'm willing to suspend is amazing.

I found him. I went all the way to Wapati, only to be told that I can't gamble for what I've already lost. And before I could get more out of him, the piece of shit walked down the slots and into thin air.

Caroline stifles a moan. Her forehead is drenched. Nascha sensibly places a cold compress upon her and nods at me with a *let's do this*.

I turn toward the sink and unbutton my cuffs, roll them four times, past the elbow, and start soaping up. The entire room smells like a high school science lab, and I wrap myself in it, huffing it like it might trigger medical muscle memory and take me away. Right now, my job is my security blanket, and without it, I'm nothing but a shaking mess.

23

GRANT ROMER

The Gambler walks toward us, and the water rolls slowly in his wake. He's scenting something, like a hound dog. Chaco hops up onto my shoulder and chirrups low, and the sound draws his attention, and for a second, he pauses, like he's surprised to see us here.

"That's far enough," I say.

He cocks his head and smiles a wide smile that cracks his lips and folds the dirty, sun-scorched skin at the corners of his eyes.

"Strange," he says. "I have won this place, but..." He licks his finger and tests the air. "But it is not yet mine. I have raked the table clean, but I am thinking perhaps a jewel fell between the cracks."

His speech is strange and dusty. The way he stands, reflected in the flat glare of the water, he looks blurry, like he ain't all there. He pauses, eyes wide, waiting for an answer I don't have.

After a moment, he asks again, holding out his fingers and rubbin' 'em together like he might magic a coin outta thin air. "My jewel. Have you seen it?"

"I got no fuckin' idea what you're talkin' about."

"Careful," Chaco says to me, knowing I'm gettin' riled up.

Damn right, I am. This asshole wearing the skin of a dead man has drowned my home. He's knocked my whole family over. He's killing my unborn sister by just bein' here.

I step to the edge, meaning to jump down, but Chaco quickly chirps, "That water is his. Do not enter it."

I'd kick something if there was something to kick, but I got nowhere to go and nothin' to hit.

"Are *you* my jewel?" he asks, looking at me skeptically. "Keeper that was?"

"I ain't no jewel, you maniac."

He picks a dried bit of skin off the center of his upper lip and ponders it before flicking it into the water. "No," he says. "I suppose not."

He stands on his tiptoes in the water, rising maybe another half an inch, and sniffs again. By now, Kai and Joey have joined me on either side. The Gambler ranges slowly to the right, stepping in a crisscross like he's circling a deer, bow out, string taut.

A cold wind brushes our backs, and it carries smoke from the lacquered pot his way.

He sniffs again. "What is for dinner, my friends?"

"Get the hell out of here," Kai says. "That's what's for dinner."

"You put the fire in the pot," he says slowly, showing that sick smile again. "Clever."

"The fire is not yours," Joey says, his voice a rumble. "It is ours. Our story burns inside it. Your story is over."

The Gambler opens up his arms. "And yet, here I am."

He breathes deep, taking in more than the smoke, like

he's draining the air itself. He leaches the life from around him with every step, leaving a dark mark where he's been, like a scorch that slowly fades. I see now why no new life would want to be anywhere near him, why my sister wouldn't want to come out into a world where he's at work, grabbing things, calling her a *jewel*.

"My story ends when I say so," he states flatly. "And I do not say so. Yours, though? What do you think... that you will live up on that box forever? Fed by the carrion birds and the swimming rats?"

"You ain't gettin' that fire," I say. "Try to take it, and you're gonna learn that real quick."

He *tsk tsk*s like a schoolteacher, never taking those watery eyes off me. He ain't blinked once. "I don't want the fire. I want the fire out. And I want *you* to be the ones who see it die."

He looks over his shoulder, where the distant sky is a swollen purple bruise. He looks back and raises his ratty eyebrows. "I can wait in my water longer than you can wait on your box."

Chaco chirrups low.

Looks like our window in the eye of the storm is comin' to a close.

I think of any deal I could make. He already has the bell, along with most of the Arroyo and most of the Rez. He stole a big grip of our people, and the ones he didn't, he ripped the hearts out of and left them soaking wet. There's nothing left. Maybe I'm worth somethin'. Maybe if I give myself up, I can at least feed him long enough to buy some more time for my family.

I clear my throat, and Chaco cinches hard on my shoulder, but I ignore it. "How about we make a deal—"

Kai pushes me back and steps to the front. "So long as

we're in a standoff, how about we at least make it interesting?"

The Gambler stops his pacing and considers her. I want to consider her myself, actually—specifically, what on earth she thinks she's doin', but Joey puts a hand on my shoulder in a way that says, *Let her talk.*

"How do you mean?" the Gambler asks slowly, licking the air with the tip of his tongue.

"Let's put something on the table," she says, pushing her jet-black hair behind her ears. Mud cakes her legs and her hands. Her face is streaked with dirt that looks a bit like warpaint.

The Gambler takes in more of our air and breathes out whatever comes from his dead lungs. He smiles that cracked smile again, bleeding now from where he picked at it.

"Now you are speaking my language, Bodrey," he says. "But there are none of your cards here or your whirring slot machines. Just the water."

"There are the old games," Tsasa says from where he's sitting. He's back-to-back with Maria, who is literally propping up both twins.

Always at her post, she is.

Tsosi speaks up. "Yes. The old games. *Tsidił, Na'azhǫǫsh, Jooł.*"

The words hit the Gambler like a drug, and he steps back in the water, eyes manic.

"Or do you not remember?" Tsosi asks, sliding off the top of the pot for another crow delivery. Wafting the smoke our way... and the gamblers. "I thought that you are the one called Winner of Games."

"I remember, cousin," says the Gambler. "That is one of my names, and I am called so for good reason." He reaches into his pockets and pours chips and coins into the water. The *splunk* of each echoes around the water-logged canyon. He looks up, still dropping his chips from knotty, knuckled fingers, and finds Kai again. "What do you have in mind to wager, little sister?"

Kai looks back at the pot.

"What are you doing?" I whisper harshly.

Joey clears his throat, and I think maybe that's meant for me, but I can't let her do it. This creature in front of us —this long shadow of death—has taken way too much from me.

When Kai looks at me her eyes are clear golden brown, as clear as I've seen 'em since she came back from Knifepoint. And I imagine what she must see in me is nothin' of the sort—no gold, just bloodshot and twitchy, waiting for the next punch.

Chaco says from my shoulder, "I think maybe we should trust her, man."

I want to say I'm pretty sure everything is falling apart at the CHC. I want to say I got a handful of people I love and I'm losing them as we speak, one by one. And I can't afford to lose anyone else. But with gamblers, it's best to play your cards close to your chest. So I step back.

He sniffs the wind again and nods. "The heart of the Arroyo. Quite a boon. For that, I will stake the earth of the Arroyo." He draws his soggy, duct-taped shoes along the dead water in an arc that floats out across the whole flat and makes everything go all wavy. It's enough to make me feel sick.

But Kai only laughs. "I thought we came here to gamble," she says. "Earth for a heart? That's no wager."

The Gambler narrows his ghost eyes, and the water

stills again. "It is plenty for you who sit stranded on a box."

"So you're afraid, then," she says, turning away and moving to sit next to Tsasa.

The twins are taking careful interest in the pot and nothing else.

"Little sister, I haven't been afraid for a very, very long time."

Kai sniffs, warming her hands over the pot. "Then stake something real, something that matters."

The look in the Gambler's eyes chills me to the core. One time I was drivin' the back roads late at night and passed a mountain lion on the hunt, and my headlights caught his eyes and lit up this sort of deadly spark in them, a killer's spark. That's what I think of.

"All of my earth, then. The Arroyo. Boxes. The track lands. The mains. Even the canyons. All the water touches. How's that, little sister?"

Kai glances at me as if, once again, I might have any fuckin' clue how to proceed here. All I can think to do is stay still. Stayin' still has served me pretty well in the past when it has to. She glances back at the twins, and something passes between them that I can't understand, some conversation that started when she was a kid in the depths of these stories around the fire and that is coming to a close right now.

"Don't you want to know which games we play first?" Kai asks.

"You should know by now that it does not matter," he says, flipping a hand. "You choose."

Kai has one of her razor retorts right on the tip of her tongue, but she bites it back, which is sayin' a hell of a lot about how delicate this whole situation is. "All of your earth for the heart of the Arroyo," she says. "Agreed?"

The Gambler laughs deep down in his stolen lungs, and it rumbles but doesn't quite reach the air. "Agreed."

Kai spits in the water. The Gambler spits in the water, which seems to seal it. He rubs his filthy palms together and eats more of our air before blowing out whatever dusty crud is deep down inside him. "Let us begin."

24

OWEN BENNET

Caroline talks when she's nervous, and I clam up when I'm nervous, so I'm silent and her voice is all I can hear. She's telling me the story of when I took that bullet for her at ABQ General so long ago that I sometimes wonder if it was a dream. More than a few times, I catch myself giving that scar on my shoulder a second glance in the mirror and wonder what the hell actually happened there.

"You said you don't really remember it, right?" she asks, panting a bit.

She's breathless already though we're nowhere near where we need to be in terms of dilation. Sadler is prepping more blood bags. Nascha is gathering linen and pads. Caroline's already lost a significant amount of blood, maybe a pint since the labor started. Sadler is taking a breather. He'll swap back in soon.

I check the hospital sat link again. It's spotty, but every second I get a connection, I hit the call button for the ABQ General team. So far, I've gotten a ring and a half. Then the link dropped again. I've tried so many times that little bloody thumbprints cover the phone.

I set it aside. I need to let that go and focus on the task at hand and calming my actual shaking hands. I'm staring down at them when I realize she's asked me a question.

"What was that? Oh, yes. I mean, no, I don't remember it. Don't remember anything, really. Just that I shut my eyes and jumped. It wasn't a choice."

Her hands are white knuckled fists balled up in the bedding at either side. She's ashen, dangerously pale. But there's a spark in her eyes still, a fire deep inside that burns.

She takes the whole of me in for a moment, and I know she sees everything in my smoke. It must be lousy with fear. I can smell it on myself, that panic sweat, fear sweat. It has an acrid smell that's instantly recognizable, almost like vinegar.

"That's what I have to do now, Owen" she says. "I have to close my eyes and jump."

I'm not quite sure what she's talking about, but that's my fault. When the contractions come, everything sort of goes out the window for me, and my replies are all fairly generic. My brain is on the vitals, on the cervix, working to manually stretch where I can, adding as much pressure as I dare. My shirt is sticking to my back. The fabric at my right bicep is soaked through from wiping my brow.

Last time Caroline pushed, I felt my little girl. But I felt the flat of her back and the soft ripple of her spine, which made the moment a dizzying mix of emotions. It was first touch, but in the wrong place. She's breech presentation, and that is not good.

"Nobody's jumping anywhere, honey. You're going to

stay right here, and you're going to have a baby, and we're going to get through this together," I say.

"Don't worry," she says again. She's said this a few times now even though it's supposed to be my line, but my bravado is so false it rings hollow enough to make me wince the second the words leave my mouth. When she says it, she really *means* it.

Maybe if she saw the other end of this bed, she would think differently. "Lie back, honey. You need to conserve your energy for when it counts."

I don't know who I'm kidding. She can see what I know—how each contraction, each push, releases gouts of bright-red blood, placental blood. And even if she can't see it, she knows how many times Nascha has swapped pads. She's done the math. Caroline always does the math.

"You wanna know what I always thought was, like, a top-ten cute moment from you?" she says, breathing like she's run a marathon.

And I do. I really do. Because right now, nothing about me feels remotely competent let alone attractive. "Sure," I say.

"How after you had your shoulder repaired and you were in that sling—remember that sling?"

I do remember that sling. I wore that thing for what felt like a myriad of lifetimes. I had two, a white and a blue.

"Remember how you used to match it to your button-down?" she asks.

From somewhere, somehow, a smile comes. "I never did that," I say, pretending to be carefully at work on the south end.

"Of course you did. You'd match it to your button-down, and you'd, like, carefully put the shoulder band underneath your collar so it wouldn't ruin your lines." She snorts at this last little bit and I'm about to laugh, really laugh, because she's absolutely right although I never told her that at the time—I've always been a sucker for my lines, and I remember it being very difficult to pass off a shoulder sling in any sort of professional way. She has more to say, but her story is clipped by that slow windup of shock that I know all too well.

Contractions are incoming.

"Now's the time to push," I say because that's what OBGYN doctors say.

Caroline pushes. More blood. At some point, Nascha comes in and wipes things down, swaps things out. She wipes me down too. Sadler switches in. I'm breathing like a spent horse. Caroline is moaning, and the sound is strange, the continuous pain. Each time, it gathers in pitch until it just hits this wall, and she sputters out, heaving. Then back to square one.

It makes sense from a medical perspective. The baby's back is to the exit. Caroline can push all she wants—she's not gonna force her out back first. She'll rip apart.

Sadler is talking to me. "Get some air, Owen! Or you'll be on the floor."

I'm seeing stars at the periphery—photopsia, shifting of the gel in the eye. Nascha grabs me by the arm and leads me to the door.

"Ten deep breaths outside," she says. "And I want you to count them, Dr. Bennet. The world will hold together for ten breaths."

I'm shoved outside the room into the dark hallway, and Nascha gently closes the door behind me, trapping in all the sounds and smells and sights.

For several moments, I just stand there. I know how

much I've been sweating by how quickly I get chilled. My hair is plastered to my head, my shirt soaked through. I'm shivering. Maybe I've been shivering for a long time. Then someone puts a blanket around me.

At any other moment of my life, this would've elicited at least a some sound of surprise. But not today. I grab it on instinct. It has the soft feel of well-worn cotton but a wonderful weight. I glance at it, at the stark patterns and colors as rich as if the dye was dripped today. A Navajo rug. And the one who threw it over my shoulders is there, nodding at me as if we've been in conversation for some time and I'm not dumbstruck.

I recognize him. He was with the family out front by the baseboard heaters when the power went out. One of the Running Water men, I saw him for an irregular heartbeat. I can't remember his name, so I can't properly greet him, which bothers me but doesn't seem to bother him. He nods toward the exit, propped open very illegally but bringing in fresh air, even in the dead eye of this storm. Another smell is coming in, too, something even cleaner.

The Running Water man helps me navigate the hall, which comes into focus for my low-battery eyes one piece at a time. A lot of people are here. The Navajo are lining the walls together.

"Why is everyone here?" I ask him. "Is the front flooded?"

"No," he says. "They come to offer strength to your clan. To witness."

And that's what they're doing—just being there. No singing. No chanting. Just being. But I can feel them, feel their collective heat and their heavy presence. It helps pin the world down in the places where I feel it fraying most.

"Ten breaths," he says. "Even I know what Nascha says goes, Dr. B."

He walks with me down the hall, and people follow us with their eyes, but not like they're seeing me as the trainwreck I am. This is more like how I would watch Grant when he was a kid. Just keeping tabs.

Outside, I find the burning sage. It wafts everywhere in the still air, including inside the door. This, I suppose, was the point of this gathering of the older folk. They sing low, almost to themselves. I don't know the song, but I can feel it. Sense how it helps clear the air. How it's directed to the hospital. And Caroline's room, in particular.

Apparently, I have more help than I think.

I have no idea what to say, so I say, "I appreciate that you didn't start this sage fire inside the clinic."

I realize how that might sound coming out. But the good thing about being in a community long enough, seeing enough patients, is that they recognize that what you say and how you feel are sometimes different. When you're around long enough, people get the voice of your heart.

Running Water wafts the smoke over me. The firepit is a smoldering Folgers coffee can set under the overhang to save it from the rain, which threatens to spit again at any time. I breathe once, twice, fight back the burn, then cough. After seven breaths, I can feel the sage in my lungs. It waters my eyes and brings my blood to the surface of my skin so that everything feels hot. And since my eyes are already watering, I figure why not just keep the show going, so I start to talk.

"She's bleeding. It's enough to mitigate at the moment, but a passage through the birth canal with the tenuous nature of her placental wall will almost certainly be a disaster. I'm not sure you're aware of how much blood the human body pushes to this area during birth. It's such a vascular area. Have you ever cut your forehead and it just won't stop bleeding? It's like that but with pints of blood. And it doesn't even matter at the moment because the baby is backside first. She's breech. If this keeps up, Caroline will exhaust herself and pass out from the pain, and in addition to the blood loss, we'll need to worry about both her and our daughter's oxygen levels. Come to think of it, this end of the wing doesn't have direct access to any wall oxygen. I'm not even sure what we have on hand."

I talk like I'm on rounds at the hospital. I talk like I'm losing my mind. I'm not entirely sure some of the older folks out here even understand English. But they listen anyway.

An old woman holds out a hand, which stops my blabbering. I think she means to shake mine, like perhaps we're finally getting around to introducing ourselves after I've just word vomited all over their sage burn, but when I grasp her hand, she pulls down so that I can pull her up.

She stands and settles her stained puffy jacket around herself then pats me on the back as she heads inside.

I take a few more breaths of the sage-infused air. Then I hear the door to Caroline's room open. My head shoots toward the entrance then back to the glowing can. "That's weird. It sounded like she just went in Caroline's room," I say.

Running Water nods. "She did."

I wave the smoke away now. Maybe something else was in there besides sage.

"You said the baby wasn't in the right spot," Running Water says. "Well, my auntie whispers to these babies, Dr. B. They move for her."

I guess I did say that. I hold out my arms like I have something more to say, but I seem to have spent all the words in my brain, so I leave the open air between my hands empty and turn around. One of the men near the door holds it open for me as I pick my way back down a hallway in which the presence of the Navajo seems to have doubled in the short time I was outside.

I open the door to find this auntie listening to Caroline's stomach and Caroline looking at me like I've got something to do with all this. Before I can tell her otherwise, the auntie hitches her coat back and places a hand on either side of Caroline's belly. I step in, but Nascha holds me back with a firm hand as the woman gulps a big breath, closes her eyes, and twists like she's trying to open the hatch of a submarine.

Caroline looks more stunned than anything, especially when the woman plunks her ear on top of her stomach again.

"Oh," Caroline says, eyes wide.

I expect the worst—another gout of blood, maybe, or Caroline passing out. Instead, I see a little cruising lump of a shoulder skimming the inside of her skin like a dolphin's fin.

Movement. A turn. The baby is in the right position.

The auntie pats Caroline on her shoulder and zips her long coat back up. She pats me as well on her way out. The door closes behind her.

Caroline and I look at each other like maybe we've both collectively hallucinated the whole affair. I can see the start of what might, under other circumstances, become a wonderful bit of contagious laughter. But then the revving pain of a building contraction stops her short.

I rush to the south end of the table, grabbing fresh

gloves along the way, trying not to think about how dirty that blanket I shrugged off might be or how healthy secondhand sage smoke from a coffee can is for a birthing mother.

I know instantly that things are different. We're more dilated now—nowhere near what I've read is preferable, but babies have been born in less. And as Caroline's moans turn to groans and then screams, I reach inside, and I feel a head.

My God, that woman did it. And I don't even know her name.

My hand comes back out as red as if it's been dipped in a bucket of paint.

The door opens again, and Sadler comes in backside first, transfusion kit primed. Nascha is stacking towels and shaking loose the bucket of ice chips.

So it's about to get messy. And if anyone has to keep their head, it's me. If ever I hope to call myself a physician or a father or even a friend to this wonderful woman again, this is when I have to get it together.

As my son says: time to cowboy up.

25

THE WALKER

Dark Sky is ripping me apart on the sand where I stand. He's doing it like a surgeon, too, picking his spots and choosing the cuts. Hos and the Smoker hold me fast, and he has free reign. He takes a chunk of my hip then slices a crescent from my chest. Everything in me throbs. The pain pulses in time with my phantom heartbeat.

He's no longer boasting—no more "Let's keep him talking." This monster is nothing but business, which is how I know I'm really in trouble. When the bad guys stop talking and just get down to business, you're fucked.

I hate that I feel sorry for myself. I've come a long way and gone through a lot of shit to get cheese grated on the shores of the great beyond. Between gasping in pain and flinching for the next hit, I wonder what it'll be like to become part of the sand, what will happen to the world without me. Souls will pile up, with dead dripping out of thin places, all while I'm ground up to snuff and tucked away in a pouch or scattered to the sand.

It would be a long time until I came together again, if

ever. Maybe after a few hundred years, the rumbles that run through the ground here might jiggle the sand around enough to put a few pieces of me together, then maybe a few more. In a thousand years, I might have a foot. After another thousand, maybe a knee. Give it a million, and I could be a walking torso, scraping at the sand while the world has backed up souls beyond belief. Chaco's rules would be shattered, the balance forever destroyed. The veil and I would be out of a job on account of the end of the world.

Right now is about when I realize some exhausted part of me *wants* to be carved up into pieces so small that I can't feel anything. Then I'll have the excuse I need to sleep for a few thousand years and see what next chapter the realm of the living has. If it hurts bad enough, I might not even feel guilty about it.

The realization has a strange smelling salts effect. It brings me back to consciousness just as Dark Sky spears my right eye out of my head as sure as a blast from a .45. My body snaps back hard, but Hos and the Smoker hold on, and I go nowhere.

I always wondered what losing part of my head would be like. I wondered if I would lose myself, my memories, my thoughts—if all of it would mist out over the sand. Nope—not that easy, I guess. My head no longer drives. It hasn't since the second I flatlined back at ABQ General. I just get the pain and none of the oblivion.

"One piece at a time, Walker," says Dark Sky. "And I have all the time in the world."

I know Hos and the Smoker. I've seen their strings. They're flawed as shit, more than most of us, but they are people, my people, and they've been hijacked. Maybe that's why I let them hold me here as long as I have. But I think I'm about done suffering for their choices.

Dark Sky is stronger than me, and he's tethered to Black Bear, who is even stronger. But Hos and the Smoker aren't tethered to anything. And I'm still the Walker. I have a job to do.

I take in a breath then yank down hard with both hands. Neither man expects it. They both stagger low and collide like they're in an awkward dance, and by the time they push off each other, I'm free.

I hit the sand running. I run like I've never run before. I'm going to the only place where I know Dark Sky won't go, not unless he wants to cut his own cord.

I'm going to the river.

26

KAI BODREY

The Gambler wants us to think we're all alone up here, a captive audience to his rigged games. He splashes the rain at his feet like a happy child then looks up at us like we're frogs in a pot. He's enjoying himself. Grant is tense beside me with frustration that has no outlet. Joey looks like he's mulling over how to muster some sort of blunt force attack, maybe from his Circle or maybe from himself, even though he knows as well as I do we're not in a game of strength anymore. The twins, for their part, look like they're seeing into the past, staring at the pot like they do. Maria sees only the twins.

As for me, I'm seeing gods. Gods are all around us.

I can't tell if it's day or night anymore. I feel like these smothering clouds would capture sunlight or moonlight the same. But there's enough light to see the gods. *Bįįh* the Great Deer stands with his brothers at the edges of this new lake, watching in silence, his coat glistening. *Atseełtsoi* the Hawk perches high on the crumbling wall of the canyon, his red tail flashing in the sun. In the thick brush are flashes of *Tse'tah Dibe* the Sacred Bighorn, who I bet is the very same that trundled his way down the path back at the trading post. And above us, *Jaa'abaní* the Bat and his clan flit like dark streaks of smoke, feasting on the mosquitoes this swamp has already hatched.

We may be trapped, but we are not alone. These gods have been helping us for days now. They brought me down the mountain. They helped us save the flame. And I have to have faith that they are not done with us yet.

"What is the game of your choice?" the Gambler asks, fingertips pressed together.

"The game is Jooł," I say.

The Gambler laughs. "You do not want Jooł, girl."

"You said I pick. I say Jooł."

He crosses his arms and drops his jaw to his shoulder like every old man I've ever met in my life right before they old-mansplain some bullshit that I've known for years. "Fine by me. But I did warn you. Since you chose, I go first."

Jooł is a simple game. Every culture has a version of it. It's basically one swing in the batting cage. You hit a ball as far as you can, and farthest wins.

The Gambler plucks up Tsasa's old walking stick, left floating in our flight to the roof. He flips it end over end and takes a few big swings, cutting the air with whooshing sounds. He looks down at the water like a cat watching a tank of fish, eyes twitching here and there. He prods the mud, punches, then reaches down and pulls out a rotten knot of wood. He squeezes it like a sponge, and when he's done, he hands up both the bat and ball for me to inspect, bowing his head like a flowery waiter.

I snatch them both without touching him and turn to the twins. They take one look and nod. I know he'll add his juice when he swings. For now, these are just wood.

I toss them both back. "Don't blow it," I say. "Be a shame if you whiffed and brought all this bullshit to an end too quick."

I know it's not smart to piss this guy off, but now we're in an arrangement, him and me. Until the game is won or lost, he plays by the game rules. Trash talking is part of that arrangement, at least where I come from.

All he gives me is a crusty wink. He rolls the wooden ball in his hands before flipping it up. He cocks the cane like a baseball bat and swings with perfect timing. He absolutely mauls the ball. The sound is incredible, a *thonk* for the ages. It sails, and it sails, and it sails—past the deer, past the sheep. It splits the sparrows and scatters the crows. I feel like it could leave the lake entirely if he wanted it to, but instead it plunks right at the edge, as if to prove a point. I only know because it splashes at the last possible place to splash, so far away that I can't even hear it.

The Gambler hands the cane to me and holds up a finger while he rips another rotten bloom of wood from the water. He squeezes it into another ball the same size, muddy drippings dark as ink roll down his forearm.

He hands it over to me, and this is where he cheats.

Chaco chirrups a low warning. I can sense the ball is off just a bit—heavier somehow, but in the spirit plane, not in the physical world. He's greased it with his smoke, but I can't prove it. The funny thing is he doesn't even need to cheat. He hit his ball a hundred yards easy. I am a lot of things, strong in many ways, but swinging a bat ain't one of them. There is no way on this earth I'll hit a ball that far. I don't even think I could shoot a rifle that far.

But the gods are watching, and the game must go on.

So I grab his spirit-spitball and shoulder the bat. I toss the ball, swing the bat, and pray to the gods.

I connect. It's a high pop, the kind we used to love back at Chaco High when we'd do this with old tennis balls and broomsticks and a crowd calling for five hundred. Hos taught me how to get under the ball, and I guess I just do it on instinct.

The problem is it ain't going anywhere far. The Gambler knows it too.

It drops fast—looks like it'll plunk down in the water about fifty feet in front of us—

right up until it gets snatched out of midair by a screeching red-tailed hawk.

The thing comes out of nowhere. A screeching explosion of feathers and wingbeats that swoops in from behind like it had been timing this catch for days. Which makes sense when you understand he's not just any red-tailed hawk. This is Atseełtsoi, the Great Hawk. The one we also call Messenger, who heralds the opening act, the beginning of the show. I can feel it in my bones.

Atseełtsoi carries the wooden ball up and up and up. He makes a point of screeching again at the water's edge, where the Gambler's ball floats, right before he blows past it with a few pumps of his wings. He flares his wings and settles on the cliff's edge with the ball. I can't quite tell, but it looks like he spears it with that great hooked beak of his and holds it up high before bringing it down hard on the canyon wall.

I'd like to think it shatters.

"You cheat," says the Gambler, low and angry. His head practically boils the damp air above him.

"No, *you* cheat. That ball was soggy as hell, and you

know it. All I do is play the game. If the gods intervene, they intervene."

The Gambler walks to the edge of the double-wide with such cold fury that even Joey takes a half step back. "Don't talk to me about the gods, girl. I know all about how we intervene. I am one."

Chaco chirrups low again.

I know, buddy. What comes next is very delicate.

"She won," Grant says. "We get all this land back. All of it. The entire Rez, top to bottom."

The Gambler seems to ponder this, which is when I realize I made a big mistake. We need a judge here, a witness that can keep this snake to his word. He's gonna welch. I can see it in his eyes, which leaves me with only one choice: get ahead of it, and do better next time.

"Or..." I say, one hand on Grant's shoulder. "Or we double down."

The Gambler pauses like all true degenerate gamblers do when higher stakes hit the table. He rolls his tongue behind his hollow cheeks, mulling over the idea. "You cheated," he says. "By all rights, I can take everything and go."

Classic victim-card bullshit. As if he's had any moral high ground to stand on in generations. Behind me, Tsasa clears his throat. "Are you not Náághwiilbiihi, known to us as the Winner of Games?"

The Gambler was turning away, but that gets him.

"Old man, I have won more in my time than you can possibly imagine. More jewels than a hundred Arroyos could hold. I have won slaves for my slaves."

The twins don't look away. Neither does Maria, for that matter, which is more than I can say for myself. Then again, I'm new to this game. I get the feeling the three of them have dealt with many monsters in their time.

Tsasa opens the pot for another sage-and-twig package from a crow friend, who lands awkwardly and looks at Chaco with a nod before it takes off into the darkening distance. The rain coming in is a velvet curtain call on slow approach. We don't have much time.

"Then double down, Nááhwiilbiihi," Tsasa says. "Unless you are afraid you will lose again."

The Gambler is quick. He kicks in the sidewall of the trailer for footing and lifts himself up so that his stolen face floats level with the roof. "I never lose."

"Then bet," I say.

"I will bet my legs for your legs," he says, grinning.

"That's it? Legs?"

"My head for your head."

He wants that bet. He wants the one that will end him if he loses, like any addict. That's the bet he's been looking for. I can see it. But that's not the game I'm playing.

"My people for your people," I say.

Grant gives me an understandably horrified look. It's the look of someone who has just been gambled. But I hold his eyes and try to will him to understand that this is our only chance. Eventually, he nods—faster than I would have if the tables were turned and he put me up on the table without asking first. I'd probably be pretty pissed. But Grant's not like me, which is why I love Grant.

I sweep the rest of our crew and find all nods. The twins' look is almost a challenge to me. *You called down the gods, young one. Now they are here. What will you do with them?*

The Gambler's eyes are wide and wet, pupils as big as stones. I've seen this before too, with the junkies that came in and out of the trading post. He needs this. He's in deep. "Interesting," he says. "What is the game?"

"Na'azhǫǫsh," I say, loud enough for the gods to hear.

The Gambler grabs a fistful of water in one sweep and lets it dribble away from his fist. "I love Na'azhǫǫsh, but it is a game of the earth, stick, and hoop. There is only water now."

"Fine, then. We play the water version."

The Gambler cocks his head and stares at me, unblinking. "And what is that, little sister?"

I look out into the flat water. Filth rises and falls underneath on some strange dead current. This thing is deeper than I thought, maybe deeper than I should think. Most flood lakes don't have enough going on to jiggle a dead moth, much less keep a Tupperware bowl spinning endlessly.

"That," I say. "You see that? The bowl. First to throw a stone inside wins."

The Gambler makes a show of thinking it through hard, but I know he's already made up his mind. I could have proposed anything, and he'd be in.

"I choose the stones," he says.

Of course his cheatass wants to choose the stones.

"Only if the stones are equal," I say, as if that might change a thousand years of crazy.

He nods absently, watching the bowl spin with the eyes of an alligator spotting a struggling fawn in too deep.

Speaking of—the deer have been pretty still. They're still on the far shore, waiting for something. I catch the eye of every one of them down the line, looking for Bįįh, the Great Deer, the god among them. All of them stare right back. Maybe Bįįh is not one. Maybe Bįįh is all.

The Gambler rubs his palms together until I can smell

his skin, and only then does he plunge both hands into the water. He stands up like a lifter with a hundred pounds on each side, but all he has is a little pebble in each hand.

"Choose, Kai Bodrey."

Chaco chirrups again, short and clear. I catch his meaning—more and more, I do. And what he's saying is it doesn't matter because both are rigged.

I warm up my hands in my pockets, not super keen to choose either one, and my fingers brush something hard: *my* stone, the one the weasel gave me. I forgot all about it. I bring it out. It's smooth and flat. A little small, but my gut tells me to go with it, and I'm all about listening to my gut these days.

"I got my own, thanks."

The Gambler looks carefully at the stone. I get the feeling he's checking it in every plane he can. After a moment, he comes to the same conclusion I did when the weasel spat it out. It's just a rock. "Fine. Winner goes first," the Gambler says, and he bows until his fingers sweep the filthy water.

Grant watches me with care. He would never do anything like say, "Hey, I got a big, jacked arm, and you can't even aim a frisbee, so let me do this." If he did, I'd probably hand him the stone. But he doesn't. And neither does Joey, who has an even better arm. But both stay quiet. I think they know as well as I do that arm strength alone won't win the day here. We need help from the other side.

Hos always used to skip rocks whenever we would get enough desert water in Flatrock Canyon. Hell, he used to skip rocks even when there wasn't any water. He'd skip them right off the dirt from the steps of the trading post.

The trick was to see how many hops you could get before the canyon ate your rock.

I know I can't throw this thing into that bowl. No sense in even trying. But maybe, just maybe, I can skip it.

I wrap my pointer finger around the edge and put the flat side down, like he taught me. I bend right and wind up like I'm going for a kidney punch. I close my eyes, pray, and chuck it.

The sound of a rock skipping is something everyone knows. It's stamped on our brains. And this is no desert-dust-hiccup skip, this is flat water, rock skip central. And my stone is five, maybe six skips deep even before I can really find it, then ten more after I do. It's a thing of beauty —until it sputters, slows, and dies.

I glance at the Gambler and find him smiling back at me. I close my eyes and ask anyone and everyone for a little help. I don't think this story is meant to end here.

Something flashes in the water, a flicker of dark fur. Two tiny brown paws break the surface, and between them is my stone. The weasel I met on Crooked Snake— has to be. But it wasn't just any weasel. It was *Dlǫ́'ii*, the holy one who helped my people find shelter from the great flood long ago.

I never even see his head. He turns tail, but before he dives, he hook shots the stone right into the bowl. It's a thing of beauty, I can hear the rattle from across the pond. His tail flashes like a shark's fin, then he's gone.

The Gambler's eyes flash in anger, and his mouth turns down into a wrinkled scowl. "That is one way to do it, yes," he says. "Now for mine."

He palms the stone like he's gonna eat it—no skipping for this one. He takes one careful step back, lets the ripples settle, then launches the rock high into the air. I know what he's trying to do. He wants to pop my stone out. And his is coming in like a bomb from up high. He won't miss. I know this. The pure force from above is gonna dunk the bowl and send my stone down to drown with the rusty trucks. That's how he wins. I can see this.

Fortunately, so can Bįįh, my deer friends.

They flank the water like foot soldiers. Way more came down from the high country than I thought. I'm praying for some sort of full assault, a deer apocalypse that will trample the Gambler and drag him back down to whatever hell he calls home.

But I get nothing like that, of course. All the deer do is drink—probably forty deer, just dipping their heads in at once while the stone falls.

If one deer dips to drink, the dip makes a ripple. When two deer dip to drink, that ripple bounces. But here are forty deer, with one stone on a crash course with a floating plastic bowl. And right when that stone is supposed to hit, their ripple does too. It's not big. We're not talking a butterfly-to-hurricane thing. All it does is nudge the bowl. All it does is, well, everything.

The rock plunks an inch to the right, splashing the bowl pretty good, but it still floats while the Gambler's stone sinks.

I can't help but giggle a little. Bįįh made him whiff.

The Gambler roars in anger, rips up another stone from his feet, and pegs it sideways at the bucket, blowing it to pieces on impact. He turns toward me, his face all twisted and red. "That's twice, now, you cheat!"

"You act like I can control the deer," I say.

He shoots a dagger look at the deer, who do absolutely nothing in return except look bored. "One last game. Double or nothing," he hisses.

"Why would I?" I ask. "I won back my land. I won back my people."

"That is not all you have lost," he says, looking up at me with that snaggletooth grin before shifting his eyes to Grant. "And you—you lose much even as we speak."

Grant puts a gentle hand on my shoulder. "Careful. He could be lying. Maybe we fixed it all already. Don't risk everything you've won on account of..."

"On account of you?" I ask, turning toward him and taking his hand in mine. "How long have we known each other, Grant Romer?"

His eyes look tired. This whole mess has hollowed him out. "Long time," he says.

"How long?"

"Five years. Almost six."

I take his face in my hands. "Five years going on six going on forever. You oughta know by now that of course I'd risk everything for you. What's mine is yours, and what's yours is mine."

I turn back around to the Gambler. "You win, you get everything—all of it back. But if you lose, you undo all you've done here, and you leave this place forever."

The Gambler's eyes flash.

"And no backing out of this shit either. You agree before all the gods."

The Gambler looks around as if daring them to appear, but I don't think he can see the gods like I can. He doesn't know they're all around us. I guess when you think you are a god yourself, maybe it's hard to see the forest for the trees.

"Agreed," the Gambler says.

"The crows have heard you, Nááhwiilbiihi," Tsosi says. "They will hold you to your wager."

The line of crows still watches the water, but at Tsosi's words, one turns its head to the side and stares at the Gambler for a long stretch of seconds before settling in again. They're watching where the bowl was, now destroyed, but in its place is a single crow feather. The slick plume catches the low light and reflects it back in flashes of black.

A gust of wind cuts the air like an arrow, swirling the mist that hangs over the still water. It spins the feather around and around and sucks it straight down. The elder twins murmur, low. They look at Grant, but Grant is looking out at the water.

"What was that?" he asks, his voice small.

The Gambler grasps his hands behind himself and tilts back and forth on the mud where he stands. "It would appear that another soul has found death's back door," he says. "One I believe you know."

Grant swallows hard. I grab his hand and squeeze. I can't have him giving up on us.

"The stakes grow ever higher," the Gambler says, "and we have saved the best game for last."

He licks his bloody lips, reaches into his pocket, and pulls out a handful of Wapati casino chips.

27

OWEN BENNET

I am holding my child in my arms. She is covered in vernix and blood. But she is not breathing.

Sadler is screaming something at me. Nascha is screaming something at me. I don't catch any of it. The ringing in my ears drowns everything out. How beautiful this must be when it works. How magnificent the miracle when a child comes, and it is pink and screaming and kicking, and they ace the Apgar test right out of the gate, and the mom weeps with joy and watches fondly while the dad cuts the umbilical cord.

I know it works for millions of people, but I know it is not working for me.

"Dr. Bennet!" Nascha says, slapping me on the back and into reality, "Do what you can!"

She's doing what she can, holding the blood bag high while Sadler is making sure my wife, suddenly gone quiet, at least has a pulse. And Nascha's right. I will do what I can, but not because of this child. I will do what I can because Caroline would want me to.

I guess I'm waiting for the love to fall upon me, the

moment of transport. But something about all the blood and probable death has wiped that love away from me. I feel terribly disassociated with this being I hold, which is probably a good thing, in the very real possibility I have to say goodbye. It's a lot easier to say goodbye to a thing when you've never said hello.

I wrap the baby in one of our last clean blankets, one Nascha kept aside for this. Pink.

I push the bulb suction into her mouth like a meat thermometer and suck out a fair amount of fluid. I ask for the oxygen, and Nascha takes it off of Caroline and hands it to me. I press it to her face and count. Bulb suction again—less fluid this time. After one more, I get a dry return. Nascha is already there with the oxygen, and I count it out again, hand it back, flip the baby and rub her back. No movement. I flick the soles of her tiny feet. No response.

I flip her around again. Her head lolls like a rag doll's, and I remind myself her neck needs constant support. I tuck her into her blanket again and put her on my knees and find the line of her breastbone, still slick with fluids. I go one finger down and start compressions. The malleability is astounding, like I'm pressing into silly putty.

Neonatal compressions have to be fast—a hundred a minute, if possible. But if the lungs aren't allowed to recoil, then none of it works. I push to the limit, pressing down again as soon as her chest gets close to settled—again and again and again. I lose myself. Only Nascha hitting me with the oxygen brings me back. I pause and press it to her face and wipe my drenched brow. The oxygen mask covers the baby's entire head.

"How is Caroline?" I ask.

"Don't worry about her," Nascha says.

I count it down and hand back the mask, wet now with blood, but I don't really know which patient the blood came from. Nascha slaps a clean bulb suction into my hand, and I go to work. I crush the bulb and go deep this time, and when it pulls open again, something comes with it.

I yank the bulb out and hook a finger in to catch whatever it caught. The timing works—so much of all this relies on timing that it's terrifying—and when I pull out my finger, it's coated in mucus.

Maybe a stir from the child.

I flick her little heels and rub her back again, but she's still.

I flip her over again and restart compressions, watching that tiny chest come back up each time and willing breath to come with it for a half second before I press down again.

We're not done yet. I swear to you, Caroline, we are not done yet.

28

THE WALKER

I hit the river like a ton of bricks and brace for the touch of the souls. Both Hos and the Smoker try to follow me, but Dark Sky releases enough of his hold on them that they're confronted with the choice themselves again, and both men stagger back, burying their fingers in the sand like they can't be trusted with their own hands.

Dark Sky walks to the edge of the river and stops. His tendrils of smoke extend out over the water slowly, snakes testing the air. That tells me all I need to know: he's no more sure of this water than Hos or the Smoker.

I'm the only one that can walk the river without being destroyed. And even I don't want to hang out in here any longer than I absolutely have to. The souls that linger here are still trying to make up their minds about which path to take. I can feel their indecision each time one brushes me, like a jellyfish zap but with emotion instead of venom. One brushes my arm, and I get a rapid-fire barrage of broken images, ranging from the beautiful to the horrific. I see a sunset. A stumbling child. A terrible fall. The sound of a car wreck. An embrace. A turning away. All in the blink of an eye. And then it floats on, swirling in a current that is all its own.

"I can wait here as long as you can, Walker," Dark Sky says, but the way he's slowly pacing tells me otherwise. Sure, he could wait me out. The consequences are worse for me and for the great balance. But he won't because even though he has time on his side, he's impatient. Again and again, his tendrils test the air over the water.

I wade away from them, but they follow me, and that's when a realization hits me. Maybe that's exactly what I want.

I take a step closer to shore and really get their attention. One senses me, stops swaying, and homes in. It climbs up my wrist, leaving welted pain in its path. It's all I can do not to snap it off.

I let it wrap me and move a little closer to shore. I need the other big one, too, and maybe we can make something happen here.

"Found you," Dark Sky says.

The tendril searches my face for an agonizing stretch of seconds. *Just a little bit more.* It circles around my back and starts to wrap its razor wire around my neck, and that's when I spring the trap.

I whip both hands around the tendrils, set my feet, and yank back.

Dark Sky tumbles forward, face down into the sand. I yank for all I'm worth, back and back, again and again. He digs his claws into the sand, but I've still got him. I pull back hard, setting the slicing pain aside, putting it into a box in my mind. I'll deal with it later. This is my only chance.

His hand splashes into the water and flares away into

light. His forearm follows, all the way up to the elbow. But that's when he flares out his wings.

They start up with the sound of knives being sharpened, and the resistance doubles down. He flips upright. One hooked bug foot splashes the river and is burned away, but the balance of power is rolling back his way now.

He roars at me with all his being and starts pulling back. We're in a stalemate, but he's got the high ground. I hold on still, hoping what he's lost might unbalance him, but he's too strong, too rooted.

My mind races. I've still got the tendrils. I could just dunk them, searing them off, but I doubt he'll fall for this again. I could wrap myself in them, use my body as leverage, and see if I can grind it out. It would hurt like a bitch, but everything hurts like a bitch right now, and it's better than being shaved down an inch at a time on his terms.

I sense something: a soul, a different kind of soul. It's a beginning soul, not an ending soul. It shouldn't be here.

Dark Sky senses it as well. He glances behind himself.

A child walks out of the house, a young girl. Her form shifts as she steps. At one point, she looks like an infant and stumbles before she gets her little legs underneath her again. When she pushes herself up, she looks more like four or five. She isn't quite formed yet, still a mishmash of what could be.

I drop the smoke tendrils and, with them, all my leverage. None of that matters now because I know in an instant who I'm seeing. It's in her soul string, but it's also in her face. She's the best of them both. Caroline's fearless heart. Owen's tireless grit. She's beautiful.

And she's headed for the river. Dark Sky's laugh begins, long and low. He doesn't even have to move—he ushers her along with a mock bow, and she walks right on by with the bright curiosity of a kindergartner wandering into traffic.

Hell no. Not today.

I scramble up and out to stop her, with not a care in my head about what Dark Sky might hit me with or how. All I know is I have to keep that girl out of the river. I don't even care what her soul string has to say about it. I'm calling an audible here. She's not going in today.

I throw myself in front of her as she's about to plop one foot in like it's nothing more than a rainy-day day puddle. I catch her and sweep her up in my arms and fall to my knees at the same time. She grabs on to me instinctively, wrapping her arms around my neck. She has a strange, shifting weight to her. She goes from weighing thirty or forty pounds one second to weighing five or ten the next. But she's got weight. She's real. That's good because if it weren't for the weight, I would swear I was losing my mind again, trapped in one of those weird memories I get of things that never happened or things that might come.

The girl looks up at me, and I feel like I'm looking both of them in the face at once—like Caroline is right here and Owen is right here, like I'm holding them all. She has a question in her eyes, but I don't know if she knows how to ask it or even if she can, since she's not really born yet.

I'd sit all day with her to figure it out if I could. But Dark Sky has other ideas.

His low laugh rumbles like a rockslide. "Looks like I didn't have to wait so long after all."

I set her down on the sand again and draw her eyes to mine. "Stay here. With me."

She nods. That gives me all the strength I need to stand up tall again and face this monster. He's hurt. I can see that. He's lost a good third of one leg, some of whatever you'd call his right hand, and his main smoke tentacles are now flailing stumps that can't seem to really find me. So I got that going for me, at least.

But I know it won't be enough. Already, he's unfurling his hellish wings. He's starting up the knife sharpener and digging in. He's got another claw and more little tentacles. More than enough to do the damage he wants.

But I got something he doesn't, now. I got something I'm willing to lose everything for in a heartbeat, if that's what it takes. And I've been around long enough to know that when your mind makes that kind of decision beforehand, it has a power all its own.

I turn toward this little girl who is in the here-but-not-yet limbo, sitting on the sand, legs splayed, toes up, swaddled in some strange echo of a pink hospital blanket like a cape. "I'm serious. Don't move," I say.

She nods again.

I'm still looking at her when I rush at Dark Sky. In part, I'm trying to catch him off guard, but mostly, I don't want to look away.

29

KAI BODREY

The Gambler flicks a Wapati chip into the air, end over end, and catches it again. He holds it up between his muddy thumb and forefinger, and it seems to glitter in the gloom. "The game is Tsidił. I have thirteen chips—one side red, one side white."

He swipes at the water with one cracked boot like he's spreading sawdust, but it parts for him. Or at least it recedes enough to expose a big circle of saturated mud beneath his feet. Half-drowned worms flop and wriggle in the center. He sweeps them away too.

"Each of us gets one toss. Air to mud. Whoever has more chips white side up wins. Simple."

Simple, my ass. Caroline warned us about this exact game. I bet those chips are dripping with his smoke. I'll be lucky to get a single white chip. But we already agreed. The game must be played. Too much is riding on it.

"Winner throws first," he says, walking carefully to the side of the double-wide. He reaches up and sets the chips in a single stack on the edge with a careful click then steps away, back to the circle.

I squat down and look at the chips. Chaco squawks, and Grant says, "take the top off the lacquer pot."

Joey opens the pot, and Chaco flares his wings, pushing air across the top, turning it to smoke that wafts over me. I glance up at the Gambler, who's digging his heels into the mud, unimpressed.

"Thank you, Chaco," I say. "We're gonna need all the help we can get with these filthy things."

I pick up the chips. They're grimy and wet, but I don't get any sense of smoke or magic or whatever it is Caroline saw. I turn toward my company up here and open my hand, showing them all. The twins grumble, which is all I need to hear.

They're loaded with something, alright, and once these are airborne, there are no do-overs.

Tsosi clears his throat. "For they saw Bįįh the Deer pass right in front of them," he says in his storyteller voice.

"And Jádí the Antelope rushed past," Tsasa replies.

Back and forth they go, listing animals. These are the creatures that came for shelter during the great flood story in the *Diné Bahane'*.

"Atseełtsoi, the Hawk."

"Hazéétsoh, the Squirrel."

"Jaa'abani, the Bat."

"And in the rising waters, our people asked them for help," Tsosi says.

"'We will try,' said Squirrel."

"'Whatever we can do, we will do,' said Weasel."

Grant puts his hands over mine, and together, we cover the chips. "He's not the only one with smoke," Grant whispers. His eyes are red, but he's somehow holding on to that last bit of a smile, that same last bit he's been holding onto since I met him.

Caroline could fix this, reversing whatever juice the Gambler stuck on these things. But she's not here right now, so all I can do is rattle them around in my hands. Then, before I can think, I toss them off and out. They flip end over end, red and white, red and white, and land with a rapid-fire thunk in the soaked mud. All thirteen hit the mud flat.

Three of the faces are white. Three of thirteen—not awesome.

The Gambler makes a point of counting them all again and again. One hand points at each.

"It's three, Gambler," I say. "You can cut the shit."

He plucks each from the mud and wipes them on his filthy jeans, smiling and muttering to himself. "Tough toss," he says.

The Gambler clacks the chips in one hand. He's watching the two of us with an awful intensity—our hands and the way we lean on one another. It's like he's eating us up.

Black blood from his split lips stains his teeth as he speaks. "My turn now."

The twins are still talking. One of the great mysteries of my life is how old men can just talk bullshit through the end of the world. My father did it, my brother did it, and now they do it.

"We could use some help from either one of you any time now," I say to them with way more snark than I ever would have normally. But we aren't a bunch of giggling kids by the campfire anymore. The campfire is a handful of coals. Where we used to sit is a worms' graveyard. And this is our last chance.

They ignore me, of course. The Gambler rattles the

chips, and the sound echoes like bones clacking against each other. The elder twins speak more loudly.

"And later, when the Gambler had won them all, they gathered, and they were unhappy," Tsasa says, like we're ten again, except he points out over the still lake toward where the red-tailed hawk still watches. "The people were afraid, but Hawk said, I will help."

Tsosi clears his throat and puts his hand over the pot like it's the fire and nods to the shore where the deer army stands stock still. "And Deer said, I will help."

Tsasa looks up. "And Bat said, I will help."

The Gambler tosses the chips high—higher than me, high enough to make a point. They flip end over end, the red and white sides catching every single bit of light left. They make an eerie whistling sound in the air, almost out of range of what I can hear.

We all watch their rise and fall, and I can see right away that they're all falling flat white like they're being pulled that way by the mud and water, which means we're done for.

I'm seeing dark spots in my eyes. Maybe I'm having a panic attack and this is what it looks like when someone's vision closes in on them—little darts of black. The chips aren't spinning, just falling, but that whistle is still there. It's the strangest ringing I've ever heard.

My eyes watch the chips, but in my head, I'm fuming. *The chips never fall my way.* I've helped prop up gamblers and drinkers my whole life, but just when I finally start to claw my way out of catastrophe, just when I need a hand, I find myself losing everything to *my ancestor*. I'm *going backward*. It's enough to make me want to throw myself off this double-wide, see if I can somehow take the Gambler underwater with me.

Then something slams into a chip, flipping it red side up like a coin trick just before it hits. I can barely make it out in the low light, flopping on the mud. A bat.

Then another bat hits another chip. The spots I'm seeing aren't a mental breakdown, they're Jaa'abani. The whistling is their speech. More and more come. They're too small to grab the chips, but they can hit the damn things, and they're hitting these chips hard. I grip Grant's hand and wince for thirteen thunks, thirteen coins hit by thirteen bats.

The chips hit the ground next to them. A few flop in the mud, but most lie still. I imagine that hitting these chips all loaded up with the Gambler's cheating weight would be a bit like slamming into a brick wall for a little bat. They gave themselves up for this. Jaa'abani did.

I'm leaning so far off the roof to check the chip colors that Grant has to hold me around the waist. And Joey has to hold him by the shoulders.

Doesn't take long to count. It's one—one white chip.

The Gambler was expecting another scene entirely. I can tell by the way his broken grin falls, by the way he looks at his own hands, wondering if they're his, wondering if his smoke is still flowing or if he's gone dry.

I've been there, in that horrible unknowing, but only because he and his chief lunatic, Dark Sky, put me there. It's nice to be on the other side this time.

"You lose, Gambler," I say.

He picks up one of my bat brothers and looks at it then looks around at the sky. The bats still flit and dart, but he still seems unable to see them. He still doesn't understand. He tosses the dead bat into the water, and I say a prayer to my friend Jaa'abani, one of many, who came to help me when my people called. Just like he has done before and will do again if one knows how to ask.

"No," the Gambler says simply. "We play again."

"I am done gambling," I say. "I will take what is mine."

"No!" he screams, and his shout rips over the water, scattering the sparrows at the edges. "We are done when I win!"

His face splits at the forehead and at the creases beside his eyes and mouth. He's done talking, and he's coming for the pot.

The Gambler cleaves one hand through the sheet metal siding of the twins' double-wide and uses it as a handhold, pushing himself up high enough to kick another hole through. Joey rolls his shoulders, and Grant tenses by my side. I find myself getting low, ready to do whatever I can, knowing that we don't got much against a man who can flood our world if he wants. That kind of man is a tough takedown.

Two voices boom out as one from behind us. "Nááhwi-ilbiihi, you will hold to your word. You may play games, but the crows do not. This you know is true."

I've never heard the twins speak as one. It's always been a back and forth. Their combined voice is something out of another world, low and strong enough to ripple the waters around us. They stand together, both watching in that old-man way, arms in front, hand clasping wrist.

This time, the Gambler is the one who blinks.

Chaco slowly rises from the pot and taps his beak together with a creepy softness. He's always been great at hitting his marks. I'd think twice if I saw him, but it ain't him the Gambler should be worried about. It's the other crows. The ones that have been watching this whole thing play out with black eyed patience for days. The ones that haven't really moved since the rain started. They're the ones that turn to take in the Gambler, one by one down the line, until every single dripping beak points his way.

I've heard stories of how Danny Ninepoint disappeared. Everyone in my circle has. I bet the Gambler has too.

He thinks of running. I can see it. But then, one of those crows on the line makes that weird noise in its throat that sounds like they're tapping a hollow bone deep inside. The Gambler gets their message, same as us.

If you run, we'll find you.

He pulls his hand out of the metal, and then his foot. He splashes down again and steps away. He rubs at his ratty hair and peeling face and seems like he's physically willing his mouth to say the words he's about to say.

"So be it. It is all yours."

As soon as he speaks the words, a great popping sound echoes around the Arroyo, and the water starts to move. It's subtle, but it's happening. The Arroyo is draining. The Gambler watches with a drunk's leer.

"You go too," I say. "That was the deal. Everything you took from our people is returned, and you go."

He hears me, and he nods, but he doesn't look up. Instead, he walks toward the middle of the lake. He kicks out at the water like a child at first. Then his kicks turn into a dance, and something about the lightness of it chills me.

"That was the deal, Kai Bodrey. I've undone everything I won from our people. You own them now. They are yours to do with as you see fit."

He's way out deep now and sinking slowly, up to his waist already. His ugly smile turns dark. "The deals I made with the bilagáana are my affair."

The word hits Grant like a bullet, and the Gambler's dark smile drives it home. <u>Bilagáana</u> means foreigner, white man. Grant's been called that before, that's not what worries me. What worries me is that I only know of two other white people on this planet in a position to make a deal with this creature—his parents. And last I heard, they were getting pretty desperate.

The Gambler's lake is draining quickly now, swirling a tornado of junk all around him, spinning leaves and branches and plastic shit of all kinds. He turns when he's in the middle, faces us, and straightens his sopping jacket. "I go to prepare a new house. For a new guest. Like I said, little sister, it's not over until I win."

He stares at us, unblinking, a leering smile on his face as he holds out his arms and falls backward into the water.

The Gambler is gone. The Arroyo is draining. Dry land is already surfacing all around us. But Grant is still gripping my hand like he's drowning.

30

THE WALKER

Dark Sky and I are locked in a grapple, each gripping the other, but I'm the one losing ground. The child is in the sand behind me, watching. I know what Dark Sky wants. Her in the river. Then me, shredded to pieces. His tendrils poke at me like dirty needles, sharp and slippery and warm, everything disgusting wrapped in one feeling.

"I want you to see her go before I pick you apart," Dark Sky says, his buggy face inches from mine.

My heels give way, and I start to slide back as he presses forward. The girl watches him from my feet in that stoic way newborns have. She has no idea of the danger she is in. Of the promise she represents. What she means to people I love. What she means to me.

Dark Sky uses one of his endless limbs to lift the bell off his slick front carapace. "At first, I wanted to find a way to ring this bell and wipe you away. But I have changed my mind, Walker. If I can't trap you in a box, I will trap you in a river, buffeted by all the souls you've led through, assailed by memories even as you lose your own."

He jangles the bell. It has no clapper, but that's still a stupid move. You don't spit at the sun. You'd think someone hundreds of years old would know that.

"First, we dissolve the girl," he says.

I know he's choosing his words to piss me off. He's probably had tons of practice at this. But I'll be damned if it doesn't work anyway. I push back hard, trying to stiff-arm the big bug at his mouth. *Dumb idea.* He snaps off three fingers off my left hand in one weird shuffling of his trough of a mouth. The pain drops me to my knees. The girl falls backward on the sand, startled, and the river sluices up to her, catching a bit of her hair, which glows away into the water.

Nothing clears pain from your mind like watching a kid nearly get dissolved. Her hand is up and balled into a little fist, ready to splash down, but I grab her first. This time, I flip around and put my back toward Dark Sky. Maybe it'll buy us both a minute or two.

Wrong—Dark Sky wraps everything around us: sharp hands, prickly arms, flailing stumps of smoke, little flickering tentacles, his sheaves of wings, all of it with one goal, to toss us into the damn river, where she'll float away from me like ash underwater. Her soul won't even have a memory. When I touch it, the silence will be worse than anything I've encountered there.

I pull the girl against my chest and think of all the ways I should apologize. My heels hit the water. I skid and skid and fall ass-first into the sand. The water of the river laps around my legs.

Behind me, Dark Sky coughs.

It's one of those strange, quick, no-nonsense coughs. One I know pretty well in my line of work. It's the kind of cough when something breaks inside. A heart attack cough.

Dark Sky stops pushing. I scoot back hard and flip to my knees on the sand, still holding the girl.

Dark Sky is looking back at the house like a rug just got yanked out from under him. His hooks are still on me, but they've stopped shredding. I shrug one off, and it hits the sand in a puff of dust. Dark Sky doesn't even look at it.

"No," he says quietly. "It cannot be."

His claws start to drip pieces of themselves into the sand. His wings dissolve at the edges.

The Arroyo people emerge from the house one by one, shaking their heads and blinking their eyes clear, as he sinks inch by inch. They look around like they're seeing one another for the first time. Some fall to the sand themselves.

This can only mean one thing. Kai and the squad up top won. Whatever they did, they won. They took the games right to Nááhwiilbiihi, the Gambler, the One Who Wins, as he's known in the living world. Or Black Bear, to those of us beyond the veil. They took it to him, and they beat him.

"Hear me, Black Bear," Dark Sky says, grasping at nothing, speaking to the dead air. "Give me more time. If I've failed you, I will make it right."

I stand slowly, and I can hear things popping and cracking inside. I didn't think these bones could possibly ache as much as they do, but at least I'm still in one piece. "You didn't fail anybody, Dark Sky," I say, hitching the girl up on my hip and gently feeling out where my face got grated. The eye I lost is already coming together again. My stumps of fingers itch like crazy, which means they're coming back too.

With each word, his face melts a little more. "But... but he promised me a home. A people."

"He never cared about you. To him, you were just another chip in play. And he just got wiped out."

My words hit him hard. He looks back at the house, at the Arroyo people, and I can see the confusion in his eyes. His clan—the Air Spirit people—had a part to play in the history of the Navajo, but they played it many worlds back.

I point to the river. "Your clan went that way a long time ago."

Whatever boon Black Bear won to keep this ancient medicine man knit together is broken now, all used up. Dark Sky watches his wings float away in a line of fine sand. The sand finds the river, and the flash acts as a fuse that leads right back to him. In moments, Dark Sky is consumed and destroyed. Whatever was left of his soul was so dry and dusty that all it needed was the barest touch. The torn-up sand at our feet is all that remains as evidence he ever existed.

That and the bell.

I set the girl down very slowly. She seems not at all interested in the river now. But she is interested in the bell.

I reach down and grasp it. Hold it in my open palm and blow away the sand. I haven't held this thing since I chucked it out over the soul map. Grant found it then. I wonder if he'll be as happy to see it this time around.

I doubt it. It's a lot heavier than I remember.

I look at the girl, who is looking up at me now. She reaches for my hand, and I take hers in mine.

"Come on," I say. "Let's get you home."

The house on the sand is creaking ominously. The

wood that makes up the walls groans and pops. The sand that was the mortar is drying and flaking, chipping off onto the ground. The Arroyo folk are in a strange place. Many are clear-eyed for the first time since that Windway gone wrong back at the Rez. They're waking up from one nightmare into another nightmare. And they're in pain again, owners of their bodies once more.

I wish I knew what to tell them, wish I could help them. But I can't. I'm beyond them now. Thankfully, Hos and the Smoker are not.

"Quickly," Hos says, shuttling these lost folks one by one down the tunnel of sand. "Just keep walking. When you wake up again, you'll be home."

Some don't want to go. Hos has no time for these people, but the Smoker does. These are the ones with nothing left, the ones who are too old to start over again, the ones that were maybe looking for a dignified way out in the first place.

I used to think folks that wanted out of life were cowards. I had my life cut short by cancer. I felt like I got robbed, and I was pissed off, and I had a right to be pissed off. But the longer I work at this job, the more I understand. I wasn't robbed. I got what I got, same as everyone else. Mostly, I understand that I got no place telling someone who has come this far looking for a way out of the life they had, to walk their steps back. That walk is theirs and theirs alone.

These people have made their decision. The Smoker knows that, and he comforts them. Forehead to forehead, he sees them, really sees them. Then he says *hágoónee'*—farewell. We don't really have a word for "goodbye," not like white people do. *Hágoónee'* means something like a mix between "okay, then," and "I guess we're done for now.

See you around." This seems particularly appropriate on the shores of this river that all of us will one day float.

Bly Bodrey is one of these saying hágoónee'. At first, Hos doesn't want to acknowledge that his mother is walking toward the river. He ignores her and helps the next in line move on down. But eventually, the Smoker stops him and forces him to see. Laying a hand on Hos Bodrey is something the Smoker would never have done up top, but washing up on the shores of oblivion can change a man.

Turns out the shores can change even a man like Hos. Because when his mother reaches for him, he bursts into tears, pressing her hand to his face.

"I wanted peace for you," he says.

"I have it," she replies. "Now, it is time for you to find peace. With yourself. And with your sister."

Bly is already struggling to stay standing. Without Dark Sky's smoke propping her up, she's falling back into the same chronic-pain hellhole she was in day in and day out.

"Hágoónee', Hosteen Bodrey," she says. "I am proud of you."

"Hágoónee', mama," he replies, and his voice cracks. In that moment, I get a look at what Hos was like as a kid —a sad, scared kid trying hard to hold on to what little he has left.

Bly shuffles to the shore—next stop, the river. Hos turns away at first, and I don't blame him. Tears stream from his eyes as he helps the next of the Arroyo down the path toward life again. He tells them to keep walking when it gets dark along the path, not to be afraid.

At the last moment, he turns back to her. Witnesses his mother as she dissolves into light. His cry is soft and sad, not unlike a child's. But as Bly's soul reforms into a bobbing globe of light, his tears abate. By the time she joins the rest of the souls on their way to peace and order, I can even sense a touch of wonder in his grief.

Soon, those that chose the river are gone, and those that chose the tunnel are on their way back. Just the four of us remain: Hos, the Smoker, the girl, and me.

"Hard work ahead for you," I say to the men. "You've won back a lost clan. They will look to you for help."

The Smoker looks down the tunnel that will lead him home then back toward the crumbling house and the river beyond. "True," he says. "But maybe that's kinda the thing I need right now. To get my ass in gear, you know?"

I do know. This side of the veil gives you a lot of perspective.

"See you on the other side," he says. Then he walks away, down the tunnel, back to his future. I can hear him whistling until the sound just stops, and I know he's through.

That leaves three. Hos looks at me, but not like before, not like he wants to walk all over me. What I see in his eyes now is a good, old-fashioned "I got no idea what to do with my life" look, which is a lot better.

"Your sister did this," I say. "Kai beat Black Bear. Broke whatever hold he had over this place and these people. She had help, but she was the one who did it."

He looks down the path back to life. A hint of a smile curves the corner of his mouth. I grab his hand and hold out the bell.

"Give that to Grant," I say. "I can't take it through."

At first, he doesn't want to touch it, but I press, and he eventually takes it from me. He holds it like a trapped wasp in his cupped hand.

I look him in the eye. "Don't mess around with that. You give it to Grant. Can you do that, Hosteen Bodrey? It's step one to becoming not so much of an asshole. I'm trusting you." I almost can't believe the words coming from my mouth, but there they are.

He looks from the bell to me and tightens his grip. He nods.

"Then go," I say.

"Hágoónee', Walker," he says.

"Hágoónee', Hos."

Down he goes, head low, pushing through. I hear his heavy footsteps until they, too, just stop. He's through.

That leaves me and the girl. I have no idea what she makes of this place. Part of me thinks she's still so very delicate that none of it will stick. Maybe it's for the best. I wouldn't want to remember almost getting shoved into oblivion in the river of souls by a huge bug. There's a little bald patch on her head where the water nicked her at her hairline. It was a damn close thing.

"Your turn," I say. "Come on. I'll go with you as far as I can."

I start to walk, but she holds back. I pause and turn. Then she speaks.

"Who are you?"

It's the voice of a little girl, clear and high and pure, and the sound of it makes me tear up in an instant. I don't really know why. Maybe I was waiting until now, holding it back for hours, maybe days or years.

I clear my throat and say, "My name is Ben. I know your family. I'm a friend."

She looks down at her own body, still subtly shifting before my eyes into a million possibilities. "Who am I?" she asks.

"We don't really know yet. But we're gonna find out."

She looks down the sand tunnel, and something that passes for fear shows in some of the facets of her face. "What is that way?"

I kneel down and take both of her hands, drawing her eyes to me, Caroline's eyes. "Life. Life is that way."

"Will it hurt?"

I think hard about what I could say, what she might want to hear, but then I decide that what she needs to hear is the truth.

"Sometimes, yeah. And sometimes, the worst hurts are in here," I say, tapping my heart. "But it's worth it."

She's not sold. She's no dummy.

"You have people on that side that love you. Good people. They want to meet you."

That perks an eyebrow.

I clear my throat. "And you have me, here, on this side. If you remember anything, try to remember that." I mean to say more, but I can't. I stand and rub my eyes with my palm while she waits.

"Will you hold my hand?" she asks, holding a hand out.

"I can do that," I say, and I take it.

Together, we walk down the path. It gets dark quickly, but she doesn't comment, doesn't pull back or cry. I can feel her little hand in mine still, but her touch is getting lighter with every step we take.

Soon enough, I feel we're at the heart of the passage, the thin space at the center of the hourglass, ready to flip. And now, the girl I saw is gone. In her place is a spark like a firefly in the palm of my hand.

I've had to usher way too many of these unborn sparks the other way across the veil, to the riverside. I've never done the reverse. But I still do what I always do. I hold it up and whisper an old blessing Gam used to say.

"Walk with beauty," I whisper. And I blow a soft breath that takes it out, down, and through.

I stand there in the dark for longer than I'd like to admit, feeling the sand, feeling my tears. Wondering if I'll ever get to hold that little girl's hand again—hoping I do, hoping I don't.

I'm the last one through. And as I slip through the center, I sense a powerful presence coming the other way, just out of reach. We pass side-by-side, and the wall between us is too opaque to see, but I think I go back up as Black Bear comes back down.

31

OWEN BENNET

For four minutes, she's had no breath of her own. I would like to hand her over to a professional now. I would like to give up this burden to the people who can fix it. If I was anywhere else in the United States, I bet I could. But right here and now, that professional is supposed to be me. I'm supposed to be the one who fixes things.

Four minutes and counting.

I never stop the rhythm. Compressing, compressing, compressing. Suction out, breath in. Turn over. Heel of the hand to the back of the ribcage. The gunk keeps coming. Usually, there's an initial clear, then we deal with whatever transient tachypnea or other drainage issue presents in recovery, but we aren't getting to recovery at this rate.

The temptation to dive into foxhole faith again is almost overwhelming, to just fold myself over her little body and weep, praying to God with clasped hands to do what mine couldn't.

But that's not how I pray. I pray by compressing, suction out, breath in. Turn over. Heel of the hand thumping the back of the rib cage.

Again and again and again, and just when I think I might break, I do it again.

Compression, suction out, breath in. Turn over. Heel of the hand on the back of the rib cage, and this time, sand falls to the floor—bloody sand, maybe a quarter teaspoon. It bops off my shoe and breaks into tiny clumps. Now, I *know* that's not normal. I know of no medical precedent for something that resembles bloody beach sand coming from inside a baby. I rub it with my thumb, feeling the grit, just in case it's a weird clot I've never heard about. But it spreads like sand.

As I'm still staring at it, she takes in a huge breath, a gargantuan breath that I swear will float her to the sun. Then she belts out a piercing scream.

I don't normally deal in absolutes. Life is too gray. But I can say with absolute confidence that this scream is the greatest sound I've heard in my entire life. I would listen to it all day and all night. But Dr. Sadler reminds me we still have a very tenuous infant on our hands.

He hands me the scissors to cut the umbilical cord, and when I don't seem to know what to do with them, he holds my hand and helps me snip it. Then he makes sure he has my attention and says very firmly, "Get her to the wall oxygen! Nascha made up a makeshift incubator in 204. She'll take you up."

The clinic has only a few rooms with good, continuous wall ox. We're working on the west wing, but the piping is all a mess, and the money is always running out, so we've only been able to retrofit the east rooms.

I take the baby to Caroline. She looks weak but still has color in her cheeks. I'm not looking at a woman on death's doorstep, which will do for now. Sadler holds an oxygen mask to her face as she reaches out one finger and brushes her tiny head. The furious screams stop for just a moment, then they start up again, but Caroline still smiles.

"Look what we did," she says softly.

"I have to take her to get oxygen," I say. "But I'll be right back."

She looks at me then at the baby again. "Don't worry," she says.

I take her hand, and I take the baby's hand, and I hold the three of us like a chain for a few heartbeats before forcing myself to pull away.

Nascha holds my daughter, which is understandable. Everything is jelly—my legs, my thoughts, the world. Together, we take her, screaming and swaddled, up the flight of steps. I vaguely register a chant rising from a sizeable crowd in the foyer as we pass, and I can't help but think it premature. *Too soon, folks.* I don't know when we can start celebrating, but to be on the safe side, I'd say it's when she graduates college.

In room 204, Nascha has rigged up one of our transport bassinets with an O_2 line from the wall. She's covered most of the holes with wrapping tape but left several open up top. It's tucked and clean, and I can hear the oxygen hissing. It's not perfect, but it's a hell of a lot more than I thought I'd get, and I hope my thousand-yard stare is grateful enough.

Nascha puts the tiniest cannula I've ever seen in her nose and checks pressure and flow. She attaches leads on her front and back. She rewraps her so that she's the size and shape of a loaf of bread. Then she sets her down in the bassinet and tops it.

I look at her in awe and at my baby girl in awe. I'm feeling a lot of awe.

The vitals kick on, and we both watch for a moment, waiting for things to stabilize. We both know what to look for. Being seven weeks premature would normally put her blood pressure somewhere near eighty over fifty, with a heart rate around 120.

After about five solid minutes, that is what we get. And when we get it, we hug each other. Nascha is crying too. Nascha never cries. This whole hospital could fall on her big toe, and she wouldn't cry. "I think we may survive this one, Dr. Bennet."

Then I wipe my eyes and see Chaco. He's on the little ledge outside the window. He seems to be struggling to tell me something by flaring his feathers and cawing. When he starts tapping the glass, he even gets Nascha's attention.

She moves over to the window and slaps at it with a pillow. "Shoo," she says. Chaco just stares her down.

"Don't worry about it," I say. "It's probably exhausted from trying to find anywhere dry to land."

Chaco looks at me and taps the window again, and I see he's holding something in his beak, a casino chip. It's one of the Gambler's chips. He's staring at me now with far more intensity than something his size has the right to emote. *Can he possibly know that I visited Wapati? That I put myself on the table for this very outcome?* But nobody dealt the cards. The Gambler wouldn't accept me as a stake.

I look at my baby girl. I just now notice that she has a bit of poliosis—a white shock of hair just above her forehead. She's watching me quietly, which is a little unsettling after all the screaming. But she's breathing. And I'm breathing. And the waters have stopped. So I don't think I have anything to fear from the Gambler.

"He wouldn't take my bet," I say out loud before I remember I'm with Nascha.

"Hmm?" she asks.

"Nothing. Sorry. Just... talking to myself."

Nascha sets the pillow down and comes over to feel my forehead. "Dr. Bennet, you need to sleep. Or at least sit down. You're gonna run yourself into the ground."

"I need to get back downstairs—"

"Caroline's stable, getting oxygen," Nascha says. "I heard on the shortwave that the water is receding. Tomorrow, we can probably get the ABQ team out here with some proper equipment. You sit. Dr. Sadler and I will keep tabs on Caroline."

In typical Nascha fashion, she physically settles me into the lumpy armchair before she leaves the room.

Chaco taps on the glass again—and again.

"What?" I ask, louder than I intend.

He shakes his feathers and hangs his head, a strangely sad look for the bird. And all of a sudden, my heartrate is picking back up again.

"If he's coming for me, fine. He's coming for me. I said I'd put myself on the table. If that's what it meant to save her."

Chaco looks at me with one narrowed obsidian eye. That's not what he means.

"And anyway, he said I can't gamble for something..."

Chaco fluffs himself up and sits down in a ball, leaning against the window, as depressed as a bird can look.

"For something I already lost."

Something has gone terribly wrong.

I remember thinking that was a strange thing for the Gambler to say. He was seated at that slot machine of his, pumping it full of coins and winning. It was a constant in-and-out flow, like dysentery. I told him I wanted to stake myself. One more game. I knew he had some sort of cursed good luck, but I thought if this is my last chance to save Caroline, I would take it.

"But it's over. Chaco, look. She's here, Caroline is downstairs. Stable. We've got two heartbeats."

Chaco looks at me for five seconds that hammer like church bells. Then he shakes his head.

I'm out of the door in an instant, running back through the crowded halls, low with conversation and song. I almost fall down the stairs, caught at the last moment by the helping hand of a stranger I don't even stop to thank. Around the corner and down the hall, I blow past Nascha and Sadler conversing while they wrap up soiled linens by the laundry closet across the hall. They yelp in surprise, but I don't care. I turn the corner and find her room and only stop myself at the door because of course she's going to be there. Of course she'll be recovering. And the last thing she needs to see is me, pale as a ghost, slamming into the room with crazy eyes.

So I brush down the front of my shirt, take a deep breath, and step inside.

The bed is empty.

The bathroom is empty. The corners are empty. Under the bed is empty. The storage closet is empty. The room is empty. Everything is empty.

I dimly register Nascha and Sadler coming in after me then pausing. They're asking the same questions I am.

Asking me. But I'm not answering. They won't understand. They can't understand.

Nascha leaves again, frantic. She'll be searching up and down the halls, asking the refugees. Sadler is on the two-way radio with Dee, his eyes wide. They still think Caroline walked away somehow. Like maybe they'll find her in the break room.

Chaco flits down to this windowsill and watches me. His eye says, *"Now you know."*

And I do. I went to the Gambler with a plan to wager me for her and the baby. But she beat me to it, the other way around.

Sadler is trying the satellite phone now. He turns me around and speaks to me, but everything feels muddy and slow, blurred. This is an impressionist painting of a room now. I push his hand away and turn back toward the bed and walk to the pillow. I lay the back of one hand in the depression where her head was. It's still warm.

"This was supposed to be me, honey," I say to the place where she was. "He was supposed to take me."

I thought that maybe after so much shit luck, we'd finally caught a break. That our terrible birthing situation turned the corner all on its own. It's happened to other people in the OR. I've seen it.

I should've known nothing as good as that child upstairs—healthy, breathing, peaceful—comes free. Not when the child is seven weeks early from the bleeding placenta of a geriatric pregnancy, not when that child is in my family, which is so close to the other side.

The terrible truth Chaco is trying to tell me is that something as beautiful as that girl upstairs requires more than a wager. It requires a sacrifice. An offering to balance the scales. I don't know if she won her bet, or if she lost, but either way, she had to swap places.

I'm leaning on the bed, or maybe my legs are giving out. Either way, I put my head on the pillow and smell the echo of her already fading.

It was supposed to be me.

32

GRANT ROMER

Not long after the Gambler left, the crow feather we watched get sucked down into the Arroyo popped back up to the surface of the water. That same low streak of wind that pushed it down pushed it back, all the way to the water's edge.

The clouds are breaking up for the first time in forever, and the feather's iridescent edge catches a passing bolt of sunlight that seems to make it glow.

Chaco left for the CHC to get an update. It'll take him some time to get there and back, but I can feel it in my bones. My sister is alive. Wherever she was running away to, she came back.

But the air up here is still heavy with loss. Kai sits with her arms around her knees, staring at nothing. Joey is spinning his totem pouch like he doesn't know whether to stay or go. Maria adds twigs to the pot, and the twins murmur low. We're all uneasy. If you didn't know better, you'd think we were the ones that just lost the bet.

I hear the twins say something about people changing

places. A switch was made. Kai hears them too, and we both share an uneasy look.

We watch the water recede inch by inch, wondering what comes next, until I see a black flash on the horizon. It's the kind Chaco used to make when he pinched the sky and sliced clean through. Right on cue, there's the pop. And Chaco does come through, but not like he used to. He flops out and drops. He manages to spread his wings enough to coast to a splash at the edge of the water, where he rolls into the mud.

Joey's there in an instant, *whoosh pop*, and he carefully picks Chaco up with both hands. When I'm about to jump off the roof myself, I hear him say, "I'm alright. Just... tired. It's my first time doing that, and it's a lot harder than it looks."

I'm all set to congratulate him since this seems like a big deal, the endless-crow equivalent of learning how to ride a bike, but he shuts me up with a thought.

"Your sister was saved, but not by the games," Chaco says. "What happened here saved the Rez, not her." He's having trouble getting the words out. They're catching in his mind like mine might catch at a lump in the throat. "Caroline saved her. And it cost her everything."

I drop Kai's hand. I drop everything, I think. Somehow, I even drop myself, first to sit, then to slide off the roof. I splash to my feet in the muddy soup below. Joey brings Chaco to me and sets him on my shoulder, where he plops and leans hard against my neck.

"The Gambler gave her this," he says, unfurling one tucked claw and dropping a Wapati chip into my hand. "Said when she was ready to make a deal, to tap it, and he'd come."

I look at the chip in my hand, close my fist, and

squeeze. "And you let her? You let her bring that sono-fabitch to her *hospital bed*?"

Chaco flutters off my shoulder and lands in the water in front of me, flopping in mud up to his chest. I can sense he's scared that he won't make himself understood and a little scared of me, which makes two of us.

"She said it had to be done. Said it was the only way. I tried to talk her out of it. She said I had to keep quiet and she knew his smoke. I guess... I guess I thought she would win."

He tries to flutter up to my shoulder again, all heart-broken and wet, but I surprise myself by pushing him away. He plops back in the water, and I immediately hate myself.

"You should have told me."

Kai sloshes over and picks him up and holds him to her chest then turns that fiery eye on me. "What the hell is wrong with you?"

"Mom is gone," I say, squeezing my eyes free of tears I refuse to cry. I like the anger better. "She made a bet, and Chaco knew it, and now, she's gone."

Kai stands and takes a breath as the reality hits her too.

"Shit," she says—the understatement of the century. "Okay... Well—"

"Well what? She's gone!"

Kai snaps back at me, "And I guess Chaco took her, then? Dragged her away with his little wings? For you to be acting like this with him? Don't think 'cause I can't hear you talking I don't know you're yelling at him."

My hands are shaking. "I... I just—"

"What did I tell you about getting mad at the right things?"

My feet feel like leavin' me again. I stumble backward and sit on the steps leading up to the double-wide from what was the firepit. The twins' house is leaking. Water is spitting from every seal and drill hole and edge. What a mess—the whole thing, top to bottom.

I put my head in my hands. Everything feels tight inside, just like the dried mud on my skin. "Is she dead?" I ask.

"I don't know," Chaco says. "It's hard to say. I can still feel... something. But I don't know if it's her or an echo of her."

A sad snort of laughter bubbles up, and I can't help but shake my head. "An echo?"

"I don't know, Grant," Chaco says. "I'm sorry."

Again, I hear that pain in his voice, the hitch. Kai's right, of course, and always has been. I put my hand out for him, and he looks up at Kai then back at me. She holds him out, and he hops from her hands to my arm, then up my arm, back to my neck.

"I'm sorry too," I say.

We stay that way, the three of us, on the stoop, watching the water recede. The cold from the cinder blocks seeps up into me and makes me just want to plant there and freeze. Stay still for a couple of months. I can thaw out when everything is over.

Joey splashes deeper into the muddy crud in front of us. "Look," he says.

At first, I can't see what he sees. Everything looks weird in the weak light, still struggling through the scattering clouds.

"By the lip of the canyon," Joey says, already wadin' out farther, chasin' the water as it goes.

And now I see bodies. Bodies are emerging. They ring

the canyon where the cars and campers used to perch, curled up like they're being born from the mud. And they're moving.

It's them, the Arroyo people.

But not all of them are here—that's for damn sure. I bet we're at three-quarters strength at best.

Kai wades out after Joey, eyes searching. She splashes her way to the front lines, where the water breaks around more and more people as it pulls back.

I know who she's lookin' for. I just ain't quite sure I want her to find him.

33

KAI BODREY

I know which lump is him. For half a heartbeat, I hope it won't move. Then I'm terrified it won't move. Then he moves.

Hos groans and spits and wipes his mouth clear of sludge. He looks like a big buck caught in a tar pit, at the edge of exhaustion. Mud bubbles up from his nose and coats his hair. He looks at the mud on his hands, looks at his arms and his body. He sees the rock line of the Arroyo ridge before he sees me, and he smiles, his teeth bright white in all the dark. When he tries to sit up on his elbows, he winces and falls to his back again. "I'm home," he tells himself. He says it a few times, like a mantra.

Then he sees me and tries to get up, but his feet slip on the mud, and he slides back to his knees. "Kai!" he says, and the mud cakes his teeth and tongue until he has to spit again.

I walk over to him, and in my mind, I hold out a hand and help him up and hug him. I know that's what a normal person would do when their brother basically comes back from the dead. But somehow, what ends up happening is I kick him in the ribs and start screaming.

"You left me! You asshole!"

He lands on his side and slides a bit in the mud. He holds up his hands, probably expecting another kick, but the hollow thunk the first one made is still making me feel a little sick. Kicking people when they're down is his game, not mine.

"I know," he says. "I know I did. I knew we were in trouble up at Knifepoint. I knew it, but I couldn't stop the train. I told myself I'd rather be dead alone than have to come back to you and say I was wrong. But I was wrong, Kai. I fucked up. And I'm so sorry."

"You *fucked up*?" I say. "You're *sorry*?" I point around at the mud pit the Arroyo has become, at the people getting unearthed—the ones that came back—but mostly at the spaces between. Where homes and people should be, but aren't. "You have no idea what we've been through. What *I* have been through. Because you *abandoned me!*"

He's up on one knee now, and I could just shove him down again, maybe shove him right over the lip, back to whatever the hell place he took all our people. I turn away and walk a few paces just to make sure I don't do it.

"I didn't abandon you at Knifepoint, Kai," he says from behind me.

I spin around toward him, expecting to fire back, expecting things to go the way they always used to with us, where we'd trade broadsides until we both sank, because one corner of my mind never stopped asking that question: *Who abandoned who, really?*

He's still on one knee, shaking. "I abandoned you way before Knifepoint, way before they locked me up, even. I abandoned you when we were kids and I decided to go off and fight everything, inside and out, and left you with..." He gestures weakly at the whole world. "Left you with all the mess. Truth is, I don't know if I ever stood by you long enough to really leave you. Which makes it even worse."

He tries to get up, slips again, and plants a fist in the mud. He's holding something tightly, and it's giving him trouble.

Hands on my hips, I watch him struggle longer than I should, shuddering out breath after breath. He eventually steadies himself, but he's shaky, and this time when he stumbles, I hold a hand out. He looks at my hand and at me, and when he grabs it, I put my back into it and help him out of the deep gunk. Together, we scrabble to better footing, and I tell myself to throw his hand away once we're there—throw it away and storm off—but I don't. I hold on.

"I hated you," I say.

"I know. For what it's worth, I hated me too."

"I might hate you still," I say. But I'm still holding his hand, and I got no intention of dropping it, so I think he knows I'm lying.

"You got every right. And I know you won't believe me —maybe never will—but I promise you I'm gonna clean this up."

Hos is literally coated in mud, and his every movement sounds like a fart, and I try to fight back the smile, but it slips out. And with it comes a relief that I had bottled up. Relief I was afraid to feel in case it wasn't real. But this is real. I wipe my eyes and smear mud across my face, but I don't care.

"Looks like war paint," Hos says. "It suits you."

I don't know what to say. He's speaking from the heart for the first time maybe ever. And I'm not there yet. But I do have a smile on my face. That's something.

"Come on, then," I say. "Better get to cleaning."

34

THE WALKER

As soon as I step back into the living realm, I feel the attention of the veil snap my way. It's panicked, like a dog left alone for too long. I don't know what it thought—or if a cosmic door can think all that much—but my guess is it thought I abandoned it. The map feels the same. As soon as it can find me with its infinite GPS, it shoots so many frayed threads my way that I'm hooked like a fish from every side.

But I'm heavy. I'm really, really heavy. I'm heavier coming out of this flood than I was going in, and I was pretty damn heavy going in. So I sit on the muddy shore of the draining Arroyo and dare all the barbs to pull. I dare the veil to sweep me on my way.

"Just give me five minutes," I say to nobody.

A map and a veil couldn't understand anyway. They're natural cosmic forces that never worked a day in their lives. But for whatever reason, they don't strongarm me just yet.

I do a quick thread check, like always. Joey's there, Grant, and Kai. I sense the child returned as well, with

Owen and—I can't sense Caroline. In a panic, I thrum every single frayed thread that has hooked me, searching for her. She's not there either—not dead, then. That's for sure.

But she's gone.

I hang my head, thinking of the shape that I passed in the neck of the hourglass. Maybe it wasn't Black Bear after all. Maybe she was right there, one thin slice of reality away, going the other way. I know instantly it was a swap of some kind—a deal or a bet, and she made it to save her daughter's life. Of course she did. I should have seen it a mile away.

I put my head in my hands. "Caroline..." I say. I start to ask why she did it, but I know why. I met why in the shape of a beautiful little girl on the shores of oblivion. And the worst part is I can't even blame her. The worst part is it only makes me miss her more. I miss both the little girl I met and the woman who swapped places with her. And in the capacity I can, the way in which I am able, I don't think I've ever loved her more.

I grasp at the sand, and my hand barely feels it. I'm back to being invisible. But the crows sure as hell know I'm here. All of them in a line on what's left of the fence start cawing at once. Chaco does too, which gets everyone's attention.

Joey stands tall and pans the space where I am. He never finds me but still says, "Ya'at'eeh, Walker!" like always, before going back to digging out our people from the crud they surfaced in.

One by one, these lost Arroyo men and women are helped back to their feet. Those that can walk start heading toward the twins' place. Those that can't get help.

I wish I could say they looked happy to be here, these

newly returned, but they do not. A few try to buck each other up, but the reality is the Arroyo is a mess. The Rez is a mess. Hard to see it any other way. We're in full rebuild here.

The good news is I think I know a great crew to get it done. Joey, Maria, Grant, and Kai are cleaning people up, shoveling a path already. I see in their faces that they know about Caroline. It weighs their threads down, but they're putting on a good face for the Arroyo. I notice a few other friends too. Big Hill is back, already mucking out the yard and unearthing the fencing. I recognize other members of the Circle too—the tall African woman in the flowing robes, the soldier with his crow on his dog tag chain—they're pulling what they can back from the mud.

It's gonna take a while, but it can be done. And my people know all about the long game. If they can get through this, I can too. So I stand and make my way over to the twins' place, where they've washed off the old pit and are carefully stacking dry piñon in a cone. The crows follow me with little tics of their heads.

I stand at the edge of the pit and watch as Hosteen Bodrey takes a hesitant step forward. The twins eye him up and down then turn to Kai for final approval—quite an honor, in my mind. She nods.

Grant is messing with a casino chip in his palm. Lost in his own head, he's tapping it between his thumb and forefinger like it might do something, but if it has any power, I can't see it. The sight of Hosteen brings him around, especially when the big guy steps right up to him, all coated in mud. Everyone quiets. Grant's the one who stares him down this time. Hos tries to meet his eyes, but he just can't. I see so much shame in his string. If he wanted to, Grant could wreck it with a single hard word.

But that's not Grant.

Grant pockets the chip. "Welcome back, Hos," he says quietly.

Hos furrows his brow then nods. He holds out his hand. "This is yours," he says.

Grant knows what's in that grip. I also know he doesn't want to take it. He won't come out and say it, not with the twins and the Circle here, along with all these animals that aren't animals, and the Arroyo so bruised up, but he doesn't want to be the Keeper anymore. He hasn't for years.

I don't blame him.

I also know that Grant Romer knows what his job is, knows what his duty is, maybe more than any of us. But still, his hand wavers.

"We need you, Grant," I say. "There will come a time when all of us can clock out. But that ain't now. There's too much left to do."

Maybe Chaco relays what I say. Or maybe Grant just knows it already. Either way, he takes the bell and puts it around his neck. When it settles where it's settled for over a decade, he lets out a shaky breath.

Maria hands Hos a bristle broom. He takes it without question and starts mucking out the back. She pops an eyebrow, and I can't help but smile. I think she's gonna be a tough sell, but if Hos can win her over, he's back in for real, and he's off to a good start.

"I'm going to see Dad," Grant says, grabbing his hat and shrugging on his old waxed jacket.

Tsasa holds up a hand as he turns to go. "May I see that chip, Keeper?" he asks.

Grant pauses, reaches into his pocket, then walks over and hands it to him. Tsasa looks at it carefully, muttering.

He hands it to Tsosi, who runs his gnarled old hands along the edges and nods before passing it to Maria, who passes it to Kai.

"Your sister has come back to us, then," Tsasa says. "The swap was true." A statement, not a question.

"I believe so, sir."

"Your father is not the only one that will need your help," Tsosi adds. "The child is also in need. She is marked by the river, born from the storm." He offers a crow feather that Grant seems to recognize. It's tied to the child. I can see that much instantly.

Grant looks at Chaco, who bobs up and down, which seems to seal the deal. Grant takes it and spins it. Runs his hand along the fletching then puts it in the band of his hat. It rests against the crown like it was born there.

He tries to push his shoulders back and stand straight. He's been trying to do that for years, to walk tall through it all, but it's getting harder for him, and I think everyone can see it. Kai takes him by the arm and presses her head to his shoulder, which helps.

"But know this, also, Keeper," Tsasa says. "The girl's heart beats strong. She is a child of the rain, but the rain is part of the sky, and so she is also a child of the sky. One who soars. Thanks to the sacrifice your mother made, she may yet get the chance."

Tsosi nods as he brings the pot around, and with his brother, they usher the white coals within onto a bed of tinder in the old pit. At first, the coals are still, then the fire creeps out of them, then it grows.

The wood pops around it, already giving itself to the flame. The twins sit back in their dripping deck chairs and smile. Tsasa pats his brother's hand, and Tsosi tops it with his own.

"The Arroyo is strong," Tsosi says. "Both the land and the people. It calls many things home. It still speaks. It may be that your mother will yet hear."

That's too much for Grant, who turns away even as he nods. Kai joins him, and he puts an arm around her as they walk to where his truck is drying out on the hill.

I know what he's thinking. He's thinking it's too much to hope that Caroline might be alive, too much to put that on a wounded heart. If he lets hope in and it turns out she's left us all forever, that heart doesn't stand a chance.

And I know how it looks. Black Bear isn't about half measures. He put on the face of the Gambler because he wins. He gets what he wants, and up until now, he's always kept it. So I don't blame Grant for walling off that hope. He thinks Caroline lost her bet.

I'm not so sure.

I know Caroline. She doesn't make dumb moves. She thinks things out. She always has reasons. And I've done this job long enough to know that nobody dies in this world unless I clip a string, and I ain't clipped nothing yet.

I think she's on Black Bear's mantel, stuck in his house on shifting sand, a prize for him to preen over while he plots how to get back all he lost.

He could've just walked away. He could've taken his loss, learned from it, and moved on. If he had, we would all be done, tied up, finished. But he didn't. He screwed up. His first mistake was pissing off the wrong crew. Like I said, we can play the long game better than anyone. Caroline, with her unique sight, both here and in the spirit world, maybe best of all.

His second mistake was bringing her somewhere on my side of the world—somewhere I can walk, somewhere I can find her, and somewhere I can finish him.

I'll tell all of this to Grant, eventually. When the pain isn't so fresh and the earth around us isn't so new. When I have the strength that conversation requires. For now, it helps to keep the words of an old friend close to heart.

Nothing is lost forever.

The story of Nááhwiilbiihi, known as the Gambler, is one of the most profound cautionary tales in the *Diné Bahane'*—the Navajo origin story. He took wagers of all kinds and gambled with everyone from animals to gods. The fact that he "always wins" and still is never satisfied makes for a fascinating literary character as well.

The *Diné Bahane'* doesn't mention how Nááhwiilbiihi got his powers. He's first referred to as a "gambling god" but then unmasked as a fraud by Nilch'i the Wind, who says "I hope you realize by now that you are not one of the Holy People. By no means are you a god."

The unmasking takes place during what is described as "the greatest set of games ever" between Nááhwiilbiihi and the Wind, where the stakes are driven ever higher. In the *Diné Bahane'*, we read that the Wind was assisted by a group of animals who found clever ways to defeat the Gambler over a series of field games.

The version I wrote of this great competition is rooted in the origin story. Even though the circumstances may differ, the heart of the tale is the same. The larger lesson, of course, is that pride and greed can be your undoing. But there is a subtext as well, one I find particularly compelling: You never really know who you're gambling with. So don't play games with things you can't afford to lose.

The more I write this series, the more I see that the

overall story has been influenced (both consciously and unconsciously) by the difficult birth of my own son, and how my wife and I fought to get him healthy. Thankfully, he is thriving now, but the battle changed us both forever. During the darkest days, I took comfort in knowing we had a strong core of family, friends, and medical professionals on our side. I believe we had more than a little help from the other side as well. I like to think that somewhere out there, a Ben Dejooli was fighting on our behalf, hand in hand with our son on a distant shore.

If you or someone you care about is in a similar battle, just know that you are not alone.

As always, thank you for reading my stories. I am deeply grateful. And there is more to come.

-BBG

ABOUT THE AUTHOR

B. B. Griffith writes best-selling suspense and fantasy. He lives in Denver, CO, where he is often seen sitting on his porch staring off into the distance or wandering to and from local watering holes with his family.

See more at his digital HQ: https://bbgriffith.com

If you like his books, you can sign up for his mailing list here: http://eepurl.com/SObZj. It is an entirely spam-free experience.

ALSO BY B. B. GRIFFITH

The Vanished Series

Follow the Crow (Vanished, #1)

Beyond the Veil (Vanished, #2)

The Coyote Way (Vanished, #3)

The Wind Thief (Vanished, #4)

Child of the Sky (Vanished, #5)

Den of the Bear (Vanished, #6) - Coming Soon!

Gordon Pope Thrillers

The Sleepwalkers (Gordon Pope, #1)

Mind Games (Gordon Pope, #2)

Shadow Land (Gordon Pope, #3)

The Tournament Series

Blue Fall (The Tournament, #1)

Grey Winter (The Tournament, #2)

Black Spring (The Tournament, #3)

Summer Crush (The Tournament, #4)

Luck Magic Series

Las Vegas Luck Magic (Luck Magic, #1)

Standalone

Witch of the Water: A Novella